SEED
OF
A
WOMAN

SEED OF A WOMAN

by
Ruth Geller

Imp Press
Buffalo

Manufactured in the United States of America

Cover Design by Donna Massimo/Great Arrow Graphics, Inc.

Seed of a Woman
is Published by
Imp Press
P.O. Box 93
Buffalo, New York
14213

FIRST EDITION

I began this, my first novel, in June of 1970,
naively thinking it would take
six months to write
and another six months to publish.

For many reasons,
my mother and father are responsible
for my determination to complete the job
I began almost ten years ago.

To them, this book is dedicated.

Contents

SEED

OF

A

WOMAN

September
1969

September was a month of change. The summer days melted gradually into autumn and the air smelled like a prophecy of falling leaves. Still, it was hot. The mid-September sun glared into the windows of the university at the city's edge.

In a small office on the third floor of the Humanities Building, Assistant Professor David Sully adjusted the shade and continued pacing around the room as he defined his theories of education to a freshman with red braids. She sat in a wooden chair, her face masked with admiration. Sully walked to the doorway stopping just at the threshold, and back to the window, pulling aside the shade and gazing out.

The office might have been sufficient space for someone else, but for Dr. Sully it was confining. He stacked books, magazines and supplies in neat precarious piles on the file cabinet and bookcase. On his bulletin board there was one thumbtack to every five papers, each having one little corner jutting out to remind him of its presence and demand his attention. Yet the crush of objects was unnecessary: he kept on hand three dictionaries, many outdated messages, and enough paper clips and staples to last for years.

Sully's height, rugged features and large black moustache made him look more suited to the out-of-doors than the crowded office. His straight black hair folded slightly over the collar of his blue work shirt. The hair was long enough to appeal to his students but not so long that it might offend his superiors. Framing his head was a poster that was visible to people passing in the hall, a huge silkscreen portraying the Mexican revolutionary Emiliano Zapata standing gun in hand against a background of crimson. His large moustache, very much like Sully's, curved down around the corners of his mouth.

Sully turned away from the window, sat down in the swivel chair and stretched out his long thin body, propping one sandalled foot against an open drawer. As he leaned back he saw the woman standing in the doorway smiling hesitantly. She was waiting for him to notice her.

"I'm busy now," he said, indicating the redhead, who turned around, annoyed at the interruption

"Oh, sorry."

"Is it anything important?"

"No, not really. . . My name is Rebecca Simon and I think I'm supposed to be your teaching assistant this year?"

"Oh, fine. Be right with you."

She nodded and stepped back into the hall, walking far enough away so that no one could accuse her of eavesdropping. She leaned against the wall, glancing at the glass door that enclosed the fire hose. She avoided her eyes.

All night long devils had invaded her brain, picking at her with little pincers: 'Why weren't you more careful! Stupid. Just plain stupid. You must have wanted to get pregnant.' In the morning she'd taken a scalding bath, hoping if she were pregnant she would miscarry, enduring the agony because she felt it was a just punishment.

Afterwards she'd dressed, preparing herself with one object: to remind Dr. Sully of an appealing schoolgirl. She felt fortunate to have received a $2500 teaching assistantship in the first year of her graduate work, but was troubled that they had assigned her to assist a professor of Mexican History. She knew next to nothing about Mexican History.

She'd combed her long brown hair down around her shoulders and applied eyeliner with a practiced hand. Because her bust was small and her legs somewhat thick in the ankle, she took pains with her face. She felt that her large brown eyes were her best feature. They could be shy or seductive, maternal or childlike as the situation and her partner required, slipping from one expression and feeling to the next with an adaptability that was rooted in her desire to please. She used her thick hair as a prop, modelling for an imaginary photographer who would print the pictures representing her life, her essence, as a series of still poses.

She stared critically at her reflection in the glass; past it she could see the crushed, ordered folds of the fire hose. As she reached up to tuck back a stray strand of hair, she heard Sully call: "Come on in, I'm free now."

She and the redhead passed each other in the doorway of his office, and she sat down on the warm chair. Sully swung around to face her and said: "So you're going to be my teaching assistant."

"Yes."

He handed her the syllabus for the two introductory courses he was teaching, and explained her duties: she was to be present at all classes, take attendance, and help him grade the exams and term papers. He told her that it might be a good idea if, before classes began next week, she read the books they'd be using the coming semester. When he reached up to get the booklist, he knocked over a desk lamp. He picked it up and said: "Kind of crowded in here."

She smiled sympathetically.

"I'm afraid the Administration isn't too concerned about my needs. I applied for a research assistant as well as a teaching assistant, but unfortunately. . ." He sighed, and she noticed the worry lines that ran across his forehead.

"I'll help you in the course all I can," she offered.

"What I really need help with is my research. I wrote an article analyzing the anarchist influence on the Mexican Revolution and it was accepted by a journal that's putting out a special issue on Mexico."

"That's wonderful."

"Yes. But the problem is. . ." The phone rang, and he stiffened. "Damned phone's been ringing all morning." After another ring, he asked: "Would you?"

She had been a secretary for years and was well trained in protecting her bosses from unwanted interruptions. With an air of competence she picked up the receiver and said: "Dr. Sully's office."

"What? Who is this, is Dr. Sully there?" said a female voice with a Boston accent.

"I'm sorry," she intoned in her formalized office voice, "he's not in at the moment. May I take a message?"

"Who is this. . ."

"This is Dr. Sully's teaching assistant."

"Oh. Well. . . tell him that Elizabeth called."

"I will. Good-bye."

"Bye," the voice said, and hung up.

"Who was it," he asked.

"Elizabeth."

"Oh no." He looked at his watch. "Eleven thirty. I was supposed to. . ." he ran his fingers through his hair and sighed.

"I told her you weren't here, is that OK?"

14

"Yes, it's fine," he said, and pushed a button on the phone so that he could receive no incoming calls on his extension. He frowned. "What was I saying?"

"You were telling me about an article you're writing."

"Right. The article I'm *trying* to write. The problem is, I got a letter from the editors today and they said that though they liked it, it needs more work. If only I had somebody to help me with the research. . . They're holding space for me, but the deadline's the end of December and I doubt I'll have time to finish it by then. . ." He looked at her. "Are you interested in Mexican history?"

"Well, I. . ."

"You know, maybe if your work assisting me in the course doesn't take up too much of your time, you could do some library work for me. Sort of half teaching assistant and half research assistant. Do you read Spanish?"

She was about to laugh and tell him that out of her two years of college Spanish she only remembered phrases like: 'Where is the green pen?' or: 'I am going to school.' Instead, she heard herself say: "I'm kind of rusty. but I can do some brushing up, it won't be much trouble at all." She thought, 'What a stupid idiot, why did you go and give yourself all that extra work? Now you have to go and learn Spanish all over again and do the guy's Goddamned research. Not knowing Spanish would've been a perfect excuse. You're just a fool.'

"That'll help me alot." he said. He looked into her eyes and smiled gratefully, and seeing those soft lips and weary eyes, something tugged inside of her.

Nevertheless, she knew she should disentagle herself and began, "The thing is, I don't really think I'll have that much time. . . I mean, I haven't even registered for my classes yet and I just moved to town and I'm not really settled. . . And since I'm on an assistantship I'll have to keep up my grades. . ."

He was looking out the doorway. She followed his gaze and saw a man straightening up from the drinking fountain. moving slowly while his eyes scanned the room, taking in everything from the lighted but unused phone to her legs, which were bare to mid-thigh. She tried to stretch the skirt material over her knees, the motion at the same time alluring and modest. The man in the hallway didn't seem to notice. He was looking at the crimson poster in back of Sully.

Sully nodded pleasantly to the man. He nodded back brusquely and passed out of sight. Sully broke into a grin. "I got that poster especially for him."

"I don't think he liked it very much."

"I know, that's why I got it." He looked out into the hallway hopefully but the man did not reappear. He turned back to her. "Well then, it's settled. Maybe we'll work something out so that you don't have to attend both of the introductory classes since they're just about identical. That way you'll be able to concentrate on the research."

She opened her mouth indecisively, but before she could speak, he said: "You're not from around here, are you."

"No, my family's from Portland. That's where I did my undergraduate work."

"How did you end up all the way out here?"

"Well. . . I wanted to get away."

"Did you come here alone?"

"Mm-hmm."

He nodded: that was the information he wanted. "I admire someone who can move around by themselves, someone who can say, 'I'm going here,' or 'I'm going there,' and then do it. Not all people are like that. Some people are insecure. They can't get by in life without leaning on other people, clinging to them. They're totally dependent. And when one person stifles another, it can be very destructive."

He seemed to be speaking about someone in particular, but she thought it would be rude to question him. "I know. If you don't rely on yourself, then you're sunk."

"Yes. Independence is very important. Especially for a woman. I know that it's hard coming to a new town, meeting new people. After. . ." His lips were pursed into a "w" sound, but he changed his mind and said: "after I came from Chicago, I got to know people quickly, and that was good. But," he said, looking deeply into her eyes, "it's also important to leave yourself open to new experience."

Flattered, she smiled and nodded in agreement.

"Sometimes I feel that I've been here long enough. . ." He gazed out the window. "It's as if my heart yearned to move on. To another city," he added, glancing at her. He crossed one leg over the other so that his foot hung in space. He lit a cigarette, and his eyes rested on the phone. "Sometimes. . . sometimes I feel trapped," he said, but there was almost pleasure in his voice. He sat tight and stiff. Only his toes moved constantly, drumming like fingers, as though they were trying to run away from his foot. They strained and pulled, pointed and arched in a constipated agony of escape. Fascinated, she stared at his toes while his words blurred over her unheard.

By the time she left his office forty-five minutes later, she felt that she knew him quite well. He had joked about the History Department hierarchy and explained the political climate of the university. She had asked him questions about his research, and convinced herself that helping him would be the intellectual challenge of her lifetime. She was pleased that she had kept his interest for so long. She liked him: he spoke to her as to an equal.

As she was leaving, he said: "Very interesting conversation. We should continue it sometime."

"I'd love to. See you in class next week, Dr. Sully."

"Dave," he corrected, and handed her the list of unpublished dissertations she should read for his article.

"Dave," she said, and pointed to herself: "Becky."

She had it all planned: she would get her period, and she and David would have a meaningful relationship based on intellectual understanding. Slowly they would become friends, then lovers, and finally. . . She let her mind drift off into fantasy. Elizabeth, whoever she was, faded away.

As soon as she left his office she went to the ladies room, closed the stall door behind her and checked for her period. It hadn't come but now she was confident that it would. The year, she told herself, would be perfect.

She ignored the vague uneasiness in the back of her mind and tried to be enthusiastic about all the extra work she would have to do. She went to the library and got three books on reviewing Spanish. If she were to share David's interests, she first had to learn the language.

Classes began and Becky found they were unbearably boring; one day sitting in her Philosophy of History course, she realized that she wanted to scream. She thought most of the graduate students were mindless flunkies, but she played the same smiling games, pretended the same interest in picayune arguments, and laughed at the same dull jokes told by the same dull professors. The exciting life she had looked forward to all summer, the life of stimulating intellectual discovery, did not exist. For the next few years she would be nit-picking for insignificant facts in thick books with tiny print.

Each class led into a labyrinth of work. She saw no point to any of it unless she took a diet pill and then everything seemed to click. But with so much work to do she depleted her small supply of pills in a week and was left with an irrelevant pile of books. Quickly she lost interest.

At home she daydreamed over her books and had to drink stronger coffee and more of it in order to keep herself alert. Her eyes had become accustomed to passing over words that never reached her brain. She was so expert that she could read a sentence, paragraph, page or even chapter, and all the while her mind was far away in daydreams. She daydreamed about the home she'd have someday when she was married. She daydreamed about sex.

The coffee she drank only filled her with nervous energy, and sometimes she masturbated as she studied. Reading *Methodology of Research* was like reading hard core pornography. The letters swam before her eyes and turned into penises vaginas bellys breasts thighs. Legs intertwining. Lips sucking. But after her orgasm she always came back to that empty room and *Methodology of Research*, and felt so disappointed she wanted to cry.

In the library she fell asleep over the huge dusty volumes of bound journals that contained research for Sully's article. Once she cut her finger on a page as she turned it—page one thousand two hundred forty six. She watched the blood well up in the tiny slit and licked it clean and blew on it to cool it. She was glad of the pain. It reminded her that she was alive. It jolted her back into the real world. She got up and made a whole procedure out of washing her finger and finding a bandage: it was a good excuse to be away from those books. But as soon as she returned to them her eyes began to droop. She tried to wake herself by searching for obscene words in the Spanish-English dictionary.

She grew to detest the library and to resent the hours she had to spend pouring through the dictionary, translating the articles word by word. The time consuming and tedious translations drained her. At the end of the month she and Sully were to have a formal meeting to review her teaching assistantship, and she resolved to tell him that she was unable to continue doing his research.

Looking forward to seeing him was the only thing that made school interesting. But the reality of their casual meetings never measured up to her fantasies. He was pleasant and polite, and talked about his work and university politics. He held out to her an impression of his unhappy relationship with Elizabeth, but he never went any farther than ambiguous complaints that stopped in mid-sentence and trailed off into sighs and weary looks. She was afraid to ask questions but concluded from his scattered comments that while he and Elizabeth lived together, they were not married. Becky attended his introductory classes that were held in the large lecture halls seating four hundred. She took attendance and sat in the back of the room watching him move around the podium as he lectured. Sometimes he made jokes about the University Administration. He was friendly with his students and they liked him. The freshman with red braids watched him closely, and when he smiled at her. Becky was annoyed to find herself so jealous.

In the meantime she settled into a routine. She got up in the mornings, went to classes, studied, picked up her paycheck, paid her bills, and worried that her car would break down. She made continual plans to sort through the cardboard box filled with old letters, pictures and diaries, but never got around to it. She ate and dieted compulsively. She waited for her period. She tried not to feel lonely.

She constantly carried one or two books in her large pocketbook. She read when she drank coffee between classes at the Cavern, the dim, sprawling, low-ceilinged cafeteria in the basement of the Student Union. She read when she ate lunch at the downtown Grant's. She even read one Monday night during intermission at the movies, peering at the hardly visible words, pretending interest because she was alone.

She got a letter from her mother and wrote back, sounding bright and cheerful. Her letters to her family were like progress reports: I read this, I did that. But the absence of news of a boyfriend was conspicuous. She imagined they scanned her letters for news and not finding it, thought: When is she going to settle down and get married. Her parents were proud that she had put herself through the university and was now attending graduate school, but they questioned the value and purpose of all that education.

They had not planned for her to go to college, and in fact had not planned her birth. She was born late in their lives when their three sons were seventeen, fourteen and twelve. By the time she was in high school, her brothers had already accomplished whatever they considered to be worthwhile: they each had families, and jointly owned a successful roofing company. The fact that they expected little from her led her to expect little from herself. Her life seemed preordained: she would marry someone very much like her brothers and become very much like their wives. At seventeen, she couldn't imagine a future more dull.

There seemed to be two ways out, the army and college, and she had no illusions about the army. When she informed her parents of her decision they were pleased. But when she told them the cost of tuition and asked for the thousand dollars they had saved for her wedding, their attitude changed.

The next four years were grim: Becky attended classes at night, and during the day worked as a "gal Friday" for a local muffler installation company in order to pay for tuition, books, transportation, clothes, miscellaneous expenses, and ten dollars a week towards her mother's grocery bill. The thousand dollars remained in the bank, growing in importance to become the center of their arguments, the symbol of their goal and hers.

She was determined to graduate with honors. Her brothers teased her, mocked the piles of books stacked in her room, told her that she was wasting her time and would end up after four years still working for the muffler installation company. She in turn used her education to intimidate them: she laughed at their ignorance of facts and theories she had learned in school but believed she had known all along.

When she was a senior she realized that they might have been right: her B.A. in History seemed unlikely to do anything but provide her security in her job as "gal Friday." If she had married a doctor or lawyer she would have had a ready made status. But she was single; and not wanting to face her brothers' smug attitudes for the rest of her life, she applied to graduate school, planning to go as far away as possible.

During those four years she'd had a series of brief, inconvenient affairs with a series of uninvolved, uninteresting men. Though she'd lost her illusions about sex when she lost her virginity at sixteen, she was still saving her love, her self, for The Man, who as yet had not come along. This past summer she thought she'd met him in Doug, and hoped that he would ask her to cancel her plans to attend graduate school so far away. But he did not. It was an affair like all the rest: no promises, no plans, no commitments and not much sex. The sex they did have gave her little pleasure. It was something he did and she observed. When her period did not come at the end of August, she couldn't quite believe it: she had thought of herself as an innocent bystander.

She had continued packing, and tried to hide her unhappiness. She was moving to the other side of the country, leaving more than her home.

She knew vaguely that she had lost something in college: a pride in what she was, an easiness about where she came from. She was continuing a pattern her father started when he changed the family name. She was filled with a thirst for movement and progress, although she didn't know what for or to where.

In her letters to her family all of the unimportant things in her life became important, and all the important things ceased to exist. She didn't write to them that she was lonely, and afraid of being pregnant.

Her period had not come. She tried to ignore it, hoping to show whatever force inside her that held it back that she didn't care. She was like someone who strolls away whistling, hands clasped behind their back, but always watching out of the corner of their eye. Sometimes she searched for it, inserting her finger into her vagina to coax it down. Every movement in her belly made her pull away her underpants to look; she was continually disappointed.

At night in bed she worried about being pregnant. Without sleep the nights were long, and often toward three or four she'd pour a drink. She'd lay in bed staring out the window at the only tree she could see from her apartment. It was an old tree, and some of its branches were dead so that it looked like winter before its time. But it was her tree, and onto it she projected the forests of the world.

Toward the end of the month she met with Sully. She decided to be firm about not doing his library work, and reassured herself that the decision was a fair one: she was being paid to help him teach, not write articles. She might even laugh and say: 'You know, Dave, slavery was abolished over a hundred years ago.' His response would be:

'Of course, Becky, I understand. I was going to suggest you do less work. You're quite ambitious to have done so much already.'

But the meeting did not take place as she'd planned. Sully had worries of his own. October 15th had been designated as the Vietnam Moratorium, a day devoted to discussion about the war in Indochina. A group of students and teachers had organized a teach-in and Sully was one of the two main organizers. At that point the teach-in had run into snags: the film had gotten lost in the mails, and a friend of Sully's who worked in Scheduling told him that the men's gymnasium was in fact available the afternoon of the 15th, but not for a teach-in on Vietnam.

When Becky walked in he was sitting with his chin in his hands, frowning. He'd been trying to get ahold of the other organizer for over an hour but so far was unsuccessful. He began a long complaint, the point being that he was the only one willing to take any responsibility.

Becky tried to sympathize with him. She told him she'd been involved with an anti-war group in college. They had done volunteer work for a local congressional candidate who ran on an anti-war platform, so she knew how disheartening people's attitudes could be.

She was in the midst of describing her canvassing experiences when he picked up the phone and said: "Excuse me, I have to make an important call." He dialed a number and drummed his fingers impatiently until someone answered. "Paul?" he said, but his face fell when he heard the voice. It was Justine.

"Oh, hello Justine. . . He's not? And you still don't know where he is. . . He didn't call or anything?. . . Well, when he gets home, could you give him a message?" He spoke slowly and distinctly: "Tell him that David Sully called, and said that he's supposed to track down the film for the teach-in. You got it?. . . Sure?. . . OK, tell him not to forget. Thanks."

He hung up the phone. That done with, he seemed less edgy, and talked about the events of the teach-in. "You should go," he concluded, "you'll learn alot about the war. As a matter of fact, a group of people in the History Department are going canvassing door to door after the teach-in. You ought to try it."

She opened her mouth to repeat what she'd said about her work with the peace candidate when the phone rang. She listened to Sully defend his teach-in involvement to someone from the History Department, almost forgetting the purpose of her visit. Ignoring a feeling that it was the wrong time to mention it, she suggested to him when he hung up the phone that she was overworked.

"Overworked!" he said, and as if providing a dictionary definition of overwork, launched into a description of his anti-war activities. He glumly cursed the Post Office for delaying the film and the University Administration for vetoing use of the men's gym. Suddenly he stopped. "I'm sorry, I guess I *am* overworked," he said with such bad-boy charm that she laughed.

They concluded the meeting amicably, but she left his office still feeling his disapproval, as if he alone were responsible for ending the war in Vietnam and she was worried about her petty schoolwork. She resolved to do his research, and spent the afternoon at the library.

Before she went home, she walked to the lavatory and checked for her period. It had not come. She stood before the mirror, combing her hair and trying to think clearly. If she was pregnant she would have to get an abortion. But she had no money. She imagined calling her father and

26

saying: 'Daddy? You know that thousand dollars you've been saving for my wedding. . .'

But even if she had the money, she had no idea how to find an abortionist. They were not listed in the Yellow Pages. There was no one she could ask. She would have to do it alone. And if she died in the process, then that was just her tough luck, wasn't it. At least she didn't live at home; by the time her mother saw the body, someone would have cleaned it.

She could not keep her mind off her body, and despised herself for this, because what did it really matter. In the vastness of the universe, her fate seemed incidental, her little tragedies irrelevant and meaningless.

She decided to forget about the whole thing, and fluffed her hair to give it some bounce. She drove home, concluding that in this new mood of confidence and cheer she would trip.

Her friend Ginny had given her a psilocybin tablet as a going away present; she dug it out from its hiding place at the back of the cupboard. She stood poised with a glass of water in one hand and the tablet in the other. She knew the drug would exaggerate any mood, and as her present mood was one of desperation, the trip would be unpleasant at best. Immediately after reaching this conclusion, she shrugged, popped the pill into her mouth and swallowed it.

'It'll work out for the best,' she thought. 'I'll end up jumping out the window and then all my problems will be solved.'

She sat on the lumpy living room couch, waiting for the trip to begin. The night air was balmy and cool, the nostalgic cool of autumn. It would have been a perfect time to go for a walk and breathe in the fragrance of the changing season.

27

But she felt trapped. The apartment seemed disjointed. She wanted to put everything in order but didn't know where to begin. The cardboard box of mementos sat in the corner of the room, waiting for her attention. No matter where she'd moved it, it was in the way. Finally she picked it up and shoved it into the farthest corner of the large closet.

Soon her jaw felt tight. The grains in the wood floor were clear and sharp, and she followed the lines as though they were a maze. The room was bright with soft tingling explosions. She felt a tickling start at the base of her neck and spread throughout her body. She had the feeling that someone was coming, and she was tense with anticipation.

There were no sounds of car doors slamming or foot-steps on the stairs. She thought that the doorbell might be broken, and she walked into the bedroom, under which was the entrance to her apartment. She opened the window to listen. As the sounds of the neighborhood invaded her room, an outer eye saw herself, and she smiled sardonically. 'Miss Popularity,' she mocked, 'thinking she's getting gentlemen callers on Wednesday evening. No one's coming, what's the matter with you.'

She lay down on the bed and stared at the ceiling. She felt hidden in a dark cave, and at the same time exposed on a vast plateau for all to see. She told herself to relax, but the apartment was like a tall hostile mirror that stared at her no matter where she turned. Her heartbeat felt a fraction of a second out of tune with her body and she kept glancing down at her belly as if at any second it would burst into a full-blown pregnancy.

Her mind kept focusing on her uterus, which she pictured as a drawing in a medical book, complete with arrows and captions. She thought that if she concentrated hard enough she could sense the egg and know if it was fertile and growing or ready to die and pass out of her body. At first she imagined a cell, dividing and re-dividing rapidly, then a sterile and withered amoeba. But always it was a microscopic machine that sent persistent tension up her spine to the base of her skull.

She decided a bath might bring on her period, and she undressed by the filling tub. The sight of her body was repulsive, for the flesh seemed to hang in loose folds from her bones. 'Please let me get my period,' she prayed, 'please let me get my period.'

Unexpected tears filled her eyes, but she blinked them back. 'Bitch,' she thought. 'You're ready to cry now when it's too late. You should've thought of that earlier.' By command the tears retreated. She set her mouth and stepped into the tub. Carefully, inch by inch, she lowered herself into the hot water. She looked down. The egg was there. She imagined it multiply, and multiply again. It was like a cancer gone mad.

"Get out!" she cried. "Leave me alone. Oh please. . . ." Her voice ricocheted from the bathroom walls and lashed at her skin. The light blinded her eyes.

She wanted to reach into her belly and rip the growth away. But her own body protected it, and at this moment there was no way to destroy it without destroying herself.

She was tired. Hot baths were supposed to bring on late periods but all they did was dry her skin. She washed quickly, dried herself and put on a robe.

She had to talk to someone, to hear the sound of a human voice. She sat at the kitchen table and poured herself a drink.

When she could stand the silence no longer, she phoned her friend Ginny, who was at school in Portland.

They exchanged greetings. Ginny chided her for not writing; and Becky said she'd found a dreary furnished apartment that was driving her to drink. Then she said: "How's that old bastard what's-his-name."

"You mean the poor soul that you abandoned for the life of academic adventure?"

"Yeah, that's the one. How is old Doug. He may be up for the Father of the Year award."

Ginny was silent. "You're kidding," she said at last.

"Nope. Yours truly, Rebecca of Sunnybrook Maternity Ward." She laughed but her voice was brittle.

"How late are you."

"Four weeks."

"That's not so long." Ginny said doubtfully. "You were never regular anyway. Were you?"

"Who knows. . ."

"Have you taken anything?"

"Nope."

"You're not going to have it, are you?"

"I don't know what I'm going to do. You got any extra coat hangers lying around?"

Ginny had often joked about the time she'd aborted herself with a coat hanger and almost died; but now her voice was serious: "I wouldn't advise *that* trip if I were you."

"No. . . I'll figure something out. Maybe my period's just late."

"Yeah. Maybe it's just late. You know, what with moving and all. . ."

"Maybe so. . ." Then she brightened and said: "Speaking of tripping, I took that tab of psilocybin you laid on me."

"Now? When you're so worried about your period? That's smart, that's really smart."

"Oh well... Why not..."

She tried to feel comfort from Ginny's voice, but after they said good-bye she was left with the hum of the telephone. She went to bed, and in the darkened room she watched the multi-colored designs on the bare white walls moving incessantly, forming patterns she'd never seen but felt she knew by heart.

She continued to wait for her period. Every day, every fifteen minutes if she was at home, every class break if she was at school, she shut herself in the bathroom or the lavatory stall and examined the fluid, inspecting it carefully, thinking she saw flecks of blood. Once, in a rush, she scratched the inside of her vagina with a ragged fingernail.

She slept little. She didn't cry at all: if a sob threatened to break out she coughed it down. She did the things she felt she had to do.

She made silent little jokes about killing herself; and then, at the end of the month, she got her period.

October
1969

The morning of the Vietnam teach-in, Paul Denton gave his Introduction to Philosophy course the homework assignment: write a paper on "Let's Make a Deal" as an extension of ruling class ideology. Several students groaned but none were surprised: they had come to expect unusual assignments from their teacher. On the first day of class he had told them that this would not be a traditional philosophy course: "You are not here to study a philosophy that has meaning in some little corner of your brain. You are here to study a philosophy that has meaning to every aspect of your daily lives." He was a strict teacher and demanded serious work from his students but few had dropped the course.

Paul leaned against the cold radiator under the window and stroked his dark beard. He was fairly short, but his body was thick and gave the impression of competence. At twenty-six, his hairline had already begun to recede and his belly indicated the beginnings of a paunch. Yet he was intensely charismatic: each semester one or two students embarassed him with their infatuations. He tried to discourage this behavior, though it amused him and he looked forward to telling Justine about each new admirer. He shared most everything in his life with Justine except his politics.

Paul was a driving force in the campus anti-war movement, and a veteran of the New Left. As an undergraduate he was involved in the Civil Rights movement, and as a first year graduate student he travelled to Ann Arbor to participate in drafting the Port Huron Statement that later became the basis for S.D.S., the Students for a Democratic Society. He often spoke of quitting school and beginning a community organizing project, but he was at present a third year graduate student. He was writing his Ph.D. thesis on "Hegel and Dialectic Materialism," and would receive his degree in the spring of 1971. The part he most enjoyed about graduate school was the opportunity to teach, and he spent a great deal of time planning classes, reading background material, and talking to students.

When everyone in the class finished writing down the assignment, he asked if they had any questions. No one spoke. He smiled and looked around the room, holding their attention with his eyes, waiting for them to guess what he was going to say. "There should always be questions," he pronounced, his tone mocking that of a pompous professor.

A student in the back of the room held up his hand. "I have a question."

"Yes?"

"Am I going to get an A?"

Everyone laughed. Paul waved his hand dramatically toward the blackboard as though he were Monty Hall, and drawled: "Behind one of these curtains is an A. Behind another is a B. But behind the third is an F. You can either choose one of these curtains or take the incomplete you already have."

The students laughed and gathered their books and papers together. As Paul watched them his face relaxed into the tired and strained look that had settled there in the past few weeks. Although he and David Sully were supposedly taking joint responsibility for the teach-in, the main duties fell on Paul. Sully meant well, but as he repeated over and over, he couldn't stand pressure. The result was that in many cases Sully's name was used since he was a faculty member, but Paul, the graduate student, did all the work.

Three students lingered behind. One was Paul's favorite. a sophomore with a quick mind. It was he who had asked for the A. The second was a pre-law student whose main goal was to receive the highest grade with the least amount of studying. The third was a freshman with long red braids who acted as if she were completely smitten with Paul: her mooning eyes followed him constantly and she hung on his every word. He was kind, but on the whole ignored her.

"You going to the teach-in?" the sophomore asked.

"Sure." Paul put his books in his bookbag and the four of them walked toward the gymnasium where the teach-in was to begin at eleven.

The university was located on the outskirts of the city. It was isolated and self-sufficient: it had its own dormitories, eating facilities, movie theaters and police force. Whatever went on in the city, the university remained untouched. Likewise, what happened in the university would not spread to the city.

In the newer section of campus stood the Montgomery Science Center, an unobtrusive structure surrounded by rhododendron bushes. The Department of Defense provided funds for this building and what went on inside of it: Project Rhododendron. The supposed purpose of Project Rhododendron, stated in a vague seventy page paper, was to develop effective insecticides to aid the agriculture of Vietnam. But the rumor among radicals was that the true purpose of Project Rhododendron was to develop chemicals for use in the Vietnam war.

Catching sight of the Center, Paul pointed towards it and shook his head. "How can the University Administration think we're so naive to believe the Pentagon would spend several million dollars on a project that's supposed to help the Vietnamese farmers."

As he spoke, the sophomore listened eagerly, and the pre-law student stifled a yawn: he had heard all this from Paul before. The redhead looked at Paul sharply, her dreamy expression replaced by something calculating. Paul noticed the change and was relieved. The girl's flirting had made him uncomfortable.

The sophomore spoke bluntly: "I think if Project Rhododendron is as bad as you say, we ought to burn the whole damned thing to the ground."

Paul held up his hand. "Wait a minute, Mark, not so fast. I think that if you took the time to analyze both the situation and the effect of your actions, you'd find that burning down Project Rhododendron wouldn't be such a good idea."

"Why not?"

Paul paused to consider his answer. Mark was filled with youthful exuberance, and was extremely impressionable. Paul hoped Justine would catch some of that political enthusiam, and to that end he'd invited Mark to visit them. Mark and Justine had spent the evening discussing her stereo equipment, and politics were pushed aside. But Paul was determined to give her a solid foundation in Marxist theory, and he felt sure that she would begin the process of change during their proposed trip to Cuba with the Venceremos Brigade.

He said to Mark: "At this point in history, the consciousness of the masses is not sufficiently advanced for such an action. You'd turn people against you. What you want to do is educate them so that when the time comes, they'll understand what you're doing and support you.

As Mark reflected on this, Paul turned to the pre-law student. "What about you, what do you think."

He had been daydreaming, and blinked to clear his head. "Um. . . yes. I agree, definitely."

Paul frowned, uncomfortable with the power he had over his students, annoyed by the lies they told him to get good grades.

They neared the one building that stood out from all the rest. It was Mellon Hall, the building that housed the office of the University President, Dr. Hamilton Ward. Though small, Mellon Hall was imposing, decorated outside with gables, turrets and huge tinted windows, and inside with thick carpets and expensive paintings. Among the offices, Ward's was the plushest: the carpets were the thickest, the paintings the most expensive. And against the window on an antique table stood a gnarled bonsai tree reputed to be over one hundred years old. It was Ward's pet, a gift from his wife when he took over the Presidency ten years ago. Mellon Hall was off-limits to students. Only the year's most promising horticulture student came regularly to tend the bonsai tree. Surrounding Mellon Hall were giant chestnut trees that dropped their ripe prickly burrs to the earth below.

As Paul and his students passed under the chestnut trees, Executive Vice President John Frick stood beside the bonsai waiting for Ward. While his eyes followed Paul, his hand reached out and absent-mindedly twisted a twig of the bonsai back and forth until it broke off in his hand. The tree quivered, and was still.

The door to the office opened and Ward walked in holding a disorderly sheaf of papers and looking flustered. "Sorry, John, the files were misplaced. I don't know what's wrong with Shirley, she's never been this disorganized before." He knew that Frick didn't like him, and in an effort to bolster a sense of cameraderie, he smiled and said, "Maybe she's going through the change."

The Executive Vice President made no response.

Embarrassed, Ward cleared his throat and sat down at his desk. He noticed that his bonsai had been looking a bit peaked lately. "Are you ready to begin?"

"Yes, I'm ready." Frick said. "I definitely am ready." He turned away from the window, glancing down once more as Paul walked up the steps to the gymnasium.

The morning of the teach-in, Becky went to the doctor.

When she first got her period at the end of September, she was elated. Once again her body was her own. But as the blood diminished, she felt a faint itching. She thought the discomfort was only another bid for attention. She had wasted an entire month worrying about her body and was determined not to waste another month. Unaware of her determination, the infection worsened. She tried to ignore it, telling her body: 'Leave me alone. Stop bothering me.'

When she finally accepted the fact that she was ill, she would not call a doctor. She knew the infection was due to all the searching she had done for her period. 'It's your own fault for poking around in there,' she decreed, and set herself to suffering.

By the second week in October the entire area burned so she could hardly walk. The infection was like a guilty secret, and she treated it herself, coating it with corn starch. That crunchy sound and cool feeling brought to mind a childhood summer when her mother patted her with corn starch. She thought of it as an old fashioned remedy that would surely work. It didn't, and by the time she was able to get a doctor's appointment on the morning of the teach-in, the pain had established itself as a part of her daily life.

She imagined the doctor would be like the stern but kindly physicians who practiced on television. But when after a two hour wait she finally sat across from him, she knew that he would never remember her from one visit to the next. His posture was perfect and his diction impeccable, but his breath smelled like stale coffee and cigarettes, as though underneath that perfectly groomed exterior he was rancid. The gold-sealed diplomas were proof of his medical authority; and the framed photographs of his wife and children, proof of his humanity.

He interviewed her brusquely and handed her over to a nurse who took her to a small examining room. Becky undressed, wrapped herself in a sheet and sat down on the table, listening to the doctor as he examined a woman in the next cubicle. The nurse returned and arranged her so that she lay back with her feet in the cold metal stirrups, her legs spread wide apart like a frog, her buttocks poised just at the edge of the table. She draped a sheet over her so that her naked body was visible to whoever cared to look, but when Becky glanced down she saw only the white triangle of sheet. The nurse aimed a gooseneck lamp directly between her legs, turned it on, and left.

Becky stared at the white triangle and at the metal top of the gooseneck lamp. She listened to the doctor's voice coming from the next cubicle: "Yes. Yes. Fine, fine. . ." She was afraid her body had played a trick on her, and as soon as he came in, the redness would disappear, the itching exist only as an echo of her hypochondriac imagination. He would find nothing wrong with her and say: "Yes. Yes. Fine, fine. . ." and send her home to the pain. She felt between her legs. It burned at the touch. She rubbed it quickly so that it would still be red.

When the doctor walked in he was brisk, confident, and in full control of the situation. She lay there like a bug on its back.

"I think I have a sunburn," she joked, referring to the light. She was immediately sorry: his smile was icy.

He pulled up a low stool, adjusted the light and peered into a place in her body she had never seen. She felt the cold metal of the speculum and heard his bored judgement that she had an infection, his mechanical description of the medication. He gave her the prescription for the birth control pills she had requested, but when she expressed doubt about their safety, he became impatient.

"I wouldn't worry about the birth control pills," he reassured, "the side effects are minimal. Just use the medication for your infection, abstain from sexual contact, and come to see me in a week."

The office visit came to twenty dollars, and she spent another nine at the drugstore for the birth control pills and the medication, beige almond shaped suppositories she was to insert twice a day. Altogether it cost almost thirty dollars, which was about half her weekly salary. She knew that if she kept getting sick, she'd have to give up her car.

She went home to insert the first of the tablets, and left for the teach-in.

The Vietnam teach-in was held in the women's gymnasium which was smaller than the men's. It was just as well: the room was only half-filled, and of those present, many seemed to have strolled in out of curiosity. They stood on the outskirts of the room looking more interested in the people than the teach-in itself.

Becky sat down on a section of the highly polished hardwood floor near the bleachers, and smoothed her skirt under her legs. The night before she had washed her hair, and the auburn tones caught the glints of sunlight shining through the high windows. She had secured her hair loosely on top of her head with a large barrette as though with one swift touch the barrette would snap open, and her hair fall sensually around her face. It could never happen. Too many small pins kept it all in place, hidden to preserve the illusion of natural sensuality. One loose lock trailed down her neck and several small wisps of fine hair curled around her face. Although she looked attractive, her appearance was overshadowed by the expression in her eyes that said: Please be nice to me. . . It was the kind of look that Bryce loved because he could answer: No.

Bryce Dedham stood by the exit sign watching her. He was slim and straight featured and he knew that women were attracted to him. He slouched against the wall with his hips jutting forward, aiming his eyes at various women around the room, nodding if he recognized them. Bryce gave the impression that he loved women and had supreme confidence in himself as a man. Every woman he saw, he saw under him, moaning. It never failed to amaze him that each and every woman had such a honey-warm place between her legs, a place whose purpose it was to provide him pleasure, a hiding place where he could refresh himself in order to return and conquer his world anew.

He had made Becky uneasy from the first time she'd seen him sitting in the Seminar on the Enlightenment. He was slumped in his seat, his face a picture of undisguised contempt. She felt she could either share that contempt or be its object. She sat near him and when he smirked at something the professor said, she caught his eye and smiled as though the two of them were in on a private joke about the world. At the second class he spoke to her.

She hadn't noticed him when she walked into the gym, but now she felt a persistent warmth on her back, and when she turned she saw Bryce staring insolently at her. His eyes were victorious because he'd made her turn around merely by staring, and she smiled to congratulate him on his victory.

Right before eleven, Paul Denton walked into the gymnasium. He paused in the doorway, scanning the crowd. He was disappointed; he'd hoped there would be more people. The sophomore stood on his one side and the pre-law student on the other. The redhead, seeing Sully at the front of the gym, discreetly moved away from Paul as though she had come in alone.

A few feet away from Becky, two women stood against the wooden wall of folded bleachers. The taller one had dark, serious eyes. She was watching Paul. "There's Justine's husband," she said quietly.

The shorter woman glanced at Paul and nodded. "Justine's not coming, is she?"

"No, she's at work. But wait'll you meet her, she's fine people."

Paul saw the two watching him but he didn't acknowledge them. He walked to the front of the gym, greeting several people on the way, and began to tell Sully about some last minute changes.

At eleven the teach-in began. Paul placed his hands on the podium, his eyes moving across the audience, and began to speak. His popularity at political rallies was due to his knowledge of politics and his showmanship. He was a spellbinder. His voice was urgent, his eyes visionary, and his hands expressive, moving always to emphasize a point. The crowd watched him, some intrigued by what he said, others enjoying the show.

"Don't accept the way things are here and now as the natural order of life," he was saying. "The only thing it's natural to is the capitalist system, and the capitalist system was designed for the purpose of making money, not for the betterment of life. And if you want a better life, you've got to do something to change things!"

"Right on!" several voices shouted in response.

The slang phrase was unfamiliar to Becky, and she turned to the man beside her. "What?"

He looked at her.

"What did he say?"

"Right on."

"Right on what?"

"Right on, man," he sneered, "just right on."

"Oh, right on," she said as if she'd known all along what he meant.

Paul was speaking: "And that's what the Vietnamese people are trying to do: they're struggling against a system that will exploit their labor, steal their lands, and in the end destroy them. The ruling class of the United States is not interested in bettering the lives of the Vietnamese people. It's interested only in one thing: profit. It's interested in the tin, the copper, the oil, the bauxite in South East Asia, just as it's interested in the natural resources all over the world, resources that belong to the peoples of this earth but are controlled by the ruling class of the United States and other imperialist countries. But it will not continue this way much longer."

Paul paused and a long haired man from the crowd raised his fist and yelled: "Right on!" There was some agreement from the more radical in the crowd.

The woman with the dark eyes leaned over and whispered: "In two years Tony the Tiger'll be saying 'Right on.' You know?"

The other nodded in agreement. "Sure. But the question is: Will the Jolly Green Giant be saying 'Off the Pig'?"

She smiled and listened to Paul.

"The United States is waging an all-out war against the people of Vietnam, using the most sophisticated weaponry known to man. In March of 1969 the total bombardment in Vietnam and Laos reached 130,000 tons a month. Nearly two Hiroshimas a week. Defoliation has been carried out over an area the size of Massachusetts. The U.S. knows, and the world knows, that Vietnam is in fact the "theater of the Pacific." All the struggling Third World countries will see the might of U.S. imperialism, just as the world saw its might when the U.S. dropped atomic bombs on Hiroshima and Nagasaki in 1945, bombs that were unnecessary because Japan had already surrendered, bombs that established the United States as the foremost imperialistic power of the post-war era."

He paused to wipe moisture from his forehead and

when he spoke again his voice was low, growing toward a climaxing shout: "But the Vietnamese will not be defeated. For every man who is killed, there is one man to rebuild a bombed road. Two men to rebuild a destroyed hospital! Three men to rebuild a demolished school—" He hesitated, holding his listeners suspended on the peak of his words, about to say: 'And four men to fight!'

The dark-eyed woman smiled. "I wonder what happened to all the Vietnamese women. They must've gone on vacation." She spoke quietly, almost in a whisper. But in Paul's dramatic pause the room was silent and her voice carried.

Those within earshot turned, and others farther away saw the movements and craned their necks, whispering: "What is it, what happened."

Somebody snickered, and the woman was conscious that she was a target. She put her hands in her pockets, hunching her shoulders as if to ward off blows.

"Oh save us, it must be fem lib come to take over the university!" a man near the podium shrieked in falsetto. There was scattered laughter.

"I'll liberate you, baby!" another man called. The one next to him said something under his breath and there was the deep sound of male laughter.

Becky laughed. She tried to exchange amused smiles with the man beside her but couldn't catch his eye.

The woman opened her mouth to state exactly what she thought of his liberation, but Paul held up his hand for silence and said: "No, it's true. My wife Justine is in women's liberation and I understand that *every* man has to struggle with his sexism."

He directed his comment to the woman, smiling magnanimously, but when she didn't smile back gratefully, he flushed and spoke to the crowd in general: "Women's role in ending the war is very important. As a matter of fact there's a women's liberation group on campus, one of whose main purposes is to discuss the war. It just began meeting recently and if anybody's interested, she should check the. . ." He paused uncomfortably because he thought he sounded like a commercial, then continued: ". . . the campus newspaper for information." That done with, he cleared his throat and resumed his speech.

When Paul was finished, David Sully got up to speak. The students liked him and they clapped enthusiastically. He pretended not to notice: his attention could not be diverted from the serious matter of the war. He frowned, stretched his arms out, gripped the edge of the podium and began. Becky was enthralled. Her attention danced on his words, while out of the corner of her eye she watched the dark-eyed woman; she felt protective, ready to defend him against her.

When David was in the midst of his speech, Becky happened to glance at Bryce. He was staring across the room at the man who'd looked into David's office that day in September. He was standing under the exit sign, arms folded across his chest, watching David.

David slapped his hand on the podium for emphasis, and continued: "Everyone here in this room is against the Vietnam war. We are all against it. Everyone here knows that the United States is nothing but. . ."

At this, the man raised his eyebrows: he did not want to be associated with this "everyone." But he didn't care if his shoes got a little dirty, as long as he could stand around and watch Sully dig his own grave.

After Sully finished, the gym darkened for the News-reel film. On the portable screen, the projector cast images

46

of war-ravaged North Vietnam, looking from the air like a deeply pock-marked face. But the people fought to survive, building their factories underground, and setting concrete tubes in city streets to provide shelter against attack. The women worked alongside the men or in groups together, running from the rice fields to their anti-aircraft guns when U.S. planes attacked.

One woman in particular caught Becky's eye. She was standing in a ditch, passing blocks of mud they were using to rebuild a road. Her black pants were rolled up over her knees. Seeing the camera focused on her, she smiled shyly. A small scar was etched across her cheekbone. As she passed on the block of mud, she laughed outloud and spoke to the woman beside her, who laughed with her. She looked back into the camera, her confidence in herself overcoming her shyness at being filmed, and she smiled broadly. Then she returned to work.

Becky kept seeing that woman: her eyes, her smile, her mud-coated hands. She saw her face in the back of her mind, even after the movie ended and the gym lit up.

The teach-in was over. Students on the floor got up, some to leave, others to mill around the podium. Becky headed toward David but saw him already occupied, explaining something to the redhead. Her back was to Becky but from the way she stood, head slightly tilted and hands clasped behind her back, Becky could tell she was listening intently. Another woman stood at David's side. Becky caught only a fleeting glimpse before someone blocked her view, but that glimpse was enough to tell her that the woman was Elizabeth. The expression on her face gave it away: she was trying to be patient and look interested in what David was saying, but underneath was that terrible anxiety because he was talking to the redhead and not to her.

Her expression made Becky want to escape, but she was also curious. She stood there undecided, shifting her weight from one foot to the other.

She felt a hand on her shoulder and turned to find Bryce staring down at her. "Hello there," he said, his lips curved into a half smile.

"Bryce." She returned his half smile; they were fellow travellers in a cynical adventure. However, she felt uneasy flirting with him: her female parts being temporarily out of order, the flirtation could come to nothing.

Just then the two women who had stood against the bleachers passed by. Becky nodded towards them and said to Bryce: "What'd you think of the show?"

He was looking across the room. She waited a few seconds and asked: "You going canvassing?"

He shrugged, clearly disinterested. "I will if Pritchard does." He looked back across the room. She turned and saw the man under the exit sign. "I'll tell you though. . ." Bryce shook his head. "I can't figure out what Pritchard's doing here. He's a die-hard liberal, and anti-war rallies aren't quite the in thing. But I'm sure he's got his reasons. Guys like Pritchard have very good reasons for everything they do. If that bastard couldn't think of a good reason for shitting, he'd stop doing it."

Pritchard walked to the door.

"Aha, my prey is escaping," Bryce said, molding his face into a mask of youthful sincerity and humble respect.

"Don't you think you're putting it on a little heavy?" she asked him.

He winked slyly, including her in the joke of his plastic zeal. "I know when I've got a good thing going. Catch you later." He lifted his hand in a lazy good-bye, and was off.

That evening, Becky went out to canvass her neighbors

concerning their attitudes to the Vietnam war, asking the sympathetic to write protest postcards to President Nixon.

Of the twelve houses where people were willing to talk to her, only three were definitely against the war, and of these three, two would not sign postcards: they were afraid of getting involved.

As she walked from house to house, she occasionally thought of the movie she had seen, and the young woman's face. But after a time the images faded.

In the last house she canvassed, a woman lived alone in a tiny upstairs apartment. She invited Becky in and offered her milk and oatmeal cookies. The living room was like a museum, crammed full of photographs, souveniers and nick-nacks. In the background the television was tuned to Peyton Place. The woman sat down next to Becky on a doily covered sofa, and showed her pictures of her daughter in Arizona and the three grand-children she had never met. Her flowery soft smell was like delicate sachets of rose petals tucked neatly in a dresser drawer, and made Becky sad. While she ate the oatmeal cookies she watched tiny particles of dust floating in the last ray of sunset that beamed across the room, only half listening to the woman talk, becoming confused after awhile about whether she was talking about her daughter in Arizona or a character on Peyton Place. In exchange, the woman half listened as Becky talked about Vietnam. She wrote three postcards because she thought Becky "was such a nice girl to go around visiting lonely people about the war."

Becky went home, on the way dropping the postcards in the mailbox. Later that evening Bryce called and asked her out for the following Saturday. She imagined telling him about the day's canvassing adventures; and in creating a more amusing story, the characters were transformed.

The last woman became an evil witch who lured tender young maidens into her house with milk and oatmeal cookies.

Undressing for bed, she remembered what the doctor had said about abstaining from sex. She didn't know what Bryce expected. She thought of calling him and cancelling the date, but was afraid that if she did, he would never ask again.

The following Friday, two women rode home from work together. As the bus drove through the city, their bodies swayed in silent unison but did not touch. Justine gazed out the window and listened to the high school girls behind him. She and Lynne had been like that once: gossiping, conspiring, confiding.

When Lynne got her the file clerk job at the brokerage last spring, Justine was grateful. Though she knew that what had passed could in no way be revived, she thought the offer of the job was at least an offer of truce. But she came to the conclusion that the most obvious reason Lynne wanted her there was for the few times a day she could stroll by, toss papers on Justine's desk, and say: "Here, file this." Yet Lynne still sat beside her to and from work, unable to renounce the last traces of their friendship.

As the bus pulled up to the curb, Justine felt Lynne's hand on her arm.

"Hey listen, Swan, why don't we—" The diamond on Lynne's finger caught the light. She looked down at it and removed her hand.

"What were you going to say?" Justine asked.

"Never mind. It's not important."

Once more they were silent. When the bus neared Lynne's stop, she made her way to the exit. The light above the door blinked on, and Lynne turned. Her happy bride's smile was forced; her eyes were tinged with a gleam that was partly sad and partly spiteful.

By the time the bus reached the university section of town twenty minutes later, the sky was dark with the approaching storm. Justine stepped into the crunch of fallen leaves and hurried home.

As soon as she unlocked the front door, she could tell the house was empty. "Paul?" she called, and no one answered. Without taking off her coat, she walked across the living room to the dining area near the kitchenette and picked up the note on the small round table. It read: "J: Have late meeting. Will be home 11—P."

The thought crossed her mind briefly, as it did everytime she read one of Paul's notes, that he was unromantic. When they were first married, Justine had signed her notes to him with "Love" and added several X's and O's. But this and other habits of hers made him smile sadly and say: "Tina, you're such a romantic." He thought being romantic was the result of her youth or deficient education. He knew the ways of the brutal world better than she, and could not afford such frivolity.

She put down the note and walked to the 24-hour store, returning with a large bottle of Coke. As she closed the door it began to rain. She poured a glass and drank deeply.

Justine's appearance was large, soft, fair. When she and Lynne were in high school they'd given each other pet names, Lynne becoming "Ostrich," or "Ossie" for short, and Justine "Swan." Their friendship had been full of private jokes and code words, all of which they now censored from their conversations. Lynne could even keep her eyes unknowing. For Justine this was a more conscious effort, but a necessary one. A flicker of memory in Justine's eyes, and Lynne's manner became tight and malicious. Today Lynne had slipped, and Justine was glad they wouldn't see each other until Monday. Perhaps by then, things would again be safe.

Justine reminded Paul of sunshine. When he first saw her in class that night a year ago, he was charmed by her hesitancy when she asked him about philosophy, and by her gray eyes that expressed something she didn't voice. She'd sat in the back of the room and he hadn't been able to stop looking at her. He'd expected her to be short and cuddly, and was shocked to find that she was as tall as he. In fact she appeared taller because of the way she carried herself. He didn't ask her out for almost a month. There was something in her eyes that made him want her, but something in her manner that made him afraid to try.

She'd worn her hair school-girl style then, long and trailing down her back. Right after their spring marriage she cut it. Paul was opposed to the cut, but she told him that if he liked long hair so much, he should be her guest and grow his own. Paul said it was her new hair style that made her look older than her twenty-one years. Her response to this comment was a silent shrug.

As she finished the soda, the phone rang. "Hello?"

"Justine?"

"Hiya Terry. What's new."

"Nothing much. How about you."

"I'm OK. Hey, what're you doing tonight, you want to do something?" Terry didn't answer and Justine added: "Paul's got some kind of meeting."

Terry was about to say: On Friday night? but stopped herself in time and said: "Sure. You want to go to a show?"

Justine calculated: the next show would start at nine, not get out until ten thirty or eleven. If Paul were already home, he'd ask questions. Or if she and Terry returned at the same time as Paul, they might meet in front of the apartment. Paul had never liked her, and since Wednesday's teach-in he liked her even less.

At the time of the incident it hadn't seemed important, but in the subsequent hours he'd become indignant that Terry criticized him in public, especially when Sully reminded him of it twice. He'd come home late Wednesday night. Justine sat in bed with a magazine lying unread in her lap while Paul paced around the bedroom.

"Me! Of all people. The only man around here who's really struggling with his sexism! I make one little slip and she jumps on me."

"Paul, she didn't mean for anybody to hear what she said."

He stopped pacing. "When did you talk to her."

"She called awhile ago."

"Oh, so she had to tell you her side of it first, right? I don't know what you find to talk about with her. What'd she do, tell you all about the glories of her new-found celibacy?"

Not wanting to chance a similar scene tonight, she suggested that Terry come to visit, adding apologetically that Paul would be back by eleven.

"Don't worry, I'll make my exit by then. How 'bout if I pick up a pizza on my way over."

"Sounds good. But wait. I have to make Paul's supper anyway, so..."

Terry said nothing.

"Would you like a gold engraved invitation? I'm making tuna noodle casserole."

Terry cleared her throat. "Oh. Well, um... I just remembered I have this extremely urgent appointment with um..."

Justine laughed. "You jerk. All right, picky, go ahead and starve, see if I care."

When they hung up, Justine changed from her work clothes into faded jeans and a T-shirt, put on an apron and indifferently threw together the makings of the casserole. She hated tuna fish but Paul had been asking her to make the dish for weeks. The one time she tried to teach him how to cook it, he'd burned the noodles. While the casserole cooked, she straightened the apartment. Paul often said he didn't mind a mess, and told her not to bother. She replied that the apartment would look like a home if it was the last thing she did.

As it was, the living room looked like an office. Books were stuffed into the two long bookcases made of bricks and boards, and stacked on the orange crate coffee table. Paul's desk stood near the doorway, piled with scraps of papers and three huge notebooks, research for the book he hoped to write someday. A hill of *New York Times* took up one corner and although Justine had covered it with a bright piece of flowered material, it looked like an ominous, towering blob. She wanted to pack the papers away, for Paul rarely looked at them, but he wanted them left out just in case. Words covered the walls: colorful posters of revolutionary sayings, and over Paul's desk, a mass of torn newspaper clippings stuck to a cork bulletin board.

Only one thing made a difference: the stereo components which were Justine's pride and joy. The whole system had been a wedding gift from her brother Bill: he'd sold it to her for $250. She'd wanted to buy a car but she couldn't pass up a bargain like that. The whole set-up was worth over $1,000 and Bill could have easily sold it for $500.

"You're sure now," she'd said. "I don't want you to change your mind in two months and want it back."

"Yeah, I'm sure, I'm sure. You want it or not, make up your mind."

Delighted that he really meant it, she went to hug him. But Bill was always embarassed by affection or gratitude and he brushed her away and said gruffly: "Go on, get outta here, I'm only doing it so you don't have to listen to *him* all the time."

When she married Paul and moved into his apartment, she'd wanted to put the stereo in the bedroom. She replaced the mattress on the floor and orange crate nightstand with an early American bedroom set, a wedding gift from her father. The bedroom was the only room in which she felt at home. But she thought that it wouldn't be right to put the stereo there: all her things in one room and all his in the other. It was a marriage, and she had to try to make herself at home in his space and he in hers. So she put the stereo in the living room.

By the time Terry arrived, Justine was sitting on the

floor listening to a tape she'd recorded the night before. Terry carried a grocery bag into the kitchen and put it on the counter while she hung her damp jacket over a chair. She removed a six-pack of beer from the bag and separated the cans, fitting three into the frost covered freezer. "Man, does this need defrosting."

"Don't remind me."

"Yeah, but if you put it off much longer, you won't be able to shut the door. You want some more Coke?"

"No thanks, I got enough."

Terry looked at her but said nothing. A week ago she might have made a sarcastic comment about the Coke and Paul's absence, but since the teach-in she was careful what she said. A week ago Justine would have laughed and said: Yeah, the cat's away so the mouse can have her Coke, but now she kept silent.

Terry sat down near Justine on the uncomfortable couch. Paul had made it from a mattress, a door and six concrete blocks. He was so proud of it that Justine didn't have the heart to tell him how she hated it.

"How was your casserole," Terry asked.

"None of your business."

"Oh no, I can see it all now, you're going to hold that casserole over me for the rest of my life. If you want to know the truth, I had to eat at my folks."

"Yeah, yeah, tell me another one."

Terry laughed and shook her head.

"How are they."

"They're OK. But my pop's driving my mom crazy. Now that he has to sit around doing nothing all day, he takes it out on her. And she takes it out on me. She was on my back the whole time I was there."

"About what, the same thing?"

"You guessed it. She wants me to either get married or move back home. She says why should I spend money on my own place when I can live at home for free."

"Stay where you are. You're lucky you found such a cheap place."

"I know. If I was at home, we'd all end up in the nut house. But I don't know how much longer I can swing it, money's getting tight. But what're you going to do. that's life, right? Today Franklin told me he wants me to work dinner shift instead of breakfast, the bastard. I told him I already planned my whole class schedule around that goddamned job. . . I'd like to tell him to take that diner and shove it." She sighed. "How's things with you."

"OK. Guess what," she said, trying to sound happy. "Bill and Lynne finally decided. They're getting married in February." 'She lit a cigarette. After she snapped the lighter shut, she held it in her hand, rubbing her fingers over the scratches, the dent on the bottom. and the letters engraved on one side that read: Babe Haney. The lighter was worn but the letters were still clear, and Justine ran her fingers over the name slowly, like a blind person reading something loved and familiar. "February fourteenth," she added.

"Valentine's Day, how nice. They've been going together a couple of years, haven't they."

"Mm-hmm. They started dating when we were seniors. But they knew each other before that, Lynne moved down the block when we were freshmen. . ."

"Hey, did Bill get laid off?"

"Yeah. He went back to his 'other job.' "

"He did? Hey, do me a favor: tell him I'm looking for a cheap tv. Nothing fancy, you know. as long as it works."

"Sure, I'll tell him."

"I hope he's careful."

"Bill? He never had any trouble before."

"How's Lynne feel about it."

"How do you think she feels. But what can she do."

"She can tell him to quit doing that shit."

"Sure, that'd be the day. He'd tell her to mind her own business. Listen, in that marriage there's going to be one boss and that's him. I'd never marry a guy like that, being his sister was bad enough. Lynne is nuts. But she made her bed, so now she's got to lie in it."

"Yeah, well I'd rather lie in it alone than with somebody who's trying to run my life."

"Sure, but she's not like that." Justine stood up. "The rain stopped. Let's go outside." She removed the Sunday *Times* from the stack of newspapers, and spread it on the top of the concrete steps. The cool air smelled of wet leaves; black clouds moved rapidly across the sky. Surrounding them was a complex of buildings for university couples: two story four apartment units.

When she first moved in, Justine often sat on the steps in the evening. It was not like her old neighborhood where people sat on the front stoop on warm spring evenings, hot summer nights, and cool nights like this, catching the last of being outside before winter set in. Few children played on the lawn and no old people gathered to talk. She muffled her longing for her home and tried to get Paul to sit with her. But he was always too busy and she ended up sitting alone, staring at the movements of the leaves and the clouds, the passing cars, or an ant making its way across the concrete, carrying a crumb or the body of a dead comrade.

She didn't like sitting alone: she thought too much of the past. She was happy that Terry was here tonight. She looked at her friend and smiled. "Nice out here, isn't it."

Terry nodded and looked up at the sky. She was tall and lanky, and her long slender fingers sometimes caused people to remark that she should play the piano. But she didn't need instruments: filled with vibrant energy, she seemed always on the verge of her own music. It was in her body and her smile, but most of all in her eyes. She was twenty-one, a junior in nursing school, but her appearance hadn't changed much since she played girl's basketball in high school. She still pulled her long straight brown hair back with a rubber band, and wore jeans, sweaters and sneakers. All of this dismayed her mother. When speaking to her daughter, Mrs. Devlin's frequent theme was: "How do you ever expect to find a husband when you. . ." It was one reason Terry had left her family's home three years before. The other reason her parents didn't know and would probably never know. Her father had a bad heart; telling them would do no good.

Suddenly she grimaced. "Oh pain. Damn, I got my period today. What a drag. It's so heavy lately, I can't stand it. I'm going broke, buying those damned Tampax."

"I know," Justine replied. "Forty-five cents for a box of ten, what a rip-off."

"And what a drag. Five days and then two days spotting. That's a week. A whole goddamned week. Then for three weeks I'm free, everything's cool, and by the end of the third week I forgot all about it, I think I'll never get it again, you know?"

Justine nodded and laughed, drawing her knees up to her chin and putting her arms around her legs.

Terry continued: "And then one day, poof! Hello, remember me? And the whole scene starts all over again."

"Nah, not me. Mine doesn't sneak up on me like that.

I know it's coming a week before. I'm swollen out like a balloon, and my insides feel like they're going to drop out."

"Yeah, I get that the first day. Like right now. Know that thing about the power of positive thinking? That's what I do. When it's over, I think: 'Well, that's the end of that.' Like it's never going to happen again. I try to convince myself that some miracle is going to happen and I'll get my period once a year. But I guess deep down inside I don't really believe it'll work. Deep down inside. . . I know. . ." She leaned back and looked up at the sky. "Man, I don't know why you did this to me, what did I ever do to you. . ."

"Uh-oh, you better watch out, remember the last time you talked to Him like that: you were staying in that cellar apartment and it flooded?"

Terry pretended annoyance that she should mention the flooded cellar, looked up at the sky and said with bravado: "Oh yeah? Just try it, go ahead, try it." Then she held her hand to her mouth and said in a stage whisper: "I'm only kidding, I didn't mean it, honest, I didn't mean it."

Justine laughed. "You're terrible. If your mom could hear you she'd have a fit."

"Are you kidding? She'd kill me."

"You better be careful," Justine warned, "you'll go straight to hell when you die, no detours, nothing, just straight to hell, one way. And you'll be standing there with your 'power of positive thinking,' you'll be going, 'No, I'm not here, I'm in heaven,' and meanwhile you're gonna be burning. . . Man! are you gonna burn. . ."

"Hey, as long as I have a package of marshmallows, I won't sweat it."

"Oh you'll sweat all right, you better believe you'll sweat."

"Shut up. I'll probably have nightmares all night long now."

They sat there talking, but after awhile the wind blew up and several drops of rain fell on them. "Uh-oh," Justine said ominously, "He heard." They looked at each other and burst out laughing.

Terry brushed a long strand of hair back behind her ear, looked up at the sky and said: "You have no sense of humor, you really don't. Come on, let's go in before we get struck by lightning."

Justine looked up at the sky. "I don't even know her. Honest. I never saw her before in my life. She walked over and sat down, what could I do?"

"Some friend you are. Thanks alot."

"Listen, we stopped being friends the minute you made fun of my tuna noodle casserole, so don't expect any favors from me. When you're drowning, I'm going to float by on my nice warm Ark and laugh right in your face."

They returned to the living room. As Justine moved across the room, Terry watched her. "You know, your face looks puffy. Are you putting on weight or do you have your period."

Justine touched her face in a smoothing motion to press down the swelling. "Neither."

"You look terrible."

"Thanks."

"What's the matter with you, are you sick?"

Justine shrugged evasively. "I don't know. Maybe my period's late."

"How late," Terry demanded.

"I'm not sure. Maybe a month."

"A month!"

The phone rang, and as Justine listened to the message, Terry watched her. Though they had known each other only a year, they considered themselves best friends. Terry was outwardly more aggressive, yet she felt that Justine was stronger, and she looked up to her. But in the subject of pregnancy, she was the wiser and Justine knew it. Terry had told her all about that year in Boston.

The moment Justine hung up the phone, Terry said: "What the hell is wrong with you! That's nothing to play with." Then she imitated Justine's unconcerned tone: " 'I'm not sure, maybe a month.' A month! If you want to have a baby, go ahead, but don't be so. . ."

Justine slumped on the couch, her arms folded across her chest, and stared resentfully at the floor. "I know what I'm doing," she mumbled unsurely.

"Oh yeah, you know what you're doing, just like I knew what I was doing. Hey, this is something you have to think about very carefully, you can't just bop along waiting for it to go away. Because it won't."

Justine blushed. "Forget about it, will you? I can't be pregnant, it would ruin everything. I'd have to quit my job, and no way could we live on Paul's fellowship, we'd starve. So don't worry about it."

"Well somebody's got to if you won't."

Justine stared at her coldly. "Will you forget about it? Did you have a good time with Maggie the other day?"

"Oh all right. But I'm telling you—" She shrugged, giving in. "Yeah, pretty good. After the teach-in we went to the Cavern. There was a whole drama going on." She smiled, warming to the more comfortable climate of gossip. "Sully was sitting there with this girl, she had these long red braids halfway down her back. . . beautiful hair, really

62

healthy. . . and she's sitting there like Sully is Tarzan or somebody, and in walks Elizabeth."

"Oh no. He doing a thing with her?"

"The redhead? Who knows. He sure as hell acts it, you should've seen him, he almost choked on his coffee when Elizabeth walked in, but he wouldn't say hello to her. I wouldn't put up with that shit. He's got her so snowed with his routine about 'non-monogamous relationships. . .' It's incredible, he's going to smash the nuclear family all by himself, right?"

"You know. . . Paul was telling me that some redhead in his class has a crush on him. I wonder if it's the same one."

"Could be. Maybe she's a political groupie."

"Poor Elizabeth. What did she do."

"Oh, she huffed around the Cavern pretending they weren't there. I called her over and she sat with me and Maggie, and the whole time she kept staring at Sully out of the corner of her eye. And meanwhile she's telling me all about this long discussion she had with him. She was handing me her usual line, you know the one: 'I'm putting so much energy into making him struggle with his chauvinism. . .' "

"So what did you say."

"I told her I don't know why she wastes her time on men, they're all stupid anyway. She's sitting there telling me something that I understand immediately but Sully wouldn't understand if he lived to be a hundred."

Justine laughed gleefully. "And she just smiled at you like you didn't understand anything, right?"

"You got it."

Justine kept peace with Paul's friends by keeping her silence, but she vicariously enjoyed Terry's outspokenness. "They came over to dinner last night," she complained.

"Sully and Elizabeth?"

"Yeah, and Susan and George."

"All four of them? You poor baby. . ."

"You're telling me. That Susan gives me a pain, she thinks she knows everything. I'm getting tired of her bullshit."

"Well, you'd better get used to it since you're going to Cuba with her. Gee Justine, you'll live in the same tent with her and everything. You'll be roomies—how super!"

"You're a riot. . . I'm not worried, me and Paul will never get picked to go. But could you imagine us sneaking off to the cane fields to make love, and then him going back to the boys' tent and me going back to the girls'? Living in a tent with a bunch of strangers, how gross. . . And he has the nerve to say *I'm* romantic. . ."

They continued talking until ten thirty when Justine began to fidget. Finally she said: "Hey pal, I hate to kick you out. . ."

"I know. He's still mad at me for what I said at the teach-in, right?"

"He'll get over it."

"Sure," Terry said doubtfully. "I guess so. You going to tell him I was here?"

"Not if I can help it."

"Then I better take the rest of the beer since he knows you don't drink."

After Terry left, Justine got into her pajamas, carried the portable television into the bedroom and at eleven thirty lay down to watch *Splendor in the Grass*. Paul came home at midnight, made himself a salad, and ate supper. She heard his chair scrape, and the cabinet door under the sink open. She tensed.

Sure enough, Paul appeared in the doorway holding the

64

empty Coke bottle aloft. He shook his head as if to say: And after all I told you. . . But he was smiling, glad of the opportunity to tell her again. "Tina, you know what this stuff does to your stomach. Do you know that if you stand a spoon up in a glass of Coke—"

"I know, I know, it rots it down to nothing, and if it does that to a spoon, think of what it'll do to my stomach." He frowned. "I'm sorry Paul, but I wish you'd get off my back about this stuff. It's my stomach, not yours. And Paul, don't call me that name anymore, please. I hate it. I'm getting so tired of asking you. . ."

Without a word, he turned and dropped the bottle noisily in the garbage. She heard the water running, and the sound of dishes being stacked in the drain. He took a shower, changed into his pajamas, lay down beside her and opened a book.

"I did my dishes," he said.

She nodded, her eyes on the screen.

He turned a page. "I said, 'I did my dishes.' "

She thought: 'What do you want, a medal?' but said: "Thanks, Paul."

"It's OK. You have a nice day?"

"What? Oh. Yeah, sure."

"How'd things go at work."

"Same as ever."

"What'd you do tonight."

"Not much."

"Stay home alone?"

"Oh Paul, before I forget, I wanted to tell you that Sully called."

"Figures. What does he want me to do now."

"He said that the bus company called, the one that was supposed to take the students down to Washington for the demonstration next month?. . . and they cancelled. Sully was all upset, as usual, and he said you should take care of it and try to find another bus company."

"I'll have to call tomorrow morning." He paused, letting his eyes wander onto the screen. "Did you watch tv?"

"What? When."

He looked at her. "Tonight."

"No, there wasn't anything on earlier. Oh, and one of your students called, Mark Weinstein, I think he said, and he said to remind you about lunch tomorrow."

"Oh yeah. Mark. What did you do before."

She pulled her eyes from the screen with effort, and said with annoyance: "Before what?"

He shook his head in disbelief. "Tina, sometimes you're such a scatterbrain I can't believe it. Your mind goes off in twenty directions at once. I'm asking you a simple question and you can't even concentrate enough to answer me. What did you do all night."

The movie was interrupted for a commercial, and Justine said: "Come on, Paul, give me a break. Why is it that it's perfectly all right for you to talk when I'm trying to watch tv, but whenever you're reading and I interrupt, you freak out."

He made a gesture of impatience, for the answer was obvious to him. It was not obvious to Justine, and she waited.

He said: "Tell me you don't understand the qualitative difference between the trash you watch on the tube and the things I read."

"That's not the point."

"It most certainly is the point."

"You mean if I was reading one of your books you wouldn't interrupt?"

"No. I wouldn't."

The commercial was over and she merely shrugged, knowing that the argument would end up with her complaint that he spent so much time at meetings and then came home expecting all of her attention. She didn't want to miss any of the movie, but neither did she want him to have the last word, and fixing her attention on the television, she mumbled: "Then you're an idiot."

He laughed outloud, shaking his head in amusement. and continued reading.

When the movie ended, a few tears rolled down Justine's face. Paul sat beside her, smiling but making no comment. After she wiped her eyes and turned off the television. he teased: "That shit is going to rot your brain."

She got into bed. "You're such a goddamned nag. Coke'll rot my stomach, tv'll rot my brain. . . I wish I could rot away in peace instead of being nagged to death by you."

He closed his book and turned off the reading lamp.

She snuggled into his arms. "You don't know a good movie when you see it. I don't know why I ever married you, you're such a dummy."

"Me!"

"Yeah. And not only that. . ." She whispered into his ear: "You're getting bald."

He laughed outloud. "That's funny coming from you, fatty." He tickled her.

"Paul, cut it out! I'm not fat. Am I?"

"When's the last time you looked in the mirror, tubby."

They smiled at each other, kissed, and made love. Afterwards, Paul kissed her good-night and fell asleep.

Outside, the rain had stopped. The only sound was the measured ticking of the clock. Justine looked off into the darkness, her body relaxed in the soft folds of the night. She lit a cigarette and found her fingers tracing, once again, the familiar letters on the lighter. Cigarette smoke drifted up in lazy layers before her. She closed her eyes and began to sing quietly, almost in a whisper: "Amazing grace, how sweet the sound, that saved a wretch like me. I once was lost but now I'm found, was blind but now I see. . ."

It was Babe's favorite song. She sang it often, as well as the others she loved so much: "Brother, Can You Spare a Dime," "Toot-Toot-Tootsie," "The Prisoner's Song." That one was Justine's favorite. When Babe sang it in her clear high voice, Justine always got a lump in her throat, and she imagined her mother as an angel, flying free over a tall brick wall: "Oh I wish I had wings of an angel. . . Over these pri-son walls I would fly. . . I would fly to the arms of my dar-ling. . . And ne-ever more I would cry." Then there was the song that always made Aunt Connie laugh: "I've been married and married and often I've sighed, I'm never a bridesmaid, I'm always the bride. I never divorced them, I hadn't the heart. Yet remember these sweet words: 'till death do us part."

'Till death do us part. Now that Babe was gone, Justine remembered things she hadn't thought of in years. She wished that Paul had gotten a chance to know Babe before she got sick, because there was no one with whom she could share the memories, no one to whom she could say: Hey, do you remember the time. . . In the months that Paul knew Babe, she had changed drastically. She'd lost her sense of humor; the pain made her irritable.

Justine had met Paul in the fall of 1968, when she attended his Introduction to Philosophy course. She was taking one night course a semester. She calculated it would be sixteen years before she finished college, but hoped the individual courses would help her find a better job. Paul's course was the third she'd taken, and she continued to waitress at Howard Johnson's, just as she had in high school. The only difference was that now she worked full-time. She'd met Terry in Paul's class; they sat together in back of the room and complained about their respective jobs. But Justine soon stopped complaining, for she became fascinated by Paul.

To her, Paul was like someone in a dream: brilliant, thoughtful, considerate, sensitive, and so intense about his beliefs that he charged her with excitement. When in October he asked her out, she couldn't quite believe it. She was shy with him, thrilled and awkward. It reinforced his opinion that she was innocent and untouched, like fresh clay ready to be molded.

Her family didn't care for him. Before that first date she had mentioned her philosophy professor at night school. They expected a distinguished man who wore a suit and smoked a pipe. Paul sported a beard and wore a sweater with a hole in the elbow. Her father said later that he looked like a bum and if she got mixed up with him she'd end up supporting him. Babe was already preoccupied with what the doctor had diagnosed as ulcers.

Bill, Jr. didn't care for Paul either. At first she and Paul had doubled with Bill and Lynne, but the two men did not get along. "It's not that I don't like him," Bill said stubbornly, "he's just not for you."

Paul was gracious to double date with Bill and Lynne but Justine felt that he was doing her a favor. She could see that Bill made him uneasy, and Lynne didn't exist for him. He considered being with her friends a chore, not as important as the time they spent with his friends.

Bill began to argue with her: a friend of his wanted to go out with her. But by then she and Paul were sleeping together, and casual dating was out.

Babe had been ill for a long time; it was clear to all of them that whatever she had was more serious than ulcers. It was only in January that the doctor got around to admitting he might be wrong, and put Babe in the hospital for an exploratory operation. The cancer was everywhere. It was too late to do anything, the doctor said, but close her up and let it go. She died in mid-January.

With Babe gone everything changed. Her father had loved Babe and depended on her. Now his life had no center. He started drinking heavily. In the house Justine tried to hold things together but he was sullen and critical, and Justine bore the brunt of his anger since Bill, Jr. was rarely at home. She felt sorry for her father, but more than that she was angry. "I was on my feet all day," she'd complain to Paul, "and after work I went shopping for groceries, and then went home and made dinner and cleaned up the house and threw in a load of clothes. And then I took the Goddamned bus to class, and the minute I walk back in the door, dog-tired, he has the nerve to ask me if I got a ride home with *you!*"

Paul was the only one Justine could turn to. She and Lynne had grown apart. Terry tried to sympathize, but Justine didn't want to confide: she had no faith in "friends" anymore. She began to think it was time to settle down.

In April Bill proposed to Lynne. They planned to be married the following year.

Paul had already asked her to live with him. She was hesitant: someplace else she wouldn't care, but not right here in town. She said no. "Well," he said, "we could get married if you want. Everybody knows a marriage license is just a piece of paper."

Paul took her to meet his parents. For a long time they had hoped he would put aside his radical ways and marry someone of their own class, a "nice" girl, perhaps the daughter of one of their friends. Justine was not their kind. Mrs. Denton took Paul aside to interrogate him. and later conferred with her husband in the kitchen. Justine and Paul were eating on the patio and could hear the urgency in their hushed tones. When Justine took a walk in the back yard, Mrs. Denton confronted her son.

"But Paul, she's Polish!" she blurted.

Mr. Denton, always the optimist said: "Only on her father's side."

To Justine they were cold, silently disapproving. They almost changed her mind about Paul.

Against both families' wishes, Justine and Paul were married. When she was with him she felt swept away. His friends, the university, it was a different world, and when the ride came around she grabbed the ring only to wake and find that she wore it on her finger. and it wasn't escape at all.

She continued doing housework, but in Paul's house instead of her father's. She took the file clerk job. Paul hadn't liked her being a waitress even though she made less money now. In September she did not register for her night class: finishing college seemed an impractical and unnecessary goal. One important difference in her life was that they lived out by the University, and she rarely saw her family. But Paul was her husband: his future and his life were hers.

It was difficult. She was a stranger in his world. It was as if she had moved to a foreign country and had to learn a new language and a new way to act. His friends often didn't understand her. When she was being serious they laughed, and when she joked they never laughed, assuming she was not witty or clever enough to have a sense of humor. As time went by she talked with them less and less.

The one way she and Paul had no trouble communicating was through sex. Paul had never met anyone like Justine. She talked freely when they made love and it excited him into a frenzy of passion. As for Justine, she always enjoyed sex because she always got what she wanted. She regulated his passion by her flow of words. She was tremendously inventive.

Paul knew that she'd had one other lover before she met him, and he told her it didn't matter. He was proud of his open-minded attitude about sex. He said he didn't want to know about a lover in her past, and believed he was generous to let her keep her privacy. In reality he was jealous, and preferred to pretend that before she knew him she had no other lover, no other life.

Once in a moment of intimacy she thought of telling him the truth. It was only a fleeting thought: she knew from experience that information given during those close moments might be stored away and later used as ammunition. What was in the past must remain in the past; to revive the memories would mean reviving the pain.

She leaned her head back and shut her eyes. She picked up the cigarette lighter and held it in the palm of her hand, touching the scratches and the letters.

She remembered one spring evening when she and Babe were standing at the sink, doing dishes. Babe was strong and healthy then, her skin ruddy and her eyes sharp, watching as Justine dried and put away the plates, silverware, glasses. At sixteen, Justine was anxious to get out of the house, and she tapped her foot impatiently as Babe made sure to wash off every spot, every grease mark. Finally she sighed and said: "Cripes, ma, why don't you boil 'em and get it over with."

"Don't be in such a rush. Someday I'll be gone and you'll be sorry you didn't spend more time with your old lady."

Justine sighed. She had not heard her. She always tuned out whenever Babe began a sentence "someday. . ." It was either: "Someday you'll have children of your own and then you'll know. . ." or: "Someday you'll understand why I'm doing this. . ." or: "Someday I'll be gone. . ."

The instant Babe had rinsed the last pieces of silverware and stacked them in the drain, Justine grabbed them, barely wiping them dry and flung them into the various silverware compartments. She tossed the towel onto the rack and was almost out the door when Babe called her. She stopped.

"Come back here. And close the door, you're letting in all the flies."

Justine grimaced, closed the door and waited. Babe stood there, one hand on a broom, the other reaching for her lighter. She flipped it open with a snap and lit the cigarette. She flipped the lighter shut and blew out the smoke. Justine sighed.

"I know you're in a rush, but I want to talk to you."

"Now? Come on ma, please. . ."

"It'll only take a minute. Now sit down and listen to me."

Justine slouched over to the kitchen table and sat down, putting her chin in her hands. Underneath her elbows she felt the cool plastic tablecloth. She stared at her mother but did not listen.

"Now listen baby, don't ever be afraid to tell your momma anything. I'm not so dumb as you think. And if something's bothering you. . ."

Justine clenched her teeth with impatience. Was *that* all her mother had to say?

"You hear me Justine?"

"I hear you, ma."

"All right, then go outside. And stand up straight! There's no reason to be ashamed of your height. You should be proud of what you are."

Then, Justine had squirmed under her mother's gaze and resented her advice. Now she would give anything in the world to look into her mother's eyes and hear her voice again.

She glanced at Paul sleeping soundly beside her, and looked down at her belly. "We will be a family," she whispered fiercely into the dark, "we will."

Saturday night was Becky's date with Bryce. Although she was positive that she would not sleep with him, she didn't use any medication all day Saturday, and when she took a bath Saturday evening, she douched. She laughed to herself and thought: 'You must be pretty desperate to sleep with him on the first date,' and was ashamed because she felt she was desperate. She told herself once again that she would not sleep with him, and stopped thinking about the fact that she was preparing to do precisely that.

He had told her they were going to the movies to see *Z*, but when he picked her up he said: "We're going to my place. My roomate's there with his chick."

Bryce lived near the university in an apartment decorated with large violent posters of The Rolling Stones. In the non-functioning fireplace were scattered some Marvel comic books, which Bryce proclaimed were his only true love. In the far corner a man wearing corduroy jeans and a tie-dyed t-shirt fiddled with the stereo components, trying to get the perfect sound. A woman with long silky hair sat cross-legged on the floor rolling a joint.

Bryce walked across the room, settled himself onto the couch, picked up a *TV Guide* and began to read. Becky stood in the doorway. The man and woman smiled at each other and the woman said to Bryce: "Thanks for introducing us to your girl, Dedham." Her tone was flirtatious, and after she spoke she continued looking into his eyes while she slowly licked the glue on the cigarette paper.

The man's eyes flicked to her and Bryce before he turned his back on them both and continued adjusting the stereo.

Bryce shrugged and kept reading.

Still facing the stereo, the man said to Becky: "I'm Tom and that's Melissa. Have a seat."

Becky sat down on the other end of the couch before she realized she had forgotten to introduce herself. She opened her mouth, but Bryce said: "Hey Tom old buddy, put on some Stones."

Tom selected an album. By then Melissa had rolled four joints and lined them up on the coffee table. They lit one and passed it around, listening to the Stones sing "Under My Thumb." When the record was half over, Melissa stood up, stretched sensually, and left the room. She returned with a bottle of wine, three glasses and a peach.

Bryce laughed. "You still on your health kick?"

She stuck out her tongue like a defiant little girl, and poured out some wine. She didn't drink her own wine; instead, she took little sips of Tom's or Bryce's, sipping always in the middle of a sentence at the most interesting part: ". . . And I was in the middle of this airline terminal, can you dig it? an airline terminal surrounded by fifty million people, and this bald freak came up to me carrying this duffle bag painted with these weird day-glo designs—it was incredible, you should've seen it, it was really incredible—and he tapped me on the shoulder and I turned and he said. . ." Sip.

Melissa and Tom were a couple. With a watchful eye toward Bryce, Tom called her "Mel" and ruffled her hair; she teased him and he laughed good naturedly. Melissa was about Becky's height and weight, but Becky felt awkward and clumsy next to her.

Bryce and Melissa talked about skiing. Bryce, leaning back and stretching his legs, bragged about the chances he had taken, and the dangerous slopes he had run, the close calls he had been in but always surmounted. Melissa, holding her hand to the side of her face and laughing, joked about her falls, spills, bumps and bruises; the time her skis caught on one another and tripped her; the time she almost fell off the lift.

Later in the evening Bryce spied the Monopoly game. "Hey, you bastard, you hid it from me."

"No, I didn't hide your precious Monopoly game," Tom said.

"I'll bet. Come on, let's play." He stood up.

"Come on man, we've played Monopoly every night for the past two weeks. I don't want to play."

"Sure you do. Becky?"

"Uh, sure, I guess so."

"Well Mel doesn't want to play," Tom countered unsurely, "so it's a draw."

"Yes she does. Don't you, Missie." Bryce spoke the name intimately but stared at Tom, challenging him. Tom looked away, then laughingly gave in.

They played a few rounds. Becky kept wondering how to tell Bryce about the infection. He watched her make her moves, and she felt that she was doing everything wrong. When she landed on Park Place, he mocked: "There she goes, buying Park Place. Man, I've heard of being hard up for property, but this is too much."

She didn't buy it. Realizing she'd made a mistake, she bought the next street she hit. Unfortunately for her that was Mediterranean Avenue where the rent was only two dollars.

On his next turn Bryce landed on and bought Park Place. Since he already owned Boardwalk he was now eligible to build. He built two hotels.

Becky was sure that the next time around she would land on Boardwalk or Park Place. She did. Bryce whooped for joy. The rent was two thousand dollars. She tried to smile like a good sport and handed him one thousand dollars and a note for the rest. "How did your canvassing go?" she asked, as if losing didn't bother her.

He nodded slowly, pleased with himself. "Not bad. I bet you can't guess who I went with."

She assumed he'd gone with Pritchard, but not wanting to spoil his surprise, asked: "Who?"

He threw the dice and landed on Community Chest. "Faaar fuckin' out!" he cried, slapping his thigh. "It's the Grand Opera opening, folks, and I'm hereby authorized to collect fifty bucks from every player. Ok, you peasants, pay up, come on, hand it over." He rubbed his hands together like an evil miser.

Melissa laughed and said: "Who are you supposed to be, Scrooge McDuck?"

Becky thought: 'How come I never say anything like that,' and handed Bryce fifty dollars.

"Now. . . What was I saying," Bryce continued. "Oh yeah. Canvassing. I went with Pritchard. That guy has it made, man, he's loaded. Do you know how much that guy makes?"

"No. How much?"

"Twen-ty thou-sand dollars," Bryce said, as if it were a prayer. "And he doesn't do shit, either."

"He doesn't teach?"

"Yeah. Independent Study and Thesis Guidance. Big deal. What he really does is sit around and churn out articles that will make the man, by the time he reaches the ripe old age of forty, a nationally reknowned authority of bullshit. Pritchard knows where it's at, and if I play my cards right, when he gets there he'll save a place for me. And the man is such a fucking asshole, all you have to do is suck up to him and you've got it made. Which I do, since he's heading my committee. Which is why my dissertation, when you get past the words, isn't fit to wipe your ass with." He looked at Becky. "I wouldn't be sharing my secret with you except by the time you pick your committee I'll be long gone."

Tom, who had been half listening, smiled and said: "Dedham, you're the very spirit of generosity. Pure, unadulterated good will, that's what you are."

"Ah fuck, if you had any balls you'd be doing the same thing instead of working your ass off at that fool dissertation."

"Bryce," Melissa said, finally taking a bite of the peach and chewing it a few times, "you're a lazy bastard."

"Sweet thing, I may be lazy, but I get what I want." He smiled as he reached over and pinched her quite hard on the cheek.

"Hey, cut it out!" she said and slapped him the way a "girl" slaps: wrist limp and shoulder leaning away from the motion. He laughed, reached out and gave her flesh another twist. Her cheek was red and she looked to Tom for assistance. But Tom pretended to be engrossed in the roll of the dice. After all, he and Bryce were friends, what could he do? his expression said. Melissa sat there rubbing her cheek and frowning, but soon Tom teased her back into good humor. He did not want her angry at Bryce.

Apparently Bryce was not finished with her. He watched as she ate the peach, sucked the pit clean, and dropped it carelessly into her shirt pocket.

He snickered. "Sweet thing, your friend Tom has been dragging you over here for two months, and in that two months you've saved at least a dozen peach pits. I never asked why, because I assumed it was some moronic reason. But at this point my curiosity knows no bounds."

"It's *not* a moronic reason."

"Well then?"

"I plant them."

"Where."

"I don't know. Wherever I am."

"You mean you just push them into the ground, just like that?"

She nodded.

"I hate to break your bubble, my dear child, but they won't grow."

"Bryce, a seed always grows."

"Not if it's got a pit around it, Missie dear. Not if it's encased in a shell."

She didn't answer.

Becky opened her mouth to volunteer the information that if the shell were cracked even a bit, the seed would germinate. But Bryce was looking at Melissa, shaking his head with humorous despair. Becky did not want to be in the midst of a statement and find that no one was listening. He threw the dice and she kept quiet.

By the time the game was over Becky owed Bryce twelve thousand dollars. While she was putting on her coat, Melissa went into the bedroom and Tom said to Bryce: "Hey Dedham, you coming back tonight?" His tone was overly casual.

Bryce shrugged. "Maybe," he said, and walked away.

In the car he motioned to her. "That was some game, old Monopoly master."

She slid under his arm, laughing at how badly she had played.

In front of her house he kissed her, wrapping her in his arms and covering her mouth with his lips. She knew that she had to tell him about the infection but waited until he paused in the kiss.

"Bryce?"

"Mmm. . ."

She opened her mouth but the words stopped short. Vaginal infections didn't fit in with adventure. The adventurous woman never cared about her health but remained miraculously healthy. Vaginal infections made her think of mold. He would never want to sleep with her again. He might think she had VD. She wished she could be like Melissa: flirtatious, bantering, easy with all situations.

She stared out at the glow of the street lights that formed a circle of golden scratches on the windshield.

"Hey Bryce. . ." She spoke hesitantly, ashamed that these mundane matters should spoil the romance of sex. "Listen. . . uh. . . I just began the pill. You know, the birth control pill? And it's not. . . see, when you take it in the beginning, you have to wait seven days the first time, and it's not seven days yet, so. . ." She laughed, as if it were all so foolish, and then looked up at him anxiously, waiting for his reaction.

He said: "I wouldn't worry about it."

She didn't know what he meant. Did he mean that he wasn't worried because they couldn't make love, or she shouldn't worry when they made love. "Well. . . I only wanted to make sure you understood. . ."

"I understand. How 'bout going upstairs, it's getting cold down here. Brr. . ." he said to show her that he was cold, and reached for the door handle.

". . . that we can't make love. I mean, I only wanted to make sure that—"

His hand paused dramatically on the handle, and he stared at her with his mouth open. "Is that all you think I want?"

She imagined herself saying: Well as a matter of fact, Bryce, yes. But she protested: "Oh no, of course not."

"I wanted to have some coffee, that's all."

"Of course you can come up, I only wanted to make sure that you understood so you wouldn't be angry. . ."

"Angry?" He smiled: how could he ever be angry at her.

Upstairs he relaxed on the couch and she stood in front of the stove waiting for the coffee to perk. She'd forgotten to buy coffee that day and what she made now would be the last of it. Tomorrow she would have nothing to drink for breakfast. She thought: 'Why can't he pretend to drink hot water instead.'

She carried the two mugs into the living room. Bryce lay on the couch with his feet up. He reached for her wrist with one hand and the mug with the other. He took a token sip and put the mug on the floor, pulling her down. "Com'mere," he said. She sat down facing him. "Why don't you put that down before it spills." He nodded with his chin at her coffee. She sighed and placed her mug next to his.

He kissed her, slipping his hand under her blouse to calculate the geography of her bra. At first his tongue explored her mouth gently and she responded; then it drove deep to conquer her throat.

She broke free. "Hey. Bryce. . ." He nodded sleepily and covered her mouth again, sucking in her lips. She broke free again, laughing nervously at the smacking sound of the interrupted kiss. "Hey. Bryce. Come on there. Remember I said. . ."

"Did you know how soft you are? I bet you didn't know that."

"Yeah, I'm soft like a bunny rabbit, right? But what about what I said, remember?"

He looked at her as if he'd forgotten and then said: "Well.   it'll be all right. . ." She felt his hands pressing against her back. "Come on," he urged, "come on."

She put her hands on his chest as leverage. "Listen Bryce. . . there's this other thing. See, I have an infection. . ." Immediately his body was still. "It's not VD

82

or anything, it's not contagious, it won't hurt *you*, it's just something women get sometimes. . ."

He sighed, and made a pretense of releasing her as he said: "Well if you don't want to. . ."

"No, no, it's not that I don't want to. . ." And she thought: 'But I don't want to, I'm not even hot.' She said: "It's only this infection. it hurts. You know? It really does. . ." For an instant, hearing the plea in her voice she doubted that it hurt. A voice inside her said: 'Oh come on, it doesn't hurt that much. Don't be such a baby.' But she did have an infection, she reassured herself, she had gone to the doctor only a few days ago. "It does," she repeated, "it hurts." At this, his lips spread into a slow, nasty smile. She knew he was thinking that the pain made it exciting. It frightened her and she said in a voice that she thought was rational and calm: "Listen, how about next week. I have to see the doctor one more time, and then I should be OK. OK? And the pills will take effect by then too. OK?"

He pouted and let go of her back. His hands had been sweaty and her skin was chilled and clammy. "Sure, and then next week you'll say the same thing. All right. If you want to be that way." His face was sulky.

"Come on Bryce, now you're being silly," she teased.

"Silly!" He said the word with disdain: it was clearly a word he never used. "You're the one who's being silly. I'm not asking for the world, you know. Shit, I don't know what you're so uptight about."

"Uptight!?"

"Yeah, uptight. Unless. . . if you don't want to. . ."

She panicked. "No, I want to, I definitely want to. . ."

"Well then?"

"But you said you understood about the pills and

all. . ." But by this time, both the pills and the infection seemed like mere excuses of a frigid woman. The pills were probably effective today, she was being picky and tightassed about it. And as far as the infection went. . . Well, it wouldn't kill her, would it?

"I understand about that," he said. "You're the one who doesn't understand. . ." Her skirt had ridden up, and Bryce placed his hand on her bare thigh. ". . . what you do to me."

Her body was poised on the edge of protest, but she didn't know what to say, and she sighed. In that sigh, the light went out of her.

"It's all right, Becky," he said tenderly.

She didn't know what he meant. It would be all right because he wouldn't try to make love to her? It would be all right when he did because she didn't really have an infection? It would be all right because he loved her and would nurse her back to health? Or take care of her if she got pregnant? "It'll be all right," he repeated. "Come on."

She pulled away and he put out his hand and unbuttoned the top button of her blouse. "Bryce!" she said, but her voice sounded seductively reluctant. "I really don't want to. . ."

It was the old game and it excited him. She was the shy maiden, he was the rake. She held back but he stood up, pulling her hand, coaxing gently.

As he stood, his foot knocked against the mug, and coffee splashed out. A little brown stream flooded the narrow space between the floor boards, sugaring the splinters.

He gave her a little shove toward the bedroom. He was smiling; he knew her type. If you pushed hard enough they'd end up doing just about anything. Standing by the bed, his face became sincere and loving. He embraced her.

Over Bryce's shoulder, Becky saw her tree framed by the window and outlined in the moonlight. She closed her eyes, and her fingers became leaves that brushed against each other in the breeze. Her body swayed gently on her firmly rooted legs. In her veins sap flowed, warm and healing. She felt that she was protected from the cold and would bloom again in the spring. 'It's all right,' she whispered silently to herself, 'it's all right.' He pulled her down to the bed.

She kept saying no. But to Bryce a woman's no was only a teasing way of saying yes. And after awhile she thought that too.

She argued weakly. She knew that the more he coaxed, the more he put his ego on the line. Eventually she would have to give in or risk losing him. She reached a point where she didn't care. 'It'll be over soon,' she thought, 'that's all.'

Fully clothed they lay in bed, Bryce on top, pinning down her arms and laughing. He was a warrior and he liked his women to fight. At one point she went limp and he stared at her, annoyed, then shook her arm slightly like a cat coaxing a dead mouse to come alive so that it could play some more.

He stripped down her underpants and entered her. "You're dry," he said critically, having expected her to be juicy wet with passion. She lay quite still, telling herself that it felt good.

It didn't. It hurt. It burned. It itched like a thousand mosquito bites scratched to blood.

"Come on," he breathed, "don't be so stiff."

"Bryce," she whispered, "it hurts." But he took her

pain for passion, and pumped all the harder. She thought she must be insane: if it hurt, he wouldn't do it. Yet he did it, therefore it must not hurt. If it hurt, she wouldn't let him do it. Yet she lay still under him.

She felt that her body did not belong to her: she was watching it all from outside the window, curious yet unaffected. She tried to think of it as being a joke she had heard somewhere. She tried to turn it into an amusing anecdote in which there was no pain or humiliation, but only detached cynicism.

He wouldn't come and she felt her insides raw and sore. She thought if she pretended excitement it would help him out. She tried to become excited by his masculinity and by her powerlessness. He took her and she gave herself to him. When she, pretending to be overcome by passion, writhed under him, he stared hard at her. "Don't move," he commanded. His fantasy had changed: now he wanted her to play dead. She lay still. And all the while she felt the walls, and his weight, and slowly became numb.

In her mind she fantasized telling it as a funny anecdote to a friend: 'I swear to God, I felt like a Sabine woman. I mean macho is cool, but I mean really now. . .' But there was no friend to wisecrack to tomorrow, no one to help her buffer reality. And so she wisecracked to herself, the stream of chatter flowing on until Bryce came and collapsed on her, and then it snapped like a tape recording speeded up until it split in two.

After a few moments he rolled off and propped himself on one elbow. "That wasn't so bad, was it? You did OK for someone with an infection." He smiled to his Becky, the wanton woman, never able to resist a good fuck, even if it hurt. Especially if it hurt. He lit a cigarette.

"I'm. . . I'm going to get. . ." She cleared her throat. ". . . a glass of water." She couldn't say she wanted to wash. He might think it was lusty for a woman to leave his seed there like an earth mother, even though it would drip coldly down her thighs.

In the bathroom she avoided the mirror. She washed between her legs like a nurse bathing one of many patients. She washed her face. She was unmoved by the hysterical laughter that echoed in the corner of her brain and the image of her face swirling in the sink water, being sucked down the drain.

She returned to the bedroom. He lay on his back with his hand behind his head. He held up his cigarette and she got him an ashtray. She lay down beside him stiffly and closed her eyes.

Bryce looked down at her, his lips curling in contempt. Her very presence made him feel such disgust that for a moment he wanted to kill her, not as an act of violence but as an act of erasure. He wanted to erase her existence from his world.

Becky felt sick. She wanted to be away somewhere, anywhere, only not inside this body. She wanted to die, to disappear. Eyes closed, she held her body rigid, stretching her throat upwards towards him.

He spread his fingers around her neck, gently at first. Then he pressed. All his being concentrated on his curved hand, all hers concentrated on her throat. Skin to skin, pulse to pulse, closer and closer they pressed as if this, and not what they had done before, were the act of union.

At the same instant Bryce drew away his hand and Becky opened her eyes. They didn't look at one another. She stared across the room while he stood and dressed.

He was annoyed with himself. He felt that that kind of

thing was all right for a joke, but in all seriousness he had to think of his career. Why fool around with that kind of feeling when things were going so well for him. 'Jesus Christ,' he thought, 'if you want to kill somebody, why the fuck don't you go to Vietnam.'

He laughed and said to Becky: "No, you didn't do too bad at all. The next time you go back to that doctor, you tell him that you were examined by an expert and he pronounced it in A-1 shape."

He left soon after, saying he'd call. But she knew from what his eyes said that he wouldn't. She tried to recapture the camaraderie she thought they'd shared, but saw in his eyes that if there was a joke, it was on her.

She sat on the bed until she heard his car drive away, then moved to the couch and curled into a tight ball as if protecting a wounded animal in her belly. She tried to soar above herself, but sunk in quicksand all night long.

The spilled coffee left a mark. Becky covered it with a throw rug, but as it was the rug had been placed strategically, and moving it exposed a deep scar of forgotten origins in the wood. Between the two the scar was worse and she replaced the rug where it had been. The stain became a part of the living room decor.

All day long she felt groggy. The night before seemed

unreal and her head felt surrounded by a heavy, dulling cloud. She warmed the leftover coffee but at the first sip she gagged.

She tried to study but her mind kept slipping into fantasy. In her fantasies, Bryce felt guilty and ashamed. Their relationship was one of deep commitment and the incident had brought them close together as though they had shared a painful experience. After a few pages she'd wake to realize that she had understood nothing.

Thinking that something would get through, she turned back the pages and began anew. But once again she understood nothing. All through the day, the shadow of the night before loomed like an enormous bird ready to swoop down on her.

That night she sat home alone. She thought of taking a tab of mescalin. She wanted to feel moving colors that glowed inside her eyelids, to enclose herself in the soft cocoon of her sensations, to curve her body into a flowing circle that grew and merged into itself. But she was afraid that the colors would slash at her eyes, the cocoon might smother her, and the circle of herself spin into an infinite, breathless vertigo.

The experience with Bryce caused a minor relapse, and she dreaded the return to the doctor. When he examined her, his attitude became distinctly sexual. He peered at her over the white triangle of sheet and smiled disapprovingly. It was as though he had wagged his finger and said: Naughty, naughty girl. Couldn't you wait? She was ashamed, and felt like a sex-crazed bitch in heat. She wanted to defend herself, but even if she knew what words to say, she knew he would believe none of them.

November
1969

Bryce did not call, and Becky felt that her only alternative was to forget him. This was impossible: she saw him every week in class, and his eyes constantly reminded her of that night. She tormented herself with what she should have said, should have done, coming always to the conclusion that she had only herself to blame.

She felt vulnerable: without a man or dreams of one, she had nothing to protect her from the small realities that wore down her ego. And David Sully was a convenient man on whom to hang all of her pre-pasted fantasies.

One day in the second week in November she met with Sully at the Cavern to discuss his paper on the Mexican Revolution. Because she was unable to be aggressive, she created an atmosphere within which he could be aggressive. She smiled at him longingly. She wet her lips with the tip of her tongue and leaned toward him seductively.

It was going along fine until she forgot her main objective and happened to disagree with him about something he had said in class. His vehement response stunned her: she thought he was joking and tried to tease him until she understood that he was quite serious: he did not like to be contradicted. Sully liked his women to be independent, to have minds of their own, to argue with him. Up to a point. He also liked them to understand independently by the use of their own minds that in objective reality he was right. Opinions were one thing, reality was another.

The conversation left a strained feeling between them, and Becky knew that she had to make a choice.

After his next lecture, she waited until everyone had gone before she left her seat. He stood behind the podium, rearranging his notes. She said: "You know, I've done a lot of thinking about what you said in class, and I think I finally understand your point."

He looked skeptical.

"I mean the main reason I disagreed," she continued, "was because I hadn't really thought the question out fully."

He smiled. "You know, there aren't many people who can admit it when they're wrong. I respect you for that."

They left the building together, good humor restored. Outside it was drizzling lightly.

"Well. . ." She looked up at him. "See you in class."

He wore no jacket, and his blue cotton work shirt was damp against his shoulders. "You know," he said, "I'd like to go out sometime. I mean really go out, not just for coffee. Would you like that?"

"Sure. I'd love to."

"Great. The only problem is. . . right now it's hard because of the Washington Moratorium. It's been alot of work trying to organize the busses and make arrangements, and as it gets closer to the fifteenth there's more and more work and responsibility. . ." His voice was hoarse with exhaustion. "So it might be hard to find time until afterwards."

She shook her head sympathetically, wishing he would get to the point since she was getting wet.

"Are you going to Washington?" he asked.

"Well, I—"

"I'd like to see you down there," he said softly, and paused. "It's an important opportunity to show political solidarity against the war. There's going to be alot of groups there—the Vietnam Vets, YAWF. . . there's even supposed to be some Weathermen. And I think some women from the women's liberation group are going. Maybe you'd like to go with them."

She wrinkled her nose. "No, I'm kind of independent. I'd rather go alone." This was a lie, for she'd decided against going to Washington precisely because she was afraid of going alone.

"Yes, you are independent. That's what I like about you." He gently touched her arm, but immediately withdrew his hand, giving a quick guilty glance around the parking lot. "I think going to Washington will be a valuable political experience for you. And you don't have to worry about going alone. . ." He smiled reassuringly. "I'll be there."

By noon of Friday, November the fourteenth, the demonstrators descended upon Washington, D.C. National Guard trucks passed yellow school busses filled with out of town demonstrators, and they stared at the Guardsmen, wondering if they were under orders to shoot. One by one the busses pulled up to the large brownstone church that served as a meeting place. One by one the passengers stepped out into the crowd milling around the church. The atmosphere was morbidly festive, like a carnival that at any moment might explode into a war. Many people laughed together or greeted old friends from distant cities with enthusiastic shouts. Others, some of whom had been in Chicago for the Democratic National Convention the previous summer, were strained and apprehensive. They silently watched the crowd or stood in small groups trying to decide upon tactics in case of tear gas or violence.

The air was cold. The wind scraped up the city dirt and the dry brown leaves and swept them into small whirlpools that flew against the yellow busses and settled on the ground, only to be lifted up by the wind again a few seconds later.

Inside the church in a large meeting hall, the organizers tried to keep the confusion to a minimum. People deposited their knapsacks in a pile against the wall, stood around and talked, sipped coffee from styrofoam cups or ate peanut butter sandwiches. Some stood in a long impatient line, waiting to use the one bathroom. Up on a platform a man repeated into a microphone: "Clear the floor. . . This floor is to be used for organizing purposes only. . . If you are standing around talking, please clear the floor. . ." Small card tables were lined up against the wall, and organizers stood behind them providing information about housing, march routes, and arrest procedure. A harried medic tried to explain to a small group of people how to treat tear gas sickness. Some listened curiously; others made defiant jokes.

In a small alcove Paul and David sat talking and Elizabeth stood against the wall, arms folded across her chest. She was small boned and slender, just over five feet. Although she hated David to call her "Squirt," she habitually accentuated her size: when she walked into a room she headed for the largest chair into which she could curl; if her feet didn't reach the ground, she kicked them back and forth in a child-like manner. She stood on tiptoe when it wasn't necessary.

She was a careful person and didn't like risks. She let few people get close to her. Asleep she was all elbows and knees, and it was a year before David had stopped teasing her about the bruises she gave him at night.

She was neat and precise. and cut her straight dark hair·bowl-shaped so that it looked like a shiny helmet. She trimmed it herself once a month. Her round wire-rimmed glasses were always spotless. Behind them. her worried eyes scanned the faces in the crowd. searching for Susan and George.

David stood up. "I'm hungry and I can't handle a peanut butter sandwich right now. Let's go find something to eat."

Elizabeth and Paul agreed, and the three of them made their way across the floor to the high double doors. Just as they crossed the threshold, David looked down and saw Becky standing below in the crowd.

She'd been standing there a full five minutes, not sure exactly what to do now that she was here in Washington. She'd pulled her hair into a single practical braid. and wore a heavy sweater, bell bottom jeans. a navy blue pea coat and winter boots. She carried a knapsack slung over her shoulder; rolled up tightly inside were an extra pair of underpants, a toothbrush. eyeliner and comb. and a blanket. She had not brought the medicine: her infection had almost disappeared. Besides, if she used the medicine her underpants would be a mess. She would have to wash them. With disgust, she'd pictured herself marching in a vast demonstration. the drying underpants pinned to her knapsack like a banner.

She felt like a fool standing alone in the midst of groups, and she was afraid. She was considering taking the next train home when she looked up to the top of the steps and saw David. For a moment she was delighted, but she saw in his eyes the urge to turn away.

David felt trapped. He had meant well in reassuring Becky about Washington but somehow he ignored the fact that she might actually come here and look to him for some of that reassurance. He looked at Elizabeth and back at Becky. There was nothing he could do. He waved to Becky and she came forward.

"Dave, hi! What—" She almost said: 'What are you doing here,' but caught herself in time. "What alot of people! It's really far out!"

It was awkward. The three of them stood there jostled by the crowd. David looked from one woman to the other and they waited for him to speak.

Finally he blurted to Elizabeth: "This is. . . this is my assistant." From the way Elizabeth nodded to her, Becky knew that he had never mentioned her before. It shook her faith in his grand statements about honesty in relationships. She managed to smile. He turned to her. "This is. . ."

"Hello," Becky said, not wanting to hear how he would identify Elizabeth.

Elizabeth knew that this was more than a simple assistantship. For the past few weeks David had been acting like he had something to tell her, and now she wondered if Becky was the something he had to tell. She nodded coolly to her and asked: "Are you here with anybody?"

"Well, I. . ." Becky looked at David for direction but he kept his eyes averted.

Elizabeth nodded to herself: check. She said: "We're going for something to eat, would you like to come?"

David's mouth opened in protest, but he said nothing. There was no reason that Becky the Assistant shouldn't accompany them.

Becky strained her ears to hear while she looked the other way, staring at the water marks on the wall—long quivering stains that resembled stalactites. By the door Elizabeth folded her arms and David held his hands out to her, explaining. Becky heard: ". . . I didn't know she was going to be here, she's my assistant. Jesus Christ. you're so goddamned suspicious. Everytime. . ." She lost the rest.

When she looked again they had changed positions: now David folded his arms across his chest and Elizabeth held out her hands, explaining. He bent down and kissed her on the cheek. She nodded to Becky and left.

Becky and David spent the afternoon together. In contrast to her image of the shrew Elizabeth, Becky was agreeable, understanding, and completely at David's disposal. The knowledge that they only had a few hours alone made their time together bittersweet. The knowledge that soon Elizabeth would come between them made it all the more precious. Once, sitting on a huge rock at the edge of a park, they held hands shyly.

There were to be three demonstrations during the weekend. The first, that night, was in support of the Provisional Revolutionary Government of South Vietnam. David said that Becky had better not come with them: "Elizabeth is funny. She doesn't understand. I'll see you tomorrow at the large demonstration. Maybe we can spend some time together then."

Before they parted he gave her the address of Jim McLeod, a friend of his from graduate school. She could spend the night at Jim's apartment. He and Elizabeth were staying somewhere else.

When Becky arrived at Jim's apartment, everyone had left for the DuPont Circle Demonstration except Jim's wife and infant son. The baby had colic.

The others came back late, the bitter stench of tear gas clingling to their clothes. Jim nodded distantly to her when she explained her presence. Paul was staying there also and he vouched that she did in fact know David, but it made little difference. At a political demonstration everyone was suspect. She listened apprehensively as they compared stories of the evening's action. They said that Elizabeth had an asthma attack from the gas, and Andy Gambino, someone they knew from Ann Arbor, was arrested. Becky knew that there were things they didn't discuss because of her presence. Several times someone began to say something, looks were exchanged, and the speaker fell silent.

For the most part Paul ignored her. She had no political credentials of her own and she could not be identified as David's woman. She was David's flirtation, nothing more and nothing less, and although Paul felt sorry for her, he didn't want to become involved.

The others looked up to Paul because of his extensive political experience. He talked about Justine, who he said could not come to Washington because she could not get off work. He told them about her oppressive job and about her childhood. When he spoke of her his voice was filled with love, and Becky wondered if David would ever speak of her like that. She imagined Justine to be a tall slim blonde, cool and arrogant because she was Paul's wife.

At midnight they unrolled their sleeping bags or blankets and found space on the living room floor. At one, the colicky baby woke and began to cry.

It was cold the next morning. Becky was stiff from sleeping on the floor but didn't complain. The implication was that this demonstration was the action of a vanguard in the first stages of the revolution, and during the revolution the conditions would obviously be severe. She would have to be tough enough to endure sleeping on the floor, at least. If she showed weakness now, they might not want to include her.

The people from Jim's house met the others, including David and Elizabeth, and all of them walked toward the peace demonstration. There was no exact point at which it began—the sidewalks and streets became more and more congested until David turned to Jim and said: "Well, I guess this is it." When they walked onto a grassy mall, David saw a crowd of people to one side, and he and Elizabeth went over to investigate. Becky followed him through the crowds, ignoring the hostile backward glances Elizabeth shot over her shoulder.

Once they got there no one knew what was happening. Almost immediately other curious people boxed them in until several thousand people waited in the small space, not marching, hardly moving, just waiting for almost two hours, listening to the floating rumors: "I heard that the march route's been changed. . . The Weathermen are supposed to do an action tonight. . . Somebody told me that the demonstration is being called off. . . We're in the wrong place and they've got us roped in here. . . They're going to gas us." The wind chilled the sunny day and snapped the green and orange and red banners that fluttered against the blue cloud-dotted sky.

Becky stamped her feet, hoping it would warm her toes. She saw only shoulders and heads and banners and sky, here and there a few trees, and behind her the Washington Monument, a tall stone phallus so like the Monument to the War Dead in front of the Court House back home that she felt she had never left. She felt elated but at the same time, depressed.

David teased Elizabeth: "Got a good view?. . . You can't see much down there, can you," periodically told her what he saw, which wasn't much, and once boosted her up. She protested weakly: "Dave, let me down!" and Becky felt like an intruder in their bedroom. The sense of political solidarity she strained to feel vanished everytime she looked into their eyes. She was cold, and hugged her arms around herself while they were warmed by each other.

Later the congealed mass of people broke and the three of them walked up to the base of the Washington Monument, situated on a large slope that overlooked the speaker's stage. They saw indistinguishable figures on the stage, and heard occasional muffled sounds from the loudspeakers and the cheers of those close enough to hear what was said. Every so often someone sang. Becky didn't know what any of it had to do with the Vietnam war.

Next to her an unshaven man stood unsteadily, smiling through eyes caked with yellow sleep. "Hiii," he murmured in a syrupy voice, "I've been tripping for four days. Four days straight." He grinned and his glassy eyes stared over the crowd. "I used to be a med student but I guess I'm not anymore. . ."

"Four days? Wow. Hey, what are the vibrations of the

102

crowd. You know? Are they good or what."

He peered myopically into the distance. "The Justice Department is orange. It's blending right in with the sky. But the sky is purple. It's hard to describe. . ."

"Far out," she breathed, not really understanding but not wanting to hurt his feelings especially since he was tripping. She turned to David to tell him what the man had said, but he was bending toward Elizabeth, laughing softly in her ear. Elizabeth saw her waiting, and whispered something to hold his attention. Becky looked away.

When they were finished talking she said: "I'm going for a walk." It was as if she were saying: I'm going to commit suicide.

"Maybe you shouldn't go off," David said, but he didn't stop her.

She snorted recklessly. "I can take care of myself," she called over her shoulder. As she turned away she saw a familiar face in the crowd. It was the redhead in David's introductory course: she was lowering a camera. Becky raised her hand in a wave but the redhead looked away quickly.

She shrugged and walked down the slope. Each step took her deeper into the shifting crowd. She tried to feel adventurous, but felt that all she did was circle David. She saw herself from high above, a speck on the ground standing there aimlessly the next morning when the garbage trucks came to sweep away the empty pop bottles and discarded leaflets.

When she turned to find David, he was gone. She took a breath to call his name but it stuck in her throat. She had no right to call him: he was with Elizabeth. She walked back to the top of the slope and looked down. In the thousands and thousands of people, she knew she could never find him.

Towards the stage, the crowd swayed back and forth, arms linked, chanting hypnotically: "All we are saying, is 'Give Peace a Chance. . .' All we are saying, is 'Give Peace a Chance. . .' " A cluster of people marched past her carrying a red banner with black lettering that read: "Mad Dogs." They sang: "All we are saying is pick up a gun. . ." Their voices mocked the other singers. One disgruntled man at the rear muttered: "This is bullshit. I told you we shouldn't've come. It's a waste of time and energy. Tonight is when. . ." But he walked out of range and she couldn't hear the rest.

A young woman in an Indian print shift sat on a blanket in the midst of the movement, breast feeding her child. A long haired bearded man looked on protectively. Their placid presence was like a statement: We are part of the new world of peace. Overhead, army heliocopters hovered, making sure that everything was under control.

Becky walked through the crowd. She felt that by the existence of the demonstration, peace had already been accomplished. But war was raging in Vietnam, and she thought. the demonstration was insufficient. She felt powerless, yet understood the power that all of these people could have if they were truly united.

She walked for almost an hour. Later, at the bottom of the hill she saw the Jolly Roger, a white skull and crossbones on a background of black. It bobbed over the heads, but it wasn't until the bearer was quite near that she saw his face. It was Ronnie Nye, a student in David's introductory course. She was relieved that she would no longer be alone, and she called to him: "Ronnie! Hey Ronnie!"

"Becky!" He waved the flag wildly in response and several people turned to look.

She smiled like an indulgent mother. His clothes and

hair were unkempt. There was a resentful air about him, as though he had all the answers and only one question: Why wasn't the world asking him? Two women stood behind him. Like pioneers they wore long calico dresses and large woolen shawls.They waited silently while Ronnie bragged about his bravery in the DuPont Circle demonstration the night before. The air was sharply cold, and the two women drew their shawls tighter.

Becky knew that with Ronnie, the demonstration would be a circus, a freaky happening whose physical sensations outweighed any consideration of political tactics or purpose. With David, at least when they had been alone, it had been a walk in the park on an autumn day. With David and Elizabeth the demonstration faded, becoming merely the background of their triangle. And if she had gone with Bryce, she would have sneered arrogantly through it all.

"What's happening?" Ronnie asked her. "Who are you with?"

She looked at the two women who waited silently. "I'm. . . looking for somebody."

"Who?"

She smiled. "I'm not sure."

He laughed. "Groovy. Come on troops." He sauntered into the crowd, the women taking quick little steps behind him.

Becky felt sorry that she'd let him go: now she was alone. She would not get another chance.

That night several thousand people marched on the Justice Department, protesting the Chicago Eight trial. The demonstration was the climax of the weekend, a senior dance with gas. Not everyone would go. Those who sang "Give Peace a Chance" would read about it in the Sunday papers. For them the demonstration was over. But to those who considered themselves radical, this was the big night. They expected it to be worse than DuPont Circle. Or better, depending on the point of view. They marched full circle around the Justice Department chanting: "Free Bobby! Stop the Trial!" One group carried an orange banner with a drawing of Black Panther Bobby Seale, chained and gagged.

The shaded windows of the Justice Department stared blindly down at the demonstrators, who had stopped marching and stood tensely silent. Shoulders hunched against the chill, they adjusted scarves around their faces as protection against the gas and to conceal their identities. Some wore motorcycle helmets and a few, gas masks. Overlooking them all, government agents stood on the roofs taking pictures.

In the middle of the crowd, a group began to beat on the sidewalk with the cardboard cylinders that held their banners. Once. . . Twice. . . more and more joined, faster and faster, louder and louder until their rhythm rumbled like thunder.

Then in the twilight, a suited man appeared on the fourth floor balcony of the Justice Department. The noise ceased. Seeing him so safe and blasé like a Czar looking out over his serfs, the crowd screamed in one frenzied voice: "Jump! Jump! Jump!" as if in his jumping, the State itself would fall. He smiled and disappeared inside the building.

Angry and frustrated, they watched him close the door without looking back.

Some tried to rebuild the beating rhythm but it trailed off into silence. Suddenly a helmeted demonstrator ran to the flagpole, lowered the American flag and put up the flag of the National Liberation Front.

It broke the waiting. Everyone cheered, and a few hurled rocks or jars of paint against the building. Red paint splattered. Windows shattered. One rock got tangled in a first floor venetian blind.

By an unseen signal, a popping sound filled the air. Like animals sensing danger the demonstrators readied for flight. Clouds of suffocating white fumes rose in the air. It smelled like rotting flesh and burning metal.

They ran. But in every direction they turned, another canister exploded until those trapped in between the two buildings could only stagger and choke, blind and helpless, unable to escape.

The gas crept toward the tree lined incline that surrounded the walkway. It snapped on faces and hands, bit on eyes. Becky was hidden in the confusion but the gas sought her out as if it knew her name. Caught unprepared, she covered her face and staggered backwards into a man who was doubled over, gagging.

In the chaos, row upon row of helmeted police appeared, gripping clubs across their spread thighs. Their gas masks made them faceless. They converged upon the demonstrators.

After the police had cleared the area, two people remained. At the foot of the incline a man lay unconscious,
his open mouth breathing in the fumes of a dying canister.
On the grass in front of the Justice Department a woman
hunched over screaming, clutching at a seared and blinded
eye. Near her the Jolly Roger lay crumpled in the dirt.

Above on the grass, trash can fires burned against the
darkened sky, throwing light onto the bare trees. Gassed
demonstrators gathered in small groups, coughing and
wiping their tear-stained faces or shaking their stinging
hands in the air. Some, having gotten a second wind,
headed back toward the Justice Department. They shouted
for others to join them.

"You gotta be kidding," someone called, walking away,
"I've had enough."

Army trucks rumbled through the streets. When they
passed the homeward bound demonstrators, a few soldiers
in each truck made peace signs, or more rarely, raised a
fist in support. Becky walked toward the bus stop. Because
she was a woman alone, the peace signs sometimes turned
into beckoning fingers and the men behind them laughed
invitingly.

She stood on a street corner for almost fifteen minutes
before she figured out what bus to take. Her clothes stunk
of gas, and as she walked to a seat, the people rubbed their
eyes and glared at her. The park was dark, but here and
there they could see small fires burning. She felt numb,
and only the smell of her clothes reminded her that it
had happened.

The wine she drank back at Jim's apartment didn't cut
through this daze. The others sprawled around the
living room like the night before, recounting their adventures. They were still wary of her. The men talked, each

including his woman in the conversation by a casual hand on her knee or an arm flung around her shoulder. Becky wavered in between the talking men and the listening women, unsure of whether to be coy or cool.

She sat like a picture on the wall observing them all. She didn't understand any of it. An hour ago most of them had been engulfed by gas. When she was in it she thought it was the most horrible experience of her life. And now she sat in this apartment. They were all talking as if the revolution were at hand. But tomorrow she would return home to her apartment, her classes. If it was revolution. she thought, she was like a high officer going out to do battle, returning to a luxurious tent equipped with all the comforts of home.

She couldn't relax. After the others were asleep she would drift off to sleep and wake with a start. catching herself from falling. All night long the stench of gas from the clothes in the room drifted up into her dreams.

When she stepped onto the bus Sunday morning. the first person she saw was David. sitting alone in the front seat. Across the aisle was Paul, and next to him was his student Mark. In back of Mark sat Elizabeth.

Becky hesitated, hitched her knapsack onto her shoulders, and smiled shyly at David. Seeing her submissive smile, Elizabeth stopped talking and stared at David coldly. Becky went to a seat in the back.

Wide-eyed. David appealed to Elizabeth for mercy: But *I* didn't do anything. . .

She turned to Mark. "Tell me, Mark," she said brightly, "how does it feel to be a part of the vanguard." The tall, gangly undergraduate turned around and grinned bashfully, flattered by such attention from David's girl.

David sighed and looked to Paul for support. Paul,

the old married man, shook his head with silent laughter: Well, you're in the middle of it now, you poor bastard. That's the price you pay.

David nodded.

On the way home they discussed the demonstration, and read the articles in the Sunday papers. Someone laughed because one article talked about the "roving bands of vandals" who broke bank windows. But Paul said that it was no laughing matter: that kind of rhetoric turned people against them.

"It's too bad that Justine had to work," Elizabeth said.

Paul nodded. "It's merely one of the ways in which the ruling class controls us. We need to work, so we can't take off time to protest any of our living or working conditions. And if anyone does protest, they lose the jobs that enable them to live."

He imagined Justine hearing his words. He would have liked her to be there, but knew that he'd remember everything that happened and tell her when he got home.

The Saturday that Paul was in Washington, Justine arrived home late in the afternoon. Moving slowly and methodically, she locked the front door and went into the bedroom where she put on her old terrycloth robe and fuzzy hot-pink slippers. From the back of the closet she took an envelope which she carried into the living room with a glass of water. As the cloudy water cleared, she ripped open the envelope and spilled the pills onto the coffee table. She stared at them a full minute, and then swallowed them two by two. Just as she got down the sixth, she gagged, ran to the bathroom and vomited. She leaned over the toilet, one hand on the door jamb. Her knees were weak. Her eyes teared and she breathed heavily. She returned to the living room with another glass of water, and swallowed the remaining pills. She leaned back and waited. Her face was pale. Dark shadows underlined her eyes.

Justine was pregnant. She had known it since the end of October. Undressing for bed one night, she'd taken off her bra. Red seam marks slashed across her white shoulders. Her breasts felt like water filled balloons that had been pinned to her chest, the skin stretched taut. She cupped her hands around them, and feeling their weight, really feeling it for the first time, she began to cry. The tears splashed onto her fingers and slid down her bruised looking breasts.

That day the panic started. Her moods flew from one extreme to another. Sometimes she fantasized about a freshly bathed and sleepy infant. Other times she took hot mustard baths and douched with hot water to get rid of it. She felt secure that now she was settling down into her life. She felt trapped because her own body had imprisoned her. One minute she'd be sweet and loving with Paul, thinking about the child they were creating between them; the next, she fantasized miscarriage. Her favorite fantasy was the following: one night she'd be walking down the street and a man would grab her from behind and stab her in the belly. They'd rush her to the hospital. She would be all right, but the baby. . . "I'm sorry, Mrs. Denton," the handsome young intern would say, "but the baby. . ."

She felt that her body was not her own. One evening she and Paul saw a science fiction movie about aliens from another planet who landed on earth and took over human bodies. Paul laughed and called it absurd. But Justine understood. Her own body had been invaded by an alien force.

An alien force. A baby. It was so many things to her that in the end she stopped feeling. As the October days sped into November she went through her options coldly. She had always wanted a baby, but a baby now would entangle her into a life that had somehow happened all by itself. For the first time since her mother's death she felt that she was thinking clearly: about Paul, herself, and their life together. Yet each day her clear thinking led to a different conclusion.

One day Lynne did not come to work, and Justine took a seat on the bus next to a woman with a baby. Watching the sleeping baby made her decision until she got to work and walked up the long flight of stairs. She stood at the top step, turned, and decided to throw herself to the bottom. But her body would not move. A few evenings later, alone in the house, she stood on the edge of the kitchen counter and jumped as hard as she could onto the floor. All it did was jar her body and hurt her heels. Day by day she went through her options, and day by day she threw them out.

Coolly, she told Paul she could not go to Washington with him because she had to work on Friday. It was getting easier to lie, and though she disliked the deceptions, it was necessary. Once he knew the truth, everything would be out of her hands. He'd make the decisions while she sat by, irrelevant.

Friday morning Paul left for Washington. On the way home from work Justine stopped at the drugstore to buy the pills. Saturday morning she cleaned the apartment and put her things in order, took a bath, dressed and went to the cemetery in the south side to visit her mother. Then she came home.

A half hour after she swallowed the pills, she started shivering as though winter had settled in her bones. At the same time she felt feverish. Looking at the hot-pink slippers made her queasy; she kicked them off and made her way barefoot into the bathroom where she locked the door and sat down unsteadily on the rim of the tub. A hot flash slapped her dizzy; she pressed her palm against the smooth tile. Her head reeled and she lay her forehead on the cool sink, feeling an icy sword slide down her spine. Sweat beaded on her forehead. Cramps gripped her belly. Her body trembled. She felt that the pills were lumped in her throat and she swallowed hard.

Perhaps the pills were not what they said. Maybe they were poison and would kill her, or only half work. She pictured a twisted thing growing inside her into a mangled helpless creature. She pictured a tiny pushed-in face, a stump where a leg should have been, a head with no skull, the gray wrinkled matter exposed to the air. She stood up abruptly and stuck her finger down her throat. It was too late: she gagged up nothing.

She sat back down on the tub. She felt so alone, as if this bathroom were the universe and she was trapped within these four walls. There was no one she could go to, no one to help.

Bells rang in her ears and when she swallowed it echoed like a hollow drum. She wanted to crawl into her mother's lap and hide her face in her mother's breast.

"Mommy," she whimpered, but instead of her voice, she heard a low and distant rumbling.

She had to get out. She stood up and reached for the doorknob but her knees buckled and she sank slowly into the hard tile floor that felt like a huge, soft, welcoming hand.

Curled at the base of the toilet, she saw the ceiling high above her, far away and very small. She smelled the coldness of the floor. She was sure she was going to die, and felt at peace. 'If I had the wings of an angel,' she thought, 'then I could get out. I could get out with no problem at all.' She floated on the ocean of tile and let her body go, sweetly, lovingly, giving it up. A voice sang from the hot bright lights: 'Oh I wish I had wings of an angel, over these prison walls I would fly. . .' She closed her eyes.

When she woke late that night her body was stiff and chilled but intact. She was still pregnant. She sat up and heard a strange sound as if she'd put her ear to a large shell. 'I'm deaf,' she thought. She went to bed and after a time, fell asleep.

Sunday morning she walked around the three room apartment. There was no space for the baby. She covered her face with her hands, and a small whining sound escaped from her throat: "Anh. . . anh. . ." She squeezed her lips tight to press the sound away. Feeling sick, she returned to bed.

When Paul got home from Washington, she was lying face down on the bed. "Tina!" he called, "I'm home!"

He strode into the bedroom and switched on the overhead light. "Hi," he said. She blinked against the glare. "You look sick." He turned off the light. "What's wrong?"

She did not answer. She felt miserable: there was one more thing to hide from him.

"Have you been sick all weekend?" He sat down on the bed, frowning because she was so pale.

"Mm-hmm."

"Do you have a fever?" He felt her forehead with his palm.

"No."

"Oh. Do you want to go to sleep? I was going to tell you about Washington."

"Go ahead."

"You're sure it's OK?"

"Sure."

"Because I can tell you later if you want, I can wait until—"

"Paul. I'm getting more tired arguing with you. . ."

"OK," he said, kissed her again, and told her about the weekend's events. When he got to an exciting part, he jumped up to act out the scene. The bed shook and Justine gripped the pillow like a piece of debris that she clung to in the sea.

She held a vision before her of Justine and Paul, happy with their beautiful baby. Then she felt better. She would tell him about the baby tomorrow.

Her sleep was filled with stifled screams of mangled babies and sick dying women. She woke suddenly and found herself sitting upright, staring into the dresser mirror, her hands damp and clenched at her sides.

Monday evening when Paul got home from school, Justine greeted him with the news. He was alarmed by her haggard appearance but he hugged her tightly, repeating over and over that he loved her and would take care of her. Justine was sure that he did not want the baby.

"Why didn't you tell me before!" he demanded.

"I wasn't sure. . ."

"Are you sure now?"

She nodded.

He began pacing around the room. "You'll have to see a doctor right away to make sure everything's OK. I'll ask around at school and find the name of a good doctor. You'll have to start taking vitamin pills: we want to be sure the baby's healthy. Did you drink any milk today? I want you to drink milk. And don't do anymore heavy cleaning, I'll take care of that. . ." He stopped pacing. "Are you sure?"

"Yes."

"Hmm. . . Well! We'll have to celebrate. I'll go out. . . and get some cake and ice cream."

She nodded despondently, and stood by the window staring at the street after his car pulled away.

Paul drove carefully, as he always did when his mind was not on the road. He went to the store and came home. At the apartment door, he stopped with one hand on the key, the other holding the grocery bag. His home did not seem the same to him. He would have to share Justine. And the Venceremos Brigade: he had forgotten all about it. The selections were to be announced this week, but regardless, they could not go. The baby had ended that. He opened the door and saw her standing at the window.

Paul put his arms around Justine for what he hoped would be a comforting embrace. She hugged him back for trying, but felt no comfort. When he released her, they went into the kitchen. She scooped the celebration ice cream onto the celebration cake, and they sat down across from one another to eat.

Home after the Washington demonstration, Becky felt energized: she felt she had actually done something instead of reading about other people who had done something. She had a fantasy of quitting school, packing a knapsack and travelling around the country from one demonstration to another. She pictured herself as a gaunt dedicated revolutionary who had no family, no friends, no ties at all, but lived only for The Revolution.

Yet she was afraid that her enthusiasm might jeopardize her shaky interest in graduate school, and the day after she returned, she decided to apply for an independent study with Professor Pritchard. William Schultz, the Chairman of the History Department, was going on sabbatical next year and Pritchard hoped to replace him. Becky knew that if she wanted to work with him, now was the time to apply.

At first her only misgiving was that she had no interest in Pritchard's field, Twentieth Century German History. But that night something happened to further complicate her decision: she slept with David for the first time.

Sexually she was disappointed but optimistic. He didn't seem to know much about what aroused women but at least he was not Bryce. The act of sex symbolized to her the beginning of the "relationship." Happening so closely to the Washington demonstration, it seemed to be the beginning of something special: they would stay together at least until the revolution. And in that time she would surely teach him how to please her.

She took the birth control pills faithfully every day and they gave her little trouble outside of occasional nausea and a five pound weight gain. David didn't mention birth control; he assumed that she was taking care of it. She also assumed she should. She was a woman and could get pregnant; therefore it was her responsibility to make sure she didn't.

After class on Wednesday they went to the Cavern. Becky leaned forward, gesturing with her hands as she presented to him the problem of Pritchard's connections versus her disinterest in German History, and her ambitions versus her principles.

As she spoke, David sipped his coffee and stared blankly across the room. She thought perhaps she was presenting her dilemma in too complicated a manner, and she simplified and re-simplified until she could think of no other way to get his attention than to ask him a direct question. "Well, what do you think?" she asked and thought: 'I'll tell you what *I* think, I think you're stupid. You sound like you're asking for the guy's approval, for God's sake.' She ignored this thought, and continued: "Do you think I should study with Pritchard or not?"

"Pritchard, that bastard," he muttered. "Schultz is sending out very subtle feelers for a new position, and if he doesn't come back after his sabbatical, I'll lay you odds that Pritchard winds up permanent Chairman."

David was given to dwelling on the past, usually with regret. Now he decided that hanging the poster of Zapata on such an obvious wall in his office was a foolish stunt that could not be remedied without appearing to have surrendered. Most of the things he regretted were like hanging that poster, thoughtless acts rooted in bravado, acts that later had consequence out of all proportion to their original intent.

He sipped his coffee and wondered, once again, if there was any way that what happened back in '64 could be on his record. Pritchard seemed like the kind of person who would stop at nothing to destroy those who got in his way, and there was no telling who or what he knew. At times, David was even sorry he'd told Elizabeth. As he grew older, that whole year seemed more and more like one big mistake, and it kept creeping up from the past to loom in his future.

"Dave. . . " Becky asked, "is anything wrong?"

"Christ. I'd like to pack Elizabeth and Pritchard off for the next moon landing."

She smiled. "How come?"

"Because they deserve each other."

"David!" She laughed. "What a thing to say."

"It's true. With him it's understandable, he's just an all-American fascist prick. But her. . . I don't know what the hell is wrong with her lately, but I wish she'd get her shit together and stop taking everything out on me. I can understand that it's a sexist society, but when she accuses *me* of being chauvinistic, that's hitting below the belt. Christ, you trust somebody, and then you wonder. . ."

She would rather have settled what she was going to do about her course with Pritchard, but enjoyed David's annoyance at Elizabeth. "What's 'chauvinistic'?"

He sat back, enjoying the role of teacher. "Elizabeth is talking about male chauvinism." He gave her a humorous look as if it was all beyond him. She smiled back, but it was beyond her too. "Male chauvinism is. . . Well, it's a difficult concept to explain to you, but I suppose in a word you could say that it's a belief in the natural superiority of the male." He leaned forward. "Elizabeth is a difficult woman. I've given her alot of emotional support. Sometimes. . ." He paused. "Sometimes I get tired. I just want to rest. I want to find somebody who understands my point of view."

Becky wanted to placate him quickly. "I can understand how you feel," she said. "It's only natural to want to be with somebody who understands you. I mean, everybody has pressures and tensions. And I think a real friend, somebody you're close to, has to understand that it's difficult for you too. And male chauvinism, whatever it is, can't be all that bad. And I mean if you're really trying. . ."

"You're something," he said, looking deeply into her eyes. She assumed a shy and humble expression. "You really are."

He stubbed out his cigarette, frowning. Elizabeth was already suspicious of Becky, already making cracks about his chauvinism. But if Becky joined the women's liberation group and he was the reason she joined, it would squelch Elizabeth's incessant criticisms. It was the perfect solution.

He said: "What do you think of women's liberation?"

She didn't mind leaving the topic of Pritchard to discuss David's problems with Elizabeth, but this was something else entirely. She wrinkled her nose in distaste. "It's OK I guess."

This was not the reaction he wanted. He began again: "Have you thought about going to meetings, there's a group on campus."

"Uh. . . Well actually, I have thought about it, but I've been so busy, what with one thing and another."

"You should go to a meeting. Women's liberation is an important part of The Movement."

"Sure, why not, I'll try it out for size," she said flippantly, but he didn't smile, and she asked more seriously: "When do they meet?"

"Wednesday nights. There's a meeting tonight in the Student Union. Room 210."

"Who's in it, anybody I know?"

"Well, there's uh. . . Elizabeth, you met her, and Susan. . . you know George, don't you? And Paul's wife. Did you know she was pregnant?"

She shook her head.

"Why don't you go," he prompted.

"Sure. I'll go."

The meeting began at eight, but it wasn't until eight thirty that Becky left the library and walked toward the Student Union. She hadn't been able to decide whether or not to go, and going late was a compromise. As she walked she looked up at the second floor of the Union, lit from within by fluorescent lights.

The windows were unshaded, and the glass reflected sharply the less than twenty women in Room 210. They sat in metal folding chairs placed in a circle, listening to Susan Mather analyze the article they had read.

The group had no formal organization. Each week they read a different article and a different woman lead the discussion, or was supposed to. What happened was that Susan lead it. The previous summer she and Elizabeth had read "Women: The Longest Revolution," and in September had announced in the campus paper the formation of a women's liberation group. Already subtle political tensions had arisen. These tensions were never discussed directly; rather, Susan maintained a facade of unity by avoiding topics that might have brought them out in the open.

She felt responsible for the group's direction, and since she believed the women to be politically immature, she took advantage of every opportunity to educate them. She was sincere, dedicated, condescending and humorless.

Susan was slim and poised, with a small pinched mouth and long brown hair that she studiously ignored. She wore jeans and combat boots, and her army jacket lay in a heap on the floor. In contrast to this austere outfit that suggested battle was an expensive heavy-knit white fisherman's sweater. She'd toned down the contrast by allowing the sweater to become ragged at the cuffs, and soiled. In the pocket of her army jacket was a copy of Mao's *Little Red Book*. She quoted it frequently with an air of absolute authority, as though Mao himself had bestowed the book upon her, hoping she would aid him in educating the masses.

Susan was an experienced speaker. She knew how to build beautifully elaborate word castles, pausing at commas and semi-colons, and forging onward, leaving her listeners bewildered down on the earth below. Although a good part of the women couldn't follow her train of thought, they did not want to appear stupid, and listened intently.

Only two made no pretence. The first was the young

daughter of one of the women. She sat in a corner and scribbled on a pad of paper with a felt tipped pen. The second was Susan's dog, who she brought to all the meetings. The dog was a mongrel named Che. He curled at Susan's feet and slept.

She was in the midst of her analysis when George appeared outside the door. He was tall and burly with a mop of curly dark hair and sideburns that curved toward his jaw. He had just found out that he and Susan, Paul and Justine had been chosen to join the Venceremos Brigade.

He'd been standing there only a few minutes when Becky turned down the hallway behind him and headed toward the room. She saw number 210 next to George's head and stopped. She wasn't sure if he was guarding the women or mocking them, but he looked impregnable in either case.

" 'Scuse me," she mumbled. He looked her up and down. She smiled apologetically since she had few political credentials to offer other than getting gassed in Washington. "Is this the women's meeting?" she asked, and mentally kicked herself. Ass! Of course it was the women's meeting, couldn't she see there was nothing but women in the room?

He smirked and stepped aside, giving her barely enough room to wedge through him and the doorway. Her stomach clenched in anger. 'Why do you always have to make the worst of any situation. Why do you always say the worst thing! The absolute worst thing!'

Her face, however, showed only a smooth placid expression as she walked into the room. It was not the kind of entrance any one of her ideal women would make: striding confidently, slinking sensually, or strolling like the dreamy nature girl. In her hurry to complete the entrance without falling on her face, she stubbed her toe on the empty chair around which she was trying to maneuver. She sat down in a lump, careful to smooth her skirt under her, though she was in such a rush she almost sat on her hand.

She composed herself and prepared to judge the whole meeting as stupid. She looked around and saw many placid faces. 'They look like a bunch of cows,' she thought, and her expression changed to a smirk.

She inspected the faces with a practiced eye. Most of the women were dressed in sweaters and skirts, and some wore jeans. A few, including Elizabeth, who had acknowledged her presence by nodding, wore women's liberation buttons: the clenched red fist inside the women's symbol against a background of white.

Becky shifted her weight in her seat and opened her pocketbook, glancing surreptitiously at the hand mirror to see if her eyeliner was smudged.

Across the room Terry watched her, and when Becky looked up, Terry smiled. Becky thought of these women as ridiculous suffragette types, swinging umbrellas at poor innocent men, and recognized Terry as the one who'd criticized Paul at the teach-in. She epitomized a fanatic and Becky wanted nothing to do with her. She stared coldly at Terry and triumphantly pulled a pencil from her pocketbook, as if that was what she'd been looking for all along.

A few moments later, Justine walked into the room. She'd tried to be inconspicuous, but Susan stopped speaking and congratulated her, explaining that Justine was pregnant. She glared at Susan and bore the flurry of congratulations and questions graciously.

George took advantage of the interruption to walk up to Susan and whisper in her ear. When she announced to the group that the two couples were going to Cuba, Justine was dismayed.

Becky had expected Paul's wife to be more like Susan; Justine seemed a dismal looking creature, one certainly undeserving of Paul. She looked so unhappy with the attention that Becky felt resentful. Being married to Paul, carrying his child, what more could any woman want.

Justine glanced at Becky, and seeing the envious expression in her eyes, she smiled as if to say: Isn't all this fuss silly?

Becky half turned before she realized that Justine was smiling at her. She looked away, embarrassed.

She thought most of the meeting dull, and wondered if David knew many of the women. She created amusing anecdotes for him revolving around what they wore and said.

At the end of the meeting they discussed a demonstration to be held that Saturday in New Haven, Connecticut to protest the treatment of the Panther 13 women. Elizabeth mentioned that she and Susan had room for one more in the car, and Becky asked for a ride.

The meeting was over. Becky wandered to the front of the room and bought a set of pamphlets that were stacked on the front table. She turned to see Terry and Justine leave the room together, their heads bent toward one another in eager conversation.

In the next few days she was sorry she'd committed herself to attending the Panther demonstration. She dreaded that long car ride, but more important, with Elizabeth gone, David would be free. But backing out now would be transparent, and when the women came to pick her up on Saturday, she was ready.

The early morning wind blew across the road, rocking the battered blue Volvo. The car's springs were worn, and everytime Susan drove over a bump, Becky and Justine bounced off the back seat and landed hard. A cold draft from a crack in the rear window blew across their necks. Justine, the taller of the two, tried unsuccessfully to straighten her cramped legs.

It was Susan's car, and occasionally she turned around to make witty comments about its condition. During the ride to Connecticut she and Elizabeth discussed the differences between the women's movement in various cities and made in-jokes about George and David.

Becky listened carefully, hoping to get some political education. It was the first time she'd gotten the chance to observe Elizabeth closely. She thought her not particularly attractive, certainly not sensual. Becky thought: 'She's the little girl type. I wouldn't think David would like that type. But maybe he's tired of her. I wonder if she's any good in bed. It must be like going to bed with a ten year old. Maybe that's what he likes. I'll have to act girlish and see how he responds. . .'

Elizabeth thought that Becky was timid; she knew David disrespected women who submitted too willingly. He wanted his woman, an exceptional woman, to submit only to him, a real man. Elizabeth's family had settled in Massachusetts several generations ago, and her father had been the mayor of a small town for two terms. She had been taught to hold her head high, and when she bowed it to David, the distance was impressive. She knew how to argue intelligently and in the end become convinced only by his superior knowledge and reasoning powers. Becky had never held her head as high as Elizabeth. Her submission could never mean as much.

126

Justine and Becky made small talk for awhile. and then Justine smiled and said: "You remind me of a friend of mine. I'm not sure what it is about you. . ."

"What was her name."

"Lynne."

"How am I like her."

"Oh. . . just like that. Hey, aren't you the one Terry told me about? Did you go to Washington alone for the demonstration?"

"Yes, I did. Why. . . how did she know."

"She saw you there. She thought you were brave to go all alone, she was scared to death."

"Me? Brave? What is she, kidding?"

"Why, don't you think it was brave?"

"Well, I never thought about it before but I guess I was."

Susan had been listening to them and now said: "It was an incorrect action to go alone."

"Susan," Justine said, "you're a voice of cheer, honest to God. They ought to rent you out for funerals."

"I wouldn't take it so lightly," Susan answered. "She could've been hurt and no one would have known about it."

"Sure, I agree, but you take all the romance out of it."

"I don't think being gassed is very romantic."

"Well you ought to know since you're such an expert on gas."

Susan laughed. To her, Justine's insults were like the nippings of a little puppy.

Justine continued: "Yeah, you remind me of Lynne. We were best friends in high school. We were like that," she said, holding up two fingers tightly closed. "Ever have a friend like that?"

"Mmm. . . Yeah, I did. Her name was Kathy." Becky smiled, remembering. "We told each other everything. We did everything together, and what we didn't do together, we talked about later on. We just about lived at each other's houses. Of course, it was nothing but a childhood friendship."

"You say it like those kind aren't important. They are."

"I guess so."

"What happened, did one of you move away?"

"No, not until later. I got interested in boys before she did. so. . . I don't know, I guess we didn't have so much in common."

"That's too bad."

"Yeah. But it was no great loss, I never was much for girlfriends."

"Oh? Why not."

Becky shrugged. "I don't know. I never liked women very much. They're always worried about stupid things like. . . I don't know, just stupid things. Most women don't have a brain in their heads."

Justine stared at her. "But aren't you a woman?"

Becky laughed. "I never said I was any prize package, did I?"

Justine kept staring. "Don't you ever take anything seriously?"

Becky was about to laugh and say: No, not unless I have to, but Justine turned away to look out the window.

It was almost noon when they arrived in New Haven. Susan parked the car on the edge of a large grassy square where several hundred people milled around. The women outnumbered the men by far, and the few men were mostly black and Puerto Rican. Becky thought to herself that it didn't at all compare to Washington. It was a women's demonstration, and the Black Panthers seemed less important than the Vietnamese. She wished that she could stay in the car until it was over. It was cold outside.

Elizabeth and Susan walked away, Elizabeth giving Susan extensive instructions in case she had an asthma attack. Becky and Justine stood by the car looking across the empty expanse separating them from the demonstrators. "This is gonna be great," Justine said, putting her hands in her pockets. "Come on..."

They wandered among the people. A woman with curly hair handed them a long sheet of paper on which was typed what looked like a poem. Becky read aloud:

" '6 sisters in prison.
   3 sisters pregnant.
   2 sisters almost in labor.
   All have been accused
   of conspiracy and murder.
   None have been tried
   or found guilty.
   All 6 are black.
   All 6 are Panthers.
   All 6 are sisters.' "

"It's from W.I.T.C.H." Justine said.

"What's that?"

She read: "Women's International Terrorist Conspiracy from Hell."

Becky laughed. "Weird."

"Terry wanted to start one."

"What do they do?"

"Oh, she was telling me they get dressed up in costumes and put spells on people. No, not spells..."

"Hexes?"

"That's it: hexes. Guerilla theater."

Becky nodded and continued reading the pamphlet:

" ' WITCH knows our suppressed history:
that women who rebel are not only
jailed, napalmed & beaten,
but also
raped, branded & burned at the stake.

We women are:
in jail at Niantic
in the mud of Vietnam
in the slums of the cities
in the ghetto-sinks of suburbia
at the typewriters
of the corporations
at the mimeographing machines
of the Left
in the water at Chappaquidick
in the brutalizing beds of Babylon.

We are going to stop
all confinement of women.
WITCH calls down destruction
on Babylon.
Oppressors:
the curse of women is on you
DEATH TO MALE CHAUVINISM.' "

The last part made Becky uncomfortable, but Justine grinned. "Yeah, I dig that: 'the curse of women is on you.' Can you imagine what it would be like to be a witch?

Man, I'd go around putting hexes on people?—I can think of ten right off the bat that I'd hex. Yeah. The second I was a witch, Zap! I'd be like Samantha." she said, trying to twitch her nose, "only I wouldn't be so nice."

She heard Terry calling her from across the grass. "Come on," she said, but Becky stood still, not wanting to be associated with Terry. "I'll be right back." Justine said, "don't go away."

Becky nodded. But she didn't think Justine would return, and she drifted to a hilltop where she stood among photographers and onlookers, watching those below. The crowd had tripled in size. Some women carried red banners with black lettering that read: "Free Our Sisters, Free Ourselves;" others stood and talked. The wind cut through Becky's jacket and she felt exposed. Around her neck she wore a long green knit scarf that she wrapped twice around her throat and tucked into the front of her jacket. She watched the few men and wondered when the march would begin.

The crowd kept growing, and gradually formed five across into a line, the black women in front, the white women in the middle, and the men scattered in back. Becky came down from the hill. She didn't want to be left behind.

After a long wait they linked arms and began to move. Becky felt awkward; she didn't know if she should walk in step with someone or not, and her body, long accustomed to walking alone, felt pulled at from both sides. Once she stumbled. She felt that the men who marched in back were overseeing it all, and she was grateful to them. But when some men ran to the front, a few women near her shouted: "Get back! It's women only!" The men were black and she wondered if yelling at them had been racist. They got back.

Their bodies fell into rhythm, and soon she was a part of a massive, thousand legged animal whose body heat vibrated in the cold streets, and whose voice rolled in waves from the front to the back as the women chanted: "Out of the house! Out of the jails! Out from under, women unite!" Despite herself, Becky felt the excitement surge up from the crowd into the air.

The chants sounded different than in Washington, more like songs than slogans. At the front of the line a group of women sang: "Po-wer to the Peo-ple, power to the people, right on!" and another group sang something else, Becky caught only scattered names: Bobby, Erika; and once again: "Po-wer to the Peo-ple, power to the people, right on!" Someone shook a tambourine.

She was moving inside a domed force field that arched into the sky and enclosed them all. The pride was catching. She felt that she belonged. It reminded her of something, a movie she had seen perhaps. She couldn't quite grasp it and finally gave up: she wanted nothing to take her away from these moments.

They marched past the stately buildings of Yale University. It was the weekend of the Yale-Harvard football game, and the students and their dates stared at them: they were part of their pre-game entertainment. The women shouted, timidly at first, and then louder: "Fuck Harvard! Fuck Yale! Get the Panthers Out of Jail!" It seemed sacreligious to say "fuck" around these dignified buildings, these proper men and their dates, and Becky began to laugh.

Some of the marching women yelled: "Join Us! Join Us!" And so caught up was she that Becky imagined for a moment that the dates would fling away their rosebuds and gardenias and flood into the march. But they smiled contemptuously or hid behind their men. One stared at Becky as though she were a freak. She was momentarily stunned, and had a sudden urge to stop marching, drop the women's arms, and say to her: 'I'm not really like this,' but also: 'You should join us, it's important.'

They marched down Main street and headed toward a tall pillared building. When they reached the steps the line broke up. The women on either side of her smiled and dropped her arms.

She looked around for a familiar face and saw Justine and Terry standing on the steps laughing. Justine saw her and waved. "Becky! Hey!"

Becky grinned and waved. Justine motioned her to come over and at the same time began to walk her way. The crowd was thick between them, and watching each other wade through the people, pushing bodies gently aside with their arms, they laughed because they thought of "the meeting," so often pictured in commercials, where people run in slow motion into each other's arms.

But when there was only empty space between them, Becky caught herself and dropped her arms as though she'd only lifted them to adjust her scarf. "There sure are alot of people here. What's happening."

"Not much," Justine said. "Not much at all." She craned her neck. "What happened to Terry, she was right behind me. Oh there she is. Hey, I thought you got lost."

"Who, me?" Terry grinned. "Never."

The speeches began. A car was parked in front in the building and its roof served as a stage. A group of black and Puerto Rican men stood around the car and hoisted the black women up onto the roof to speak. They joked and laughed among themselves, and Becky felt left out.

In the windows of the surrounding buildings, Federal

agents took picture after picture. 'Of us,' Becky thought. 'Of me.' But she felt safe: she was white, and a student. 'I don't really belong here,' she thought toward the cameras.

Behind the women at the top step of the building, a man in a suit stood taking pictures. He was in full view of the crowd, not bothering to conceal himself behind a nearby pillar. He was bold: a man among women, a stag among does, made arrogant by the State and his body.

Terry saw him and pointed. "Look!" She made her way to the steps, and other women saw him and followed her.

"Hey, what are you doing!" a woman shouted.

"Yeah, get outta here!"

"Pig!"

"Pig!"

"Pig!" they screamed, surrounding him, stamping their feet and roaring: "Pig! Pig! Pig!"

At first he tried to laugh away their anger, to explain, but they squeezed him in tighter and tighter like a living iron maiden, screaming: "Pig! Pig! Pig!"

Just as they backed him up against the brick wall of the building, the man panicked and lunged forward. The women stepped apart. One grabbed his camera and whipped open the shutters exposing the film. Another stuck out her foot; he stumbled over it and landed on his knee.

He ran away and the women jeered him. They swirled into a circle dance of victory, whooping and yelling like Jane swinging through the trees for the first time.

Becky stood apart, wishing she had joined them. But she felt anonymous in the crowd, and that was where she wanted to stay, at least for now.

When the crowd began to thin, they walked back to the

car. On the way home they stopped at Howard Johnson's. The orange slated roof sloped over a world of dull food, bland piped-in music, and twenty-eight flavored dependability. If you came to Howard Johnson's you knew what to expect. In Pittsburgh or New Haven, Kansas City or Boise, Howard Johnson's fried clams were Howard Johnson's fried clams. After the demonstration it was an alien place to them.

Susan lead them to a back booth and they sat down, she and Elizabeth on one side, Becky and Justine on the other. Susan was sulking because she'd wanted Chinese food. Elizabeth tried to coax her out of her mood: "Look, Susan, look at this, did you ever see anything so incredibly bourgeois in your life?" Justine ignored her and thought: 'What a baby. She needs a good slap.' Occasionally Susan glared resentfully at Justine, as if Justine's refusal to baby her were the cause of her bad mood.

The waitress came and they ordered: Susan a hamburger plate, Elizabeth a BLT with extra mayonnaise, Becky a hamburger plate, and Justine an egg salad sandwich.

Susan and Elizabeth chatted about their men in affectionately complaining tones. Elizabeth said: "Do you know what David did the other day?" and told a lengthy anecdote. She ended with a smile: "He's going to drive me crazy," and looked at Becky as if to goad her into some comment about her own relationship with David.

Becky said nothing. The situation was clear to her: Elizabeth was part of a couple and she was part of nothing. When Elizabeth told funny stories about David or complained about him, she could only listen. She didn't have the right to moan that he was driving her crazy. If she went crazy she would have to go in silence.

Though Susan and Elizabeth kept trying to bring Justine

into the fold, she resisted, giving her full attention to Becky. At one point when Susan and Elizabeth were talking about the Thanksgiving dinner that the three couples planned to share, Justine turned to Becky and said: "What are you doing for Thanksgiving."

Becky saw Susan and Elizabeth freeze, and although she was in fact spending Thanksgiving alone, she said: "Oh, I'll probably go home."

The waitress brought the food and left. Justine looked at her sandwich and said: "Hey, this is tuna fish. I ordered egg salad." She looked around but the waitress had disappeared.

Susan said: "You ordered tuna salad."

"No I didn't. I never order tuna salad. I hate tuna fish."

"I'm sure I heard you say tuna salad. Why don't you just eat it."

"Because I ordered egg salad, that's why."

"But if you make her take it back she's only going to get in trouble."

"She's not going to get in trouble, Susan. I worked in a place like this for years, and all they do is put it aside 'til somebody else orders it."

Susan shrugged, unconvinced. "I wouldn't want it on my conscience to get the waitress in trouble. She probably works hard all day."

"Yeah, well so do I, and when I pay for egg salad I expect to get it."

"I don't see the difference. Didn't you hear her say tuna salad?" Susan asked Becky.

As Becky stammered uncomfortably, the waitress passed by. Justine hailed her and requested the change.

Susan began discussing the purpose of the demonstration as a show of solidarity with the Black Panthers. Justine listened in silence for a few minutes, then cut in: "I didn't demonstrate to show solidarity with anybody. I don't care if they're Panthers or giraffes," she said, trying her best to needle Susan. "I went to New Haven because they're going to take that girl's baby away from her. My God, she's got enough strikes against her: she's a girl, she's black, and I'll bet you anything she doesn't have a dime to her name, poor thing. And now they're going to take away her baby. . ." She appealed to Becky: "Isn't that terrible? I mean, all she has is her baby, and they're going to take it away. Poor thing," she said defiantly to Susan.

Susan explained that the demonstration was the Left's response to the repression that the government had employed to crush a movement that had done so much constructive work in the black community.

"I don't care what she's done," Justine said hotly. "Just because she's in jail doesn't mean she's a criminal."

They stared at one another with dislike. The waitress brought Justine's sandwich and she began to eat.

On the way home the four sat as before: Susan and Elizabeth in front, Becky and Justine in back.

Later, Justine fell asleep. Her head drooped, then found its way onto Becky's shoulder.

Before, if it had been a man's head, Becky might have felt something sexual, perhaps maneuvered her body until his head rested on her breast: or if it had been a woman's, she would have been repulsed, might have stiffened, and tried to push her head in the opposite direction.

But now she just felt the pleasant pressure of a warm head on her shoulder and smelled the subtle fragrance of clean hair in the dark, silent, gently rocking car.

Outside, the wind blew cold, rushing in through the cracked window. Becky's long green scarf trailed loosely around her neck and onto her lap. She picked up one end and placed it carefully around the front of Justine's neck, tucking it between her shoulder and the vinyl seat, so that the scarf formed a warm shield around them.

December
1969

Winter had come in a wind that blew cold across the hills, shaking the bare branches. The first snow fell one afternoon in the third week of December and lasted late into the night. Beneath the streetlights gusts of snow whirled, settling down to blanket the cracked sidewalks and dented garbage cans with soft white.

It was Becky's last night with David. After a movie they walked to a diner, huddling against the cold. Becky went to the ladies room and David sat at the booth.

When she opened the door to return, the waitress was calling an order to the cook while she poured a large glass of orange juice and set it down before a man who had opened a newspaper and snapped it upright. On the grill, hamburgers sizzled. Toast popped up: the cook grabbed the slices and slapped on butter.

Through this activity Becky walked smiling and composed toward David. She felt that the two of them were enclosed in an atmosphere they exuded, like the heavy smell of gardenias. They were a young couple in love. The man at the counter glanced at her legs encased in high leather boots; below her short plaid skirt, her bare thighs were red from the cold.

On the wall over the booth was a chrome juke box selector. David flipped the knob as he read the titles. He wore a green woolen shirt and black turtle-neck jersey; his skin was ruddy and his hair was tousled from the wind. Becky looked at his moustache, the shock of black hair falling across his forehead, and thought him beautiful.

She sat down and glanced at herself in the chrome. She wore a black V-neck sweater, and her hair was piled softly on top of her head. She thought they made a beautiful couple. She wanted to tell him how she felt, but knew he would take it as a question rather than a statement.

She felt surely her eyes glowed: she was a woman in love. But tomorrow it would be over; he was leaving to meet Elizabeth in Boston. Since Elizabeth had left town at the beginning of Christmas recess, Becky's life had been transformed. Now was the time to write her term papers, due in January. Now was the time to begin studying for her final exams. But she put it all aside; she thought of December as David's month.

They spent all his free time together. They cooked together, went for long walks, laughed and talked. They made love passionately and frequently, and as far as he knew it was perfect every time but one. This was the life she had dreamt about for so long: her own apartment, her own man. But she grasped so frantically at their time together it had the quality of past events, as though she were looking back from some future date when it would all be memories.

And in a way she was consciously creating memories for him as well as herself. She felt that she had to pack a great quantity of experience into this short time so that when he returned to Elizabeth, he would look back on the idyllic days with longing.

She sighed and reached for the menu.

"I already took care of it," he said. "Didn't you say at the movies you wanted a BLT?"

"David, how sweet. Thank you."

"And I remembered: no mayonnaise."

He looked at her so warmly, she didn't have the heart to tell him he'd confused her with Elizabeth. Becky liked mayonnaise, alot of it.

The waitress brought their coffee, and placed a set of silverware before him.

"What did you order?" Becky asked.

"Bacon and eggs." He adjusted the silverware so that the knife and spoon were separated the same at the top as the bottom. The fork he moved an inch to the right, leaving just enough room for the plate.

She laughed. "You're so fussy!"

"You'd be better off if you were a little fussy, too."

"Oh, I'm not so bad as I was, am I?"

He considered her question. The waitress brought their food, and as he began eating, agreed that she had improved.

Becky's apartment was basically clean, but she was extremely disorganized. One day David saw her putting away her laundry: stuffing all her underwear into a drawer, clean but unfolded and unsorted. He teased her until she yielded, arranging everything into neat piles. The first time they ate dinner together, she set things out haphazardly, standing the silverware in a glass in the middle of the table, using paper towels in place of napkins, dishing the food directly from the pots onto their plates. He taught her to line up the silverware exactly, fold the napkins, and use serving dishes. It meant more trouble all the way around, but if it made him happy she didn't really mind.

She was also "intellectually disorganized," as David said. Writing her own school papers she used no notes or outlines, but wrote it all in one draft from beginning to end.

When David brought her his paper on the Mexican Revolution to type, she opened the manilla envelope and found thirty pages covered with strained precise handwriting and a myriad of arrows pointing to small, clipped on notes. It was, in a sense, organized. But the paper was bad. She reorganized it all and rewrote many sections, changing not only the style but also using the information she'd discovered while doing the research. She was glad that she had already written the proposal to Pritchard at the beginning of December. Writing and typing David's paper took all of her time.

Her sandwich was dry and she had to wash it down with coffee. As she finished the third cup, she asked: "Did you mail your paper?"

"No, I have to stop by my office tomorrow before I leave. It'll be great to go there without running into all the Department reactionaries. By the way, did I tell you I signed my teaching contract for next year?"

She nodded. He had told her. Twice.

"I hope the paper helps me with my tenure fight next year. It ought to, all that work."

"Are you glad it's done?"

"I sure am. What about you, co-author, you must be glad too. You put alot of work into that paper."

"I sure did."

"What would I ever do without you," he asked, and stroked her hand lightly with his fingertips. "This time with you has been wonderful," he said sadly.

"Yes. It has."

"It's too bad. . ." He didn't finish the sentence but she knew he meant it was too bad that their time together was over. "Don't get me wrong, it's only that Elizabeth is a very demanding woman."

She listened to his complaint, and said: "Do you think you'll ever move out?"

Her voice was casual and the question was a logical extension of his grievance. But seeing his trapped expression, she knew it wasn't casual or logical enough. He hemmed and hawed nervously, giving her no chance to withdraw. Finally he said: "Well, it is getting a little crowded. . . And I have been thinking of moving. . ." He stopped; he stared at the knife and flipped it over and back repeatedly in a tight, insistent motion.

"Dave. . . you know, if you ever feel that I'm pressuring you, I want you to tell me. OK?"

He smiled at her gratefully and laid the knife to rest. "You're not like that. You're different. It's amazing, but you really are different. You understand me. We've got a good thing going."

She smiled weakly. They were supposed to be adults engaging in a free, mature, non-monogamous relationship. yet for all that, she felt like an old-fashioned mistress that David kept tucked away for his spare moments.

She had tried to make him jealous, mentioning men she had been with in the past and men who flirted with her now. He merely laughed and said: "You're not my property." But she felt as long as she was alone she was public property, something for men to whistle at and remark about in the street. When she was with a man, other men recognized that she belonged to someone else. Being private property, she would at least be protected.

But David went so far as to imply that he might have been relieved if she dated someone else. He mentioned that Elizabeth had gotten a ride to Boston with Paul's student, Mark, and he sounded proud when he joked about "Elizabeth's undergraduate admirer." But Becky suspected his reaction would have been different had he thought the feeling between Elizabeth and Mark were mutual. Regardless, Becky could not go in search of a second lover: her moral code defined sleeping with one man as being in love, and sleeping with more than one man as being a slut.

When they returned to her apartment they made love. Half asleep, David murmured, "Good-night, Lizzie-bee," kissed her on the forehead and turned over. Becky lay there, slightly horrified.

Her bedroom was dim, lit only by a lemon scented candle that stood in a plate on the dresser, its glow reflected in the mirror. From the living room came the low sound of music. The sheets were fresh, the blankets warm, the pillows soft. She fluffed the pillow and waited for the effect of the coffee to wear off so she could fall asleep. Fully alert, she stared at the flickering candle and wondered if going in the other room to masturbate would help her relax.

Sex with David wasn't quite satisfying. Of the few times they'd slept together in November, she only climaxed once. She didn't want him to feel insecure about his manhood, and she wove a lie with heavy breathing and a frustrated moaning she pretended was passion.

When Elizabeth left town, Becky wanted to start anew. On their first night David asked: "Did you come?" She replied: "No." At first he was depressed and implied there was something wrong with him; later he was mildly abusive and implied there was something wrong with her.

The incident threatened to ruin everything. The next night she lied convincingly. She accepted these lies as a normal part of their relationship. She'd lied before with other men; she felt that undoubtedly she would lie again. David was easily fooled by a few well placed moans, and this fact made her wonder about his relationship with Elizabeth. She thought: 'For all her talk about women's liberation, she probably fakes as much as me.'

She consoled herself with the thought that she would teach him how to please her. Soon. When he felt more secure. She believed that her own pleasure was something extra, not necessary to qualify what they did as sexual intercourse, and could wait.

The one time this extra did occur she had to work so hard for it that it didn't even feel like release. Her fantasies were sensual luscious dreams of explosive sex. Her reality remained a hard climb toward a tight, pinching orgasm.

Lying in bed, she told herself she was being morbid to dwell on her frustrations, and she turned her thoughts to a review of the pleasant evening with David.

Something bothered her vaguely, like a fly buzzing somewhere at the back of her head. It wasn't until she began to fall asleep that the picture snapped into her mind: Elizabeth sitting across from her in New Haven. saying to the waitress: "I'd like extra mayonnaise on my sandwich, please."

The next morning he left. Standing in the doorway. he kissed her good-bye and said: "I have a present for you." He reached into his pocket and took out a small women's liberation button, but as he pulled it out, another one exactly like it fell to the floor. He picked it up quickly and hid it, looking guilty.

When she was alone she sat at the kitchen table. looked at the button and felt its smoothness under her fingers. She tried to concentrate on this one, but kept picturing the one he dropped. She saw the button on the floor and that quick guilty look in his eyes.

All day long the thought nagged at her: the other button, who was it for? And the mayonnaise. . . There was someone else, she felt it for sure. There was someone else.

The pregnancy made the vows between Paul and Justine painfully clear. Irritating differences were magnified into antagonistic ways of life. They hoped the baby would bring them together, and each avoided topics and situations that might lead to conflict. Their one ongoing argument was about a Christmas tree. Neither went beyond "I want one" and "I don't want one;" for voicing reasons might lead to voicing expectations. Until the end of the month, the veneer remained intact.

Paul plunged himself into his schoolwork, studying for his oral exams which were scheduled for May. In the evenings he studied at the library, coming home after Justine had fallen asleep. She had assumed that after the Washington demonstration his political activities would taper off, but he became involved with the investigation of the Pentagon funded Project Rhododendron. George and Susan left for Cuba, and it was Paul who took on George's political responsibilities, since David was unreliable.

Paul was bitterly disappointed about missing the chance to live in Cuba. He appeased himself with the idea of creating a revolutionary living situation, a collective that would be a hub of anti-war and anti-imperialist political activity. Though he had not broached the subject to Justine, he convinced himself that her reaction would be favorable. All labor in the collective, including child-care, would be divided equally. Expenses would be shared. Surrounded by people, Justine would no longer be lonely.

For now she spent many evenings alone, but it had ceased to bother her. She was waiting for the first signs of life. As much as she had earlier denied the pregnancy, she now became absorbed in it. She found it supremely amazing that without conscious thought or planning, her own body was creating a new life. Granted that some aspects of the pregnancy were unpleasant, uncomfortable, granted that her moods were erratic, her feelings toward Paul contradictory. But there was a center, the baby and herself: now one, soon to be two separate human beings.

She imagined a future time after the baby was born when she and Paul would snuggle up and talk about their future: their future alone, not the future of the world. They would have a real home. They would be a real family.

Yet moods of despair came upon her often and they were deepened by the fact that she could not share them. She wanted her mother to hold her close, to tell her what childbirth was like and how to prepare. Lying in Paul's arms one night she started crying, clinging to him like a child. But she felt he wasn't really there, and after that she cried alone, sobbing violently, unconcerned with anyone else's feelings. She cried for herself, for the baby, for her passing youth.

In the beginning of December she went for her first prenatal check-up. The doctor reassured that she had not hurt the baby; nevertheless, she worried. He gave her vitamins that she took faithfully; he gave her a diet that she taped to the refrigerator and checked everyday. Her clothes became tight. She took to wearing loose fitting jumpers to work.

She told her family she was pregnant; no one was surprised. Though they congratulated her, she could not help but see the misgivings in their eyes.

Only Lynne seemed truly happy, and their friendship entered a new stage. Lynne stopped tossing work on Justine's desk; she became protective. One morning after she sat down on the bus, Justine became nauseous and made it to the street just in time. She held onto a telephone pole for support and vomitted a stream of half digested breakfast and stomach bile that splashed onto the icy curb. The bus was stopped at a red light and the faces looked down at her, sympathetic but squeamish. Lynne had followed her, and looked back at the faces defensively. She held Justine's arm and waited for the sickness to pass, jauntily declared that they would go to work in style, and hailed a cab.

All month they talked about Christmas dinner at Aunt Connie's. Lynne was going to try to make a pie from scratch, and Justine's first attempt at baking would be herb bread. But one week before Christmas, Paul told her that his parents were expecting them early in the afternoon of the twenty-fifth, and she remembered their agreement: last year they'd spent with her family, this year they'd spend with his.

Christmas morning she drove to Connie and Phil's to exchange gifts, then to her father's. Paul did not come. She gave her father a maroon velour pullover, and he gave her a long housecoat: blue and green paisley, tied with a tassled sash. Though it was large enough for her to wear throughout the pregnancy, it was not a winter robe: the material was a thin slippery nylon. Her father had always been impractical; he and Babe had balanced each other, her methodical planning off-setting his impulsive splurging.

As Justine admired the robe, he smiled apologetically. "It won't be warm enough for the winter. Right after I bought it, I thought of what your mother would say. You know how she was. . ."

"It's beautiful, Daddy, I love it."

They hugged one another. But the moment vanished when he remembered she was spending the day with her in-laws. He began criticizing Paul, and Justine, realizing that she did not know how to defend him, became upset and left. Ill-tempered, she went home.

As she dressed for dinner, she closed the bedroom door. She wore maternity bras now; her heavy breasts had begun to leak a slow, sweet, white stickiness that peeked out from tiny holes in her nipples. Paul thought bras were a sign of women's oppression, and especially disliked the underwired maternity bra. When he saw it, he reminded her about his friend from Ann Arbor who wore no bra through her entire pregnancy and seemed none the worse for it.

She put on a green sweater and a charcoal gray jumper, nylons and low heels, and applied light make-up. As she was brushing her hair, Paul opened the door. "How do I look?" she asked.

He stood next to her and observed them both in the mirror. The gray jumper accentuated her gray eyes. She looked stunning: clear-skinned, fresh-faced. Somber, yet very young. Paul wore his usual outfit: jeans, faded blue work shirt, U.S. Navy surplus sweater. His hair and beard were neatly trimmed. He had a stubborn look to his face, as though he were determined to cling to his unpopular ideas and expected to encounter argument.

Standing side by side they looked completely mismatched, and for a split second he wondered if maybe his father were right. Not that he would have wanted one of those conceited little snobs his father might have chosen, but someone, perhaps, whose convictions matched his own and who dressed to suit those convictions.

Justine did not look like the same person who'd walked into his class that night over a year ago. She had looked so carefree in her blue jeans and sandals, a sweater tied jauntily around her shoulders, her long hair flowing over the sweater. Since she'd gotten pregnant, she looked so settled.

She put the brush on the dresser, and held out her arms. "Well?"

"I wish you hadn't cut your hair," he said.

She dropped her arms. "I know. And I wish you'd stop telling me. Come on, how do I look? What do I have to do, kiss your ass on Main Street to get a compliment out of you?"

"You look fine," he said. "Though I don't know why you always insist on getting so dressed up." He got their coats from the hall closet.

She followed him. "And I don't know why you insist on looking like such a slob."

"I don't look like a slob. I'm just not trying to impress anybody." He opened the outside door. It had been raining, and the sky was overcast. He inspected her closely. "You're wearing make-up."

"Thank you, I'm glad you noticed."

He walked ahead of her down the pathway. "I don't know why you waste your time at those women's liberation meetings if you're going to turn around and put that shit all over your face."

She got into the car and slammed the door.

During the hour it took them to drive to his parent's house, they continued to bicker. The road was slicked with rain. He drove fast, mumbling directions to her regarding what not to do and what not to say. She was annoyed with him for not having told his parents of her pregnancy.

"It's bad timing, Paul. We can't bop in there, point to my stomach and say, 'Guess Who's Coming to Dinner?'"

"Don't worry. It'll be cool."

But she did worry. She worried as she sat in the kitchen, trying not to see the food drippings crusted on the side of the stove while she listened to Mrs. Denton talk about recipes—which didn't interest her. She worried as she sat in the dining room, pushing the food around on her plate while Paul and his parents argued about politics—which didn't interest her.

Paul announced the news of her pregnancy during the after dinner espresso. Mrs. Denton, holding her demitasse cup to her lips, set it down on the saucer abruptly. A quick look passed between his parents.

"Well well well," his father said and stood up to find his pipe.

"Isn't that. . . nice." his mother said, looking like she were about to have an attack of migraine.

The Dentons knew how to keep up a polite front, but now and then a look would escape.

Justine tried to ignore them, and examined the Oriental rug, the rows and rows of books, the pottery Mrs. Denton had collected as an art student in Peru.

Later, Paul and his father sipped their after dinner liquer. Justine had been daydreaming, and suddenly heard Paul say: ". . . we're considering home delivery. There's a doctor in town who. . ."

It took Justine a moment to realize he was talking about the baby.

Mrs. Denton was staring at Justine. "But how can you. . ." she sputtered, ". . . in a house. . . with only the two of you. . ."

Paul calmly sipped his Grand Marnier. "It won't be just us. The doctor will be there. And hopefully by then we'll be moved into the commune, and there'll be people to help."

Justine's mouth fell open but she composed herself and made no comment.

They left at seven. Stars shone against the dark sky, and the moon reflected on the ice-crusted snow. Justine breathed the crisp air deeply. Mrs. Denton placed her hands lightly on Justine's shoulders and brushed her lips briefly against her cheek. "Now do keep in touch, dear," she said stepping back.

Justine smiled past the faint look of distaste on her face. "Thank you for the dinner."

They walked down the four brick steps to the driveway. Justine felt their eyes on her back. At the car she turned to smile once more and waved as Paul backed the car out of the driveway. Mr. Denton waved with his pipe and Mrs. Denton lifted one weary hand looking as though the migraine had attacked full force.

The rain had frozen into a smooth coating around the trees, covering the tiniest branches so that each tree was an intricate design of ice. Some of the houses were strung with colored lights, and one lawn displayed a statue of Rudolph, his nose a bright red bulb.

Justine took a deep breath. "Look, I don't want to spoil the delightful time I had with your folks. . ."

She was unable to keep the sarcasm out of her voice,

and he reacted immediately: "Yeah, you sure as hell know how to ruin a perfectly good evening." He shook his head. "All this time I thought it was them, but now I see that it's you. You sat there like a goddamned iceberg. My mother went to all that trouble cooking a turkey, and you hardly touched the food on your plate. . ."

"I hate turkey. And I would've eaten the stuffing, but be serious, who ever heard of rice mixed with marshmallows."

"That's gourmet cooking," he said evenly.

"It may be gourmet to you, but to me it was plain old rice and marshmallows inside a dried out turkey. Hey, I love rice and marshmallows, but I call them Marshmallow Krispies and I wouldn't eat them in turkey."

"You could've pretended."

"I was pretending, believe me. I was pretending."

"I don't know what the hell's the matter with you. Were you trying to evoke my father's pity, or what."

"I don't know what you're talking about," she said with evident disinterest, folding her arms across her chest.

He mimicked her in a whining voice: " 'Paul won't let me have a Christmas tree.' What kind of dim-witted statement is that!"

"That isn't what I said!" she cried, slapping her hands on her thighs.

"It was damned close to it."

"And why shouldn't I say it. It happens to be true. And now that you brought it up, let me tell you something else: next year I'm having a Christmas tree, and if you don't like it, tough shit. If you think I'm bringing up the baby year after year with no Christmas tree when everybody else has one, you'd better think again."

"I'm so glad you're concentrating on the really important issues of child-rearing. You're probably going to raise the kid on Coke and cartoons so that he's mentally and physically retarded by the time he's five."

"You son of a bitch. . ."

"I can't believe how you acted in front of them," he went on. "You're always talking about family, but we spend the day with my family and look how you act."

"When I talk about family, I'm not talking about visiting other families, I'm talking about us being a family, and if you don't know that, then you're the retard."

"I don't know what the hell you want. I'm at home, aren't I? I had a chance to go to Cuba with the Venceremos Brigade but I didn't because you—" He stopped short.

"Because I what. Because I'm pregnant? Well listen, husband dear, I would've had a much better Christmas if you'd gone to Cuba, so don't feel you did me any favors. I didn't ask you to stay. If you stayed it was your idea and not mine so don't go blaming me because you missed your precious trip to Cuba. I know you don't want the baby. You go around bragging you're going to be a father and pretending how happy you are, but I know. . . That's all you need is a baby to spoil your precious plans. That's probably why you want me to have it at home, so I'll die. You'd love that: me and the baby would die together and you'd be able to go to Cuba or China or wherever the hell you want to go."

"You're nuts."

"Oh yeah? Then why are you trying to palm us off on that commune. . ."

"Justine, use your goddamned brain for once, will you?"

"Oh pardon me if I'm stupid, I'm so sorry."

He sighed. "Look, my wanting to move into a collective has nothing to do with my feelings about you or the baby. Well. . .it does, but not the way you think."

"Oh sure, I'll bet."

"Will you shut up for a goddamned minute!"

She pressed her lips together and folded her arms stubbornly across her chest.

"I want to explain and I want you to listen. The nuclear family is the basic unit of the capitalist state: the father oppresses the mother and the mother oppresses the children."

"The father *loves* the mother and the mother *loves* the children!"

He glared at her and she closed her mouth, pouting. "The nuclear family teaches people how to live in a hierarchy of oppression. Children are socialized to fit into a pecking order. They're socialized into oppressive sex roles: the father works and the mother stays at home."

"That's not exactly the case in our family, is it."

He glared at her once more, decided to ignore the remark, and continued: "The nuclear family teaches children to be competitive. They have to compete for their parents' love and affection. I want us to live in an atmosphere where there's more love, more people for our baby to depend on."

"And who are these people supposed to be that the baby is going to love and depend on?"

"Me and you."

"Obviously."

"And Susan and George. . ."

"Oh Paul. You have to be kidding. Really. I know you're not serious. Our baby is going to love Susan? Listen, if our baby is going to be the type of person who loves Susan, I want to put him up for adoption the minute he's

157

born. I can just see her when she gets back from Cuba, she'll probably be wearing a beard." She tried to laugh; she was afraid of where the argument might lead. "I can't stand the smell of cigar smoke, it'll never work out."

He was not amused.

"Anybody else?"

He hesitated, then blurted: "Elizabeth and David."

She stared at him. "No. Definitely no. Elizabeth I like. George is a little bit off the wall, but I think I could live with him. But Susan no. And David definitely no. It's going to be funny enough when his little redhead starts coming to the women's meetings, no way can I see us all living together. No. Not David. He could start a commune all by himself, why does he have to be in yours?"

"Because David and I work well together. Because David's political analysis—"

"No way. So forget about it."

"All right, we won't talk about it now. It's not even an issue at this point because Susan and George won't be back until March." He didn't tell her that David was already looking for a house, or was supposed to be. "So we'll forget about it. You can relax and stop being so uptight."

She pointed her finger at him. "Listen, when it comes to you making decisions behind my back, I'll get as fucking uptight as I want. David Sully. . . Is he one of the people you said would be there when I have my baby?" He nodded, and her eyes filled with tears. "No," she said firmly. "Never. I'm warning you, Paul, you go deciding about my life and you'll be one sorry person. That's all I have to say: you'll be one sorry person."

"All right, Tina, all right. Take it easy, you made your point. I told you we were only talking."

"Great, then that's the end of it. And if I told you

once, I told you a thousand times: don't call me Tina!"

He sighed, and they sat in miserable silence for the rest of the way home. He pulled up in front of the apartment. She got out of the car and slammed the door. Paul shut off the ignition and sat there. As Justine walked up to the front door, she thought she felt something move within her. But she couldn't stop now. Without pausing, without waiting for Paul or turning around, she unlocked the door with shaking hands and went inside.

When David left, Becky woke to her own life which was waiting where she'd left it. She worked feverishly: reading books, writing papers, studying for final exams. She woke also to winter. The first snowfalls had passed, the first exhilarating crispness, and winter settled into dampness, slush, and gray dreary days. She maneuvered her car out of tight, unplowed parking spaces and prayed that her battery would hold out one more day, one more week.

What surprised her was that after David left, she was relieved. She no longer lived in constant expectation: she could cook or read or do her laundry without the nagging feeling that what she was actually doing was filling time. The muscles in her face felt different, and she realized that those expressions of coyness or impudence, innocence or pained maturity were all very tiring. 'I should give my face a medal,' she thought. 'Or a week's vacation.'

Now her face was her own and her time was her own. She spent her days and evenings doing schoolwork, and late at night she watched television or listened to music. One night she came across the women's liberation pamphlets she'd bought in November, and she stayed up reading until dawn.

In the days before Christmas she had hoped that her father would send her part of the thousand dollars as a present so that she could fly home, but he was holding out for her wedding. Her parents called Christmas day. It was good to hear their voices, though knowing that her mother and father, her brothers, their wives and children were all gathered together made her feel farther away than three thousand miles.

The next day she went to campus and checked the mailbox in the History Department office. She found a note from Pritchard. It read: "See me 2 p.m. Jan 7." She had heard that if Pritchard didn't like one's work, he would not bother with a reply; the reply meant he had accepted her for independent study next semester.

To celebrate, she went to see *Oklahoma* at the Student Union Theater. The theater was empty except for a few people sitting in the back. She sat in the front row. Ten minutes after the movie began, several people sat two rows behind her. She glanced over her shoulder and saw Melissa, Bryce and Tom. Tom had his arm around her shoulder, and Bryce was holding her hand in his lap. Between the two men, Melissa smiled smugly. Becky slid forward in the seat, wishing that she could sneak out the side exit without them seeing her.

But Bryce saw her. At one point in the movie, a character sang the song: "I Cain't Say No," and Bryce began quietly singing along. He sang to Melissa at first, his words muffled because he was nuzzling her neck: "You're just a girl who cain't say no, you're in a terrible fix. . ." He finished the line leaning toward Becky: "You always say, 'Come on, let's go,' just when Doc says to say: 'Nix.' "

Rage swept through her. It was short lived, replaced by humiliation. Bryce was not at fault for mentioning the incident, but herself for taking part in it.

Melissa said: "Doctor? Bryce, what are you talking about?"

"Your shrink, Missie girl. Your shrink says you should say nix, and instead you're out turning tricks."

"Bryce!" She laughed uncomfortably. "What have you been doing, rifling my doctor's files?"

Tom said quietly: "I didn't know anything about it." He sounded very much excluded.

Bryce laughed. "Why should I rifle through your doctor's files when you tell me everything I want to know?"

For this, Melissa had no answer.

Becky barely heard the rest of the movie. She listened to Melissa back up further and further, providing Bryce with ammunition with which to wound her. She felt she were listening to herself.

After the movie she passed the three of them in the aisle. Tom said hello, Bryce winked, and Melissa smiled at her complacently. For a moment Becky wished that David were there, or that she could get into a conversation with them and mention his name. Then she thought: 'I'm just as bad as her.'

On the way home her mind raced. She thought about the month of December and the changes in her personality while she was with David. She thought about the pamphlets she'd read, things Terry had said, and Justine. She remembered incidents in her life she'd believed to be long forgotten. She thought about Melissa and herself, and she wondered if within her there was some continuous being, or merely fragments that men molded to themselves.

When she got home she parked the car and locked it before she remembered she had to buy coffee for tomorrow's breakfast. The street was empty. A light snowfall had covered the day's brown slush, and for a few hours it would be beautiful. She decided to walk to the A & P.

On the way home she felt warm and peaceful listening to the snow crunch underfoot, watching the white sparkles reflecting the light of the street lamps, feeling her body encased in heavy winter clothing.

As she neared her apartment she passed a man shovelling his sidewalk. "Hello," she said.

"Hello," he said and moved aside to let her pass. He stood there for a moment, one hand on the shovel and the other on the small of his back, watching her walk away. He frowned, not quite able to place her, and asked: "Who are you?"

"Oh, just a girl from up the block," she said over her shoulder, thought for a moment, and said: "No. I'm a woman." Immediately she knew it was the wrong thing to say.

He had already bent to shovel the snow but at her comment he straightened and looked her up and down with new interest. "Oh you are, are you," he drawled, as if she'd lifted her skirt and said: I'm ready, baby.

She flushed and walked away. She could feel his eyes on her back and didn't begin to relax until she heard the rhythmic scraping of his shovel against the sidewalk.

'So,' she thought, 'that's what it means to say you're a woman.'

At home she sat down and stared into the darkness. She found herself alone, which was in reality what she was: alone. She knew that deep within herself she had known it all along.

On New Year's Eve Bryce called. He said: "The three of us are having a party. Nothing special, just sit around and do our thing. I think it's going to be a first class bore and I need another victim." He laughed, implying the victim would be of boredom, but Becky knew he meant something else entirely.

"No thanks, Bryce. Not this time."

"You're missing the opportunity of a lifetime. . ."

Quickly, before she had time to consider, she said: "No."

That evening she smoked some grass and listened to music. She lay on the couch a long time, not noticing that the new year had begun.

January
1970

Vacation ended. Classes and campus activities resumed. Monday night Becky went to a women's meeting, and it aroused her interest in what she had thought would be a dead-end group.

Since Susan left for Cuba, the women seemed more relaxed. Elizabeth chaired the meeting and suggested that they attempt constructive self-criticism. No longer in awe of Elizabeth, and encouraged by the pamphlets she'd read, Becky stated that walking into the women's meeting for the first time was no different than walking into any other meeting she'd ever attended: she felt isolated and uncomfortable. If they were concerned with women and women's liberation, they should at least make an effort to welcome each new woman, explain the group and make her feel at home. To her surprise everyone agreed, and they voted her to be the "Official Welcoming Committee." The whole discussion occurred with much joking, especially by Terry, who teased Becky about her awesome title.

They decided that an immediate goal was outreach. Accordingly, they reserved a table in the large foyer of the Student Union, and signed up in hour long shifts to sell pamphlets. Becky had volunteered for the first of these shifts, to begin Tuesday.

Tuesday was her twenty-fourth birthday, and she'd invited David for dinner. Monday night she slept poorly, and knew that with an afternoon nap she'd look fresher, like a flower picked for the moment of his arrival. Instead she went to campus, for it seemed ridiculous to fill her day with him when she had so much to do.

She'd never slept well. Her nights were restless, and mined with the devils in her brain that assaulted her with memories of all her mistakes and near mistakes. Lately it was worse. In the day she might fantasize revenge against Bryce, but at night she felt powerless, as if he controlled her brain. She hoped he would not be in class Tuesday morning, but he was there, observing her with new interest. After class she was drinking at the water fountain when he came up behind her. Wiping a drop of water from her mouth, she faced him.

"You missed a fantastic New Year's Eve," he said.

She shrugged. "That's the breaks."

He cocked his head and grinned at her. "Say, I hear you're into women's lib."

She was flustered, wondering how he knew and hoping he would not challenge her association with the group.

"What's this women's lib all about, anyway. It doesn't mean no sex, does it?"

Her first reaction was relief that he'd saved her from having to define women's liberation. She almost giggled and said, 'Don't be silly,' but caught herself and said coolly: "It means no sex with you, Bryce." She touched her fingers to her forehead in a mock salute, and walked down the hall before he had time to respond or she had time to retreat.

In the parking lot she took the pamphlets from her car and carried them into the Student Union, her head held high. Several men turned as they passed her by, and that made it even better: having a strong identity as a woman made her more attractive to men.

But sitting behind the pamphlets with their obvious feminist titles, her courage waned. When a male student strolled up to the table she flirted with him anxiously. A woman approached cautiously but Becky ignored her, thinking: 'Just because I'm into women's liberation doesn't mean I don't like men!'

By noon, when another woman from the group came to

166

take her place, she had not sold one pamphlet. She went to her afternoon classes, and drove through the heavy snow to shop for dinner.

It strained her budget so that she would have to eat spaghetti for the rest of the week, but Becky prepared David's favorite foods. She cleaned the apartment until her back ached, but the evening would be perfect. Dinner was to be at seven.

At seven-thirty the phone rang, and when she said hello. she heard David whisper: "Becky? I wasn't too sure what time I was supposed to be there. . ."

"Seven." Her voice was cold.

"Seven? Oh wow, what time is it now?"

"Seven thirty."

"Oh no. Well listen, Becky, there's been a complication and I won't be able to make it over until later. I'm right in the middle of a heavy conversation with Elizabeth. I can't talk right now but I'll tell you about it as soon as I see you."

"Dave, didn't you tell Elizabeth you were coming over?"

"Of course, of course I did. I told her, I said. . . Well I don't remember my exact words, but she knows I have to go out."

"Didn't you tell her it was my birthday?"

"Well. . . not exactly. I thought that if she knew it was something special it would have made her insecure."

"It would have made *her* insecure!" She bit her lip. In that moment she changed for him. She was no longer his port in the storm; now she was just another storm. At the other end of the line there was silence. "I'm sorry, I know it's hard for you. . . Listen, I'll take care of the dinner and you take your time and get over here when you can."

"Gee Becky, you're great. OK, I'll tell you what, I'll

be over there by nine o'clock. No, by eight thirty at the latest."

She made herself laugh. "No, better make it nine, just to be on the safe side."

"OK. Nine it is."

"But you'd better be here by nine on the dot, because if you're not you'll have to eat roast beef that tastes like shoe leather."

"Roast beef, far out."

"Mm-hmm, and mushroom gravy, and mashed potatoes and tossed salad with Roquefort dressing, and chocolate cake." Before the words were out of her mouth she was sorry she'd spoken. If he didn't come now she wouldn't be able to say: Oh it's all right, I didn't make anything special anyway. . .

"Far out," he said doubtfully. There was a silence and he said: "Well, I'll see you at nine."

"OK, see you."

· She hung up the phone. The kitchen table was laid out exactly as David liked. Between the precisely laid settings, two new yellow candles waited to be lit. She looked critically at the triangular napkins beside the plates, and folded them each into rectangles.

The potatoes were water-logged, and when she lifted them out of the pot they fell apart and splashed back into the water in little clumps. She set her teeth, fished the clumps out with a slotted spoon, and mashed them with butter and milk, salt and pepper. They tasted soggy. She took the roast beef out of the oven.

At nine o'clock she put the roast, now medium rare, back into the oven, heated the mashed potatoes in a make-shift double boiler, and lit the candles.

At nine-thirty she took the roast out again and turned

off the fire under the potatoes. She sat in the living room, staring at the television, unable to comprehend what she saw because her anger was too intense. But she knew that if he walked in this minute she'd run to him, clucking because he had been out in the cruel world, poor man, and was tired and cold and hungry, and needed only her soft comforting arms and a good warm meal. She could not stop herself from peering out the window at the cars driving down the unplowed streets. She could not stop herself from picturing him standing at the doorway, his clothes caked with snow, his knuckles red from the cold.

The grease congealed on the roast beef gravy, and the mashed potatoes hardened.

At midnight she blew out the candle stubs, put away the food and went to bed. She made herself think of nothing at all. She knew that if she felt anything, thought anything, if she let anything out, it would be anger that she turned against herself. She held her body rigid.

The next day she went to meet Pritchard. He was reading at his desk, tapping a yellow felt-tipped pen on a pile of papers. Near his hand a cup of coffee had grown cold. The gray metal desk under the cup was circled with so many intersecting rings that they had merged into one smudge of coffee brown.

She introduced herself, sat down and set her face and body into a position of pleasant and eager attentiveness. He began to speak, first polishing off her proposal in a few neat sentences, then veering into his work, and from thence she was lost, for he didn't bother to touch ground in reality.

She realized that the entire independent study would be all form. The quality of her work would hardly matter. Sitting here looking eagerly attentive would matter, smiling at Pritchard, wet-nursing his ego. She let her mind wander, wondering if she should commit herself to the independent study, knowing she would learn nothing new since she already was an expert at what she was doing now. There were other professors she could work with, but none, unfortunately, with his influence. During these thoughts, which invariably lead to the dead-end of 'What should I do, what should I do?' she darted back every so often to the scene in which she was physically involved, checking on her expression, automatically giving him a smile or sympathetic frown.

As for Pritchard, his thoughts dwelt on that great historical work that would someday be written and that he was now living, *The Life of Pritchard*. He was careful to portray the essence, the very being of Pritchard. Anyone might be a source of information about the great master. Becky, sitting before him in her admiring pose, might be such a source.

At first he treated her like just another hungry little graduate student, but when she crossed one leg over another it jarred his memory, and he paused and stared at her.

The silence threw her into a mild panic, for she hadn't been listening, and knew only, from his tone, that he hadn't asked her a question. She nodded at the papers on his desk. "Is that something you're working on now?"

"Yes, as a matter of fact, it is," he said, then remembered seeing her across from Sully that day in the fall, behind them the huge poster of Zapata, between them the lighted but unused phone. "It's an article on the Second World War. 'The Relationship of the Armament Expenditure of the German Government to their Escalation of Hostilities: A Study of the Second World War.' "

"Sounds quite interesting," she said, and thought: 'Oh my God, what a jerk. If they start a war, they buy guns, right? And he gets twenty grand a year for that?'

Pritchard was well aware of Sully's reputation for extra-curricular activities with his students, and as he began to describe his research, he smiled knowingly at her.

She became aware that something in his manner had changed. She shifted in her seat and tried to tug the short skirt over her knees, thinking: 'What if he wants to sleep with me, what am I going to do. . .'

She remembered when Ginny had slept with Dr. Manally, a popular professor in the Sociology Department. Becky thought him a phony. In class he sat on the edge of his desk and leaned forward, his body aching with sincerity, his voice drenched with: Oh, if only I could cast aside this professional role. . . But he needed that role to protect him from his students, just as he needed his marriage to protect him from other women, and other women to protect him from his wife. He never quite gave himself to anyone.

Abruptly Becky thought of David, and just as abruptly focused her attention on Pritchard. But his sentences were so long, so vague and interconnected that her mind wandered.

Ginny began the relationship with the illusion that this would be The Man, who would bring out her hidden self as though she were Sleeping Beauty waiting for the Prince to kiss her alive. "He really knows me," she'd said, "he makes me feel that for the first time in my life, I'm really me."

The relationship ended with "harsh reality," as Ginny

called it. A few days after he broke off with her, Ginny sat in class observing him walk around being sincere. She said to Becky: "I mean, reality is harsh, but this is a bit much, wouldn't you say? I can't believe I actually slept with him, I must've been nuts."

Becky had nodded in critical self-recognition. Sleeping with someone you realized afterwards you never liked, that was something she knew all about.

'But if I sleep with Pritchard,' she thought, 'I'll know from the beginning I don't like him. I'll know exactly why I'm doing it.'

He was staring at her. "Don't you agree?"

"Oh yes, definitely," she said, took his last sentence, juggled it around and handed it back to him, intact.

She left his office with two points clear. The first was that they would meet Thursday afternoons between two and two thirty. The second was that he saw her as more than an intellectual protégée. As she was leaving he reached forward to shake her hand and held it while he said: "Perhaps you'll find that we have more in common than German History. . ." He smiled at her, and though he left the sentence unfinished, the meaning in his eyes was clear.

She thought: 'So this is what it's all come to.' All those days of typing and filing and answering the phone at the muffler installation company to pay her way through college, ignoring her brothers' scoffs, studying every spare moment to get high marks, winning a fellowship to graduate school. . . And now this. Pritchard. And getting a good job might not depend on how intelligent or clever she was, how hard she worked or how well she taught, but whether or not she slept with Pritchard. 'It's not fair,' she thought, 'it's just not fair.'

She walked down the hall and knocked on Sully's door, too unhappy to notice that Pritchard was watching her. She knocked once, twice, but no one answered.

That evening Sully called. He sounded exhausted, but spoke rapidly: "Becky I'm sorry about last night but everything was a mess, I'll tell you about it when I see you because it's too long to go into now. Can I come over tonight?"

"Why not?" she answered, "I'm still waiting from last night."

He laughed as if she were joking. "All right, I'll be over in fifteen minutes."

She vowed that she'd give voice to her anger, be honest with him for the first time, but when he arrived he spoke before she could open her mouth: "I told Elizabeth I thought it might be a good idea if we had a different living situation."

"You told her you were moving out?" she asked suspiciously.

He looked down at her hand and touched it with his fingertips.

"But why did you have to tell her last night?"

He shrugged helplessly. "Those are the kind of things you don't plan. Last night it reached a point where we had to talk about it. It was something that had to come out and unfortunately it came out on your birthday." He touched her on the cheek.

Inside she began to soften. It was stupid to yell at him now when she hadn't done so on the phone; and he was moving out. All the same she felt cheated.

He related the whole scene to her, and slowly the evening before as she remembered it faded away: the cooking and the waiting, the tension and the false hopes.

She felt her anger slipping and knew it was too late. She'd trip over her words, unable to explain why she was angry, and her anger itself would seem ridiculous. It was better to be silent than to feel stupid, she decided. But she felt like a pushover.

Later, he reached into his book bag and pulled out a large book with a brown and yellow cover. "Here," he said, handing it to her, "for your birthday. I hope you like it."

The book was titled: *Intellectual Pioneers of the Mexican Revolution*. She opened the cover to see if he had inscribed it. A small white card lay there: "Dear Professor: We hope you enjoy this complimentary copy of. . ."

David saw it too and took the book from her. "Wait. I forgot to write something." He put the book on the coffee table and as he bent over it with a pen, slid the card out and slipped it in his pocket. He wrote something on the first page and handed it back. She read: "For the bees who make the honey. Love and Struggle, David." The words had no meaning to her. He had once again confused her with Elizabeth.

He waited for her to thank him. She was about to protest when David's internal lobbyist began its apology in her brain: 'He's got so much on his mind. . .'

She was sick of hearing that lament, and as much to shut it up as answer him, she said: "Thanks alot."

He smiled. "This is just in case you decide to continue our research project. We make an awfully good team, you know. What do you think. . ."

When he left, she lay in bed and watched the snow fall onto the tree outside her window. There was so much she'd wanted to say to him and it all had gone into nothing. She saw herself smiling at him, being sweet and agreeable while her stomach churned with unexpressed rage.

'Oh well,' she decided, 'no sense in thinking about it now. It's your own fault for not saying anything. You certainly had the opportunity. It's your own fault so forget about it.'

She stared into the night, despising herself for what she was.

When Justine came home from work Friday and Paul told her he'd fallen on the ice and sprained his wrist, she suggested that instead of going to the movies with David and Elizabeth, they stay home. Her motives had more to do with her own emotions than Paul's wrist. She'd been feeling particularly blue that week, and Paul had been out until midnight, Monday thru Thursday. Every night she sat in the living room dreading the time she had to go to bed; every night she dreamed of Babe. Tonight she wanted to be alone with Paul, for it was one year ago tomorrow that Babe had died.

Paul said that a little sprain did not make him an invalid; he wanted to go to the movies. Just as they were leaving the apartment, however, David called and said that he was tired: he and Elizabeth were staying home.

Justine drove. She was irritable and the road was icy. As they approached the university, a car cut in front of them without signalling and Justine had to swerve.

"Fuckin' nigger," she snapped and beeped the horn furiously.

The other driver lifted his middle finger in a calm, unperturbed "fuck you" sign.

"Did you see that! Cocksuckers think they own the goddamned road," she snapped, jabbing her middle finger violently in the air.

Paul was horrified. "Justine. Don't say that."

She stopped at a red light. "What, cocksucker? I'm sorry honey, you're right. I should stop swearing or else the first words out of the baby's mouth will be—"

"No," he interrupted, "not cocksucker."

"You mean nigger?"

"For God's sake, Justine!"

"Well he was! Paul, did you see what he did? He cut right in front of me. We could've been killed."

"I don't know why you have to bring up his race. Being a road hog has nothing to do with his race."

"It most certainly does, he wouldn't do that to his own. He did it because I'm white."

"Do you mean to tell me that everyone who's black drives like that?"

"No, don't be silly, not all black people are niggers." But before the word was out of her mouth, she knew she shouldn't have said it.

"I'm glad David didn't come," he grumbled.

She made a sharp left into the main university parking lot. They walked through the Student Union and opened the door to the small theater. It was dark, and the light from the hall cut a swath of yellow down the rows of heads. The credits for the movie went on.

"It's beginning," Paul whispered.

"I know it's beginning. I'm not blind."

176

Paul walked quickly down the aisle to the second row. Justine sat next to him. She felt a tap on her shoulder and saw Maggie sitting directly behind her.

"Hiya Maggie, how you doing?"

"Not bad. Have you seen this movie before?"

"No. You?"

"Yeah, it's terrific. Wait'll you see it."

There was someone sitting next to Maggie and her presence pulled at Justine's attention. It was a woman. Her deep brown eyes looked into Justine's directly and steadily. She was smiling. Justine met her gaze and smiled back.

Paul nudged her. "Who is it?" he whispered.

"Maggie."

"Who?"

"From the women's group."

He nodded.

The movie bored her and she turned to chat with Maggie. But Maggie was engrossed in the film, so Justine talked to Maggie's friend. She sat sideways in her seat and whispered sarcastic comments. The woman laughed. Paul said: "Shh!" and Justine sat quietly. . . for a few minutes at least.

When the lights went on, they stood up.

"I guess I don't have to introduce you two," Maggie said.

"No," Justine answered, "we're old buddies by now." She held out her hand. "Justine," she said.

"BJ," the woman said, and they shook hands.

"This is Paul. Paul, Maggie. BJ. . ."

He nodded absent-mindedly to them and continued putting on his gloves.

"What're you two doing," Justine asked Maggie.

"Now?" She looked at BJ, who shrugged. "Nothing, why."

"You want to go down to the Cavern for a beer?"

"Sure."

"OK, great."

They made their way to the exit, Paul trudging unhappily behind her.

"What's the matter, Paul, did you want to go someplace else?"

"No. . . not really."

"Well then, come on."

The hall was crowded with movie-goers waiting to get in, and Justine noticed how they stared at BJ as she walked by. Maggie frowned and looked straight ahead, but BJ didn't mind at all.

She was different and proud of it. She walked confidently as though her mind and body had made a common decision. The attention only roused her thirst for challenge. She knew her rights and she had a right to be here. She picked out someone and stared back intently, a hint of smile on her lips, her eyes saying: Oh yeah? And what's *your* problem. The other person looked away. Her eyes cut a pathway through the crowd.

Justine also felt different from this homogenous gathering of students. Behind her, Paul was walking with, and obviously being flattered by a pretty undergraduate. Pretty and slim. Unpregnant. She belonged among these people. She would never embarass Paul in front of David. Justine felt bulky, awkward, and out of place.

Downstairs, they bought beers and found an empty table. When they pulled out the chairs, the couple at the adjoining table stared at BJ openly, as if demanding an explanation for her existence.

She glanced at them briefly and looked at Justine, who shrugged. "Rude," she said.

Justine nodded.

"You know what I'm going to do? I'm going to get cards printed that say, 'I do not like being stared at. I charge $1.00 for autographed pictures.'"

The couple looked indignant. Justine laughed. "Well, you might as well make money off it, right?"

"Right."

Paul had set his chair off to one side. Out of the corner of his eye he snuck a glance at Maggie and BJ, scanned the wall clock and the juice lined up on ice and some people studying a chessboard, and when he thought the two women weren't looking, his eyes wandered back to them.

Maggie took a deep breath in an effort to relax, and said to Justine: "I take it you didn't like the movie."

Justine made a face. "It was OK. But I didn't understand it. You know, all those subtitles."

"Yeah," BJ said. "I can't stand them. I can't pay attention to what's happening on the screen and read those things at the same time. Too confusing."

"I know, they don't even translate half the things they're saying. Somebody'll be talking a mile a minute and there won't be any words written underneath and you think: What? What the hell did I miss?"

"Yeah, I'd rather see a good old American movie any day. If I have to buy a ticket, I want to understand the plot. It was bullshit: they go out sailing and the girl disappears, and everybody forgets about it."

Paul faced BJ aggressively and said: "That's exactly the point. Granted, the movie was steeped in bourgeois ideology, but Antonioni was trying to represent alienated relationships."

"Whatever it was." BJ said. "it was still bullshit."

Justine was not listening to them. "That island was nice, wasn't it."

No one responded until BJ said: "Seemed kind of rocky to me. If I was going to live on an island, I'd like one with coconuts, streams, palm trees. . . and maybe a grocery store on the corner."

The two women laughed.

"I kind of like that island in the movie," Justine said. "Although. . ."

BJ smiled into her eyes. "How would you live?"

"Well. . . Justine said slowly, tilting her head and smiling back. They looked directly at each other, distinctly aware of Paul and Maggie. "I'll tell you what I'd do. I'd dig an underground tunnel and when people wanted to run away they could come to the island and I'd hide 'em out. They could bring me food or money and we'd make a trade."

"Not bad." BJ said, "you'll make out all right."

"Thanks. I know I will."

They continued talking, but Paul drummed his fingers on the table and the noise was distracting. When Maggie finished her beer, she looked questioningly at BJ. BJ swallowed the last of her beer and stood up. "We're going to split."

"I guess we're gonna go too." Justine said. "You ready, Paul?"

He nodded emphatically.

"It was nice meeting you," Justine said to BJ.

"Same here. Maybe we can get together some time. How's that sound to you. Mag?"

"Sounds good to me. Bye Justine. Nice meeting you," she said to Paul.

180

"Take it easy," BJ said to Paul.

He nodded.

Outside, he walked ahead of Justine, head down and hands in his pockets. "Hey," she said, "crabby." He kept walking. "Come on, I'm declaring a truce." She threw a snowball at him.

"Hey, cut it out! You attack me when I'm disabled and then you want a truce? Pretty sneaky tactics, as far as I'm concerned."

She put her arm through his and they walked to the car. "Come on," she said, "let's go home and have a real truce."

"Sounds good to me. I'm hungry."

She laughed suggestively. "Sounds good to me."

"No, I mean food. That dinner was pretty bad."

"Learn to cook."

"Why don't you learn to cook."

"Because someday you're going to be a rich professor and I'm going to have a cook, a maid, a butler. . . and a nurse for the baby."

"Sure. The kid'll be seventy by then."

At the car, Paul silently held out his hand for the keys. "You don't trust my driving?" she asked.

"It isn't your driving that bothers me."

She gave him the keys and he drove home awkwardly.

In the apartment, Justine poured a glass of chocolate milk and sat down at the small table. Paul went into the kitchenette to make cinnamon toast. "What do you know about them," he asked casually, opening the loaf of bread.

"Who."

"Those women I met tonight."

"Not much. Maggie's in the women's group."

He nodded. "I thought I recognized her. She's a friend of Terry's, isn't she. She was with Terry at the October teach-in."

Justine shrugged. "I only see her at the meetings. I think she studies math or something like that."

"What about the other one."

"BJ? I don't know anything about her. I met her tonight, like you. Come on Paul, you going to make cinnamon toast or not."

He put two slices of bread into the toaster and pressed down the lever. "They acted a little strange, if you want to know my personal opinion. I think there's something going on between those two."

"Maybe they're queer," Justine said, and tilted the glass up to get the last of the chocolate.

Paul frowned. "You mean homosexual?"

"You know damned well what I mean."

He stared at the toaster, and when the toast popped up, he stared at that. "You know," he said thoughtfully, "lesbianism can be a divisive force in the women's movement. It can divide women."

"What!"

"She seemed like a troublemaker to me. I wanted you to see that movie and she wouldn't leave you alone."

"Come on Paul, don't start any crap, it's almost midnight. The toast is getting cold and the sugar's not going to melt."

He buttered the toast. "Justine, I know you've gotten involved with the group. I know it means alot to you. And I'm only trying to warn you."

She smiled. "OK, you warned me."

He held the spoonful of cinnamon sugar poised over the toast. "Although, come to think of it, that ring looked like

182

a wedding band. I can't remember which hand she wore it on. . ."

"Paul, what the hell does a wedding ring have to do with the price of potatoes. Carol's married and that doesn't make any difference. . ." She pressed her lips together.

"Carol! You never told me that Carol was a. . . lesbian."

"Well I didn't think it was important. I didn't tell you she lives in a trailer either, did I?"

"But she's married."

"So?"

"She's got three grown kids!"

"Where did you grow up, Paul, on the moon?"

"And she told you she was?"

"She didn't have to. I know there's something going on between her and a girl from accounting. Anyway, it's none of my business." She stood up and put her glass in the sink. "Forget about my toast, I don't think I could swallow it at this point."

She went into the bathroom. Paul stayed in the kitchenette listening to the running water while he ate the cold toast.

Justine stood under the shower, lathering herself slowly; the water struck the soapsuds and slid down her body. Paul came in to wash; he saw the translucent shower curtain stick to her skin.

She turned off the water and rubbed herself dry with a fresh towel. Stepping out of the tub, she spread her hands over her swelling flesh and faced herself in the full length mirror that hung on the bathroom door. It was fogged with steam; through it she saw her faint image.

She felt a slight movement and shut her eyes to listen, but the baby was quiet. She sighed and continued on with her nightly ritual. She squirted lotion onto her hands and smoothed it on her neck and arms, buttocks and legs. From the medicine cabinet she took the cylinder of cocoa butter and gently massaged it over her belly, hips and breasts. It was the part of the ritual she enjoyed best; she shut her eyes, smelling the cocoa butter on her warm skin. She sprinkled on baby powder to coat the cocoa butter, and reached for the clean maternity bra. But she changed her mind and instead put on the new paisley robe, then walked into the bedroom.

Paul was sitting in bed. He watched the robe cling to the lines of her body, billowing out behind her. She reminded him of a tall proud ship. She stopped in front of the mirror and brushed her hair, pulling the brush across her head slowly, watching him in the mirror watching her.

In bed he took her in his arms. Something crossed his face that she didn't understand but she took it for passion. Just as they were about to kiss, he said: "Justine. . . she hasn't ever come to any meetings, has she?"

She knew who he meant, but asked: "Who. . ."

"That BJ woman."

"Why, do you want me to fix you up with her?"

He laughed uncomfortably. She brushed her lips across his mouth and nibbled his lower lip. "How about if I fix you up with her. OK? You two can do a thing and I'll watch. . ." She laughed, turning it into a joke: "We'll get a Polaroid and I'll take pictures. And after that. . ." She hesitated, putting her head on his shoulder. ". . .after I watch you two, you could watch us."

He was intensely aroused and wanted to make love to Justine enveloped by her words of fantasy. The vision in his mind simultaneously thrilled and revolted him.

He would not let himself go. Reacting to the revulsion, he laughed nervously and said: "Don't be disgusting. Is that any way for a pregnant woman to talk?"

She drew away. "Thanks for reminding me, for a minute I forgot."

"Oh Tina. I didn't mean it that way." He touched her shoulder.

She shrugged him away and walked to the doorway. "You're so goddamned high and mighty. You're just as prejudiced as me except you won't admit it. You got so uptight when that guy cut in front of me, and then you go around accusing people of being queer and you don't even have any proof."

"Honey. . . what are you getting so upset about."

"At least I had proof. At least I know that guy was a nigger!"

"Now look, there's no reason to use that word. First of all, the point is that if I have any prejudice about homosexuals, I do my best to try to understand it. You don't even try to understand your racism."

"There's nothing for me to understand. I'm racist and I know it. I don't know why the hell you're so worried about me. That nigger's the one who cut in front of us, you ought to go lecture him about his racism." She paused and bit her lip. "I know what I am, Paul. You don't have to tell me what I am."

"And second of all," he continued. "I didn't accuse anybody of anything. Even if they were homosexuals, I don't have anything against them. All I'm worried about is her breaking up your women's liberation group. Homosexuals should have the same rights as anyone, but not the right. . ." He saw BJ lying next to Justine, her slow, teasing fingers separating his wife's thighs while Justine looked into her eyes seductively. He rubbed his eyes and said in an even tone: "But not the right to infiltrate an already established organization."

She was silent.

"And third of all, I don't think you're disgusting. I can't understand why you're so upset."

Her eyes filled with tears. "I know you can't," she said and left the room. She sat in the living room and waited until she was calm before she returned to him.

Paul was bewildered by her outburst and blamed the pregnancy. When she lay down on the bed he murmured: "Hey baby, come here. . ." He put his arms around her and kissed the top of her head. "God, Justine, I love you. I think you're beautiful. I didn't mean anything. It's just. . . It's quite a shock for a man to picture his wife with another man, let alone. . ." He laughed to show her he knew she wasn't serious: "let alone with a woman. Come on, baby, don't be upset. Do you want to make love?"

She shook her head.

"You sure?"

She nodded.

"OK, then let's go to sleep. Maybe if we get up early. . ." He kissed her again and switched off the light.

She stared past his chest at the wall. Tomorrow. . . today. It was one year since Babe's death. All week long she sat in the empty apartment and thought about what had happened in the past year. She wished she could talk to her mother because she didn't know what to do. But she had lied even to Babe. She began weeping silently.

Paul tightened his grip on her shoulder. "It's OK, Tina. Don't cry. All married couples fight once in awhile. Sometimes it helps. . ." He thought for a moment and said uncertainly: ". . . it helps to clear the air."

Justine's air was not clear: she felt choked, suffocated. The tears dried on her face.

On the last Saturday in January, two women sat at the kitchen table in Terry's apartment. Terry was reading a large book, Justine sewing a piece of fabric that covered her lap. As she moved, the colors changed from blues to greens and back again. Terry's dog Charlie lay under the table dozing.

The women had been silent awhile when Terry sat back and said: "So do you think it's sick?"

"Don't be silly, how can love be sick?" Justine re-threaded the needle, squinting into the windowlight. A row of icicles hung from the roof, gleaming in the midday sunshine. On the window ledge stood a sweet potato plant in a Mason jar, and drops from the icicles fell past the leaves.

"I mean. . . if you love somebody, if you're in love with them, sex is a natural expression of it. Right?"

Justine knotted the thread and resumed sewing.

"Then if you're in love with a woman. . . you know? I mean. . . does that sound sick?" Terry waited for a response, then sighed and continued reading.

At three o'clock the phone rang. Facing Justine, Terry said: "Oh, hi Paul." Justine grimaced but nodded. Terry said: "She's right here," and handed her the phone.

Justine listened for a few minutes, and when she hung up, said: "I have to go. Poor Dr. Denton's all alone. I think he wants me there because in case he croaks, he's

too weak to call a priest." She resumed sewing. "Well
I'll give him another couple of minutes to suffer alone.
That way he'll have a reason to complain, otherwise he'd
have to make one up, and I wouldn't want to put poor
Dr. Denton to all that trouble."

"You're in rare form today," Terry observed. "Remind
me if I'm ever sick not to call you."

"Hey listen, I've been taking care of him for two days.
I never saw anybody suffer so much in my whole life. I
had the same thing last week and it wasn't any picnic,
but Paul's milking it for all it's worth. Today when I left
he must've called me back a dozen times." She closed her
eyes to slits and spoke in the voice of someone so sick, so
weak, they hardly had the energy to breathe: " 'Tina,
cover me please, the blanket slipped off. Tina, will you
give me some juice, I'm too weak to move.' The damned
glass is two inches from his face, two inches! What a pain
in the ass. But of course he wasn't too sick to give me his
rap about the collective." She laughed. "It might be kind
of funny watching Sully juggle his appointments between
Becky, Elizabeth and his new flame. You know what I
ought to do? I ought to call up Sully and tell him that
there's a new caucus of the women's group made up of
all his followers."

Terry giggled. "You're depraved."

"I know, Paul tells me all the time: I'm culturally depraved."

"You know. . . I've been thinking alot about Sully. I
think he's got a definite problem. And I think I've
got him figured out." She leaned forward, frowning
earnestly, and counted the points on her fingers as she
listed them: "He can't stand pressure, so he goes and
finds some new woman to relieve the pressure, but it

turns out that she has needs too, so all it does is give him another pressure, and he starts all over again." She leaned back, flipping closed the large book. "It's definitely compulsive behavior."

Justine glanced at the book title, *Introduction to Psychology*. "Oh no, I can see it all now. . ."

The doorbell rang. "Oh Jesus, it must be the ambulance come to pick me up."

Terry laughed. "No, it's probably Becky." She pushed away the book and went downstairs to answer the door.

Becky was standing on the porch, holding the books she and Terry were to discuss.

Due to the pamphlet sales, more women were attending the meetings. The "Official Welcoming Committee" had grown to three: Becky, Maggie, and Diane, a new member. Elizabeth had put forward the idea that the women's education should be integrated with a political goal. She said that since the University had ignored both the history and contemporary problems of women, it was up to the women's liberation group to provide this information. After lengthy discussion, they decided to develop a credit-free course introducing the concepts of women's liberation within a socialist framework. They designed a tentative syllabus, and several women volunteered to research each topic and compile a reading list. Becky said she would research "Women in American History," and Terry volunteered along with her. Terry was not as much interested in the topic as she was in Becky, and knew of no other way to befriend her.

Terry answered the door and they went upstairs where they found Justine sitting in the sparsely furnished but comfortable living room. Charlie lay at her feet in front of the space heater.

189

"How come you came in here," Terry asked.

"Well my God, Devlin, you only own two kitchen chairs. what do you want the poor girl to do, sit on the floor?"

"Pick, pick, pick," Terry said and turned to Becky. "Take off your coat. Make yourself at home. You want something to drink? Coffee? Beer?"

"No thanks," Becky answered and removed her coat. She now wore the women's liberation button, placing it strategically so that she could leave it exposed or flap out her collar to hide it.

"I see you got a button," Terry said. "I had an extra one, I was going to give it to you."

"David got me this one," she said proudly, draping her coat over a chair. She sat down across from Terry and Justine, took the books from her bag, and described them to Terry. Terry said little, but Justine, who continued making tiny stitches in the material, asked occasional questions.

Becky ended with: "Flexner has a great bibliography, it should help us alot. I figured there was two main areas, and we could each cover one. First of all there's the feminist movement, and then there's women in the labor movement and in radical politics in general. Take your pick."

"It's all the same to me."

"I thought you might rather do the feminists since. . ." She hesitated, and the three of them burst out laughing.

Terry stood up. "I'm going to put on water for tea. Anybody want tea?"

"Sure," Becky said.

"Yeah, I'll have a cup," Justine said. Terry went into the kitchen, and Justine asked: "Is this your first year in graduate school?"

190

"Mm-hmm."

"How do you like it."

"Oh. . . it's OK. It's not as great as I thought it would be. Alot of tedious work. But I did really well first semester."

"What classes are you taking this semester."

"I'm taking an American History course. It's really interesting, I'm thinking of specializing in it. But I'm taking an independent study with this creep Pritchard. . . He's such a jerk but I have to be nice to him because he has all this influence. I wrote a proposal, you know, for the paper I'd write?"

Justine nodded.

"And then I changed my mind, I decided I'd rather do something on the women's movement in Germany. But he said no."

"Sounds like some of Paul's professors."

"Yeah. They're all the same." She thought of David. "Most of them, anyway."

Terry stood in the doorway. "What'd you say his name was?"

"Pritchard. Maybe you've heard of him, he's written a couple of books."

"Any porno?"

"Yeah, sure: they call him Pritchard the Porno King."

"Oh yeah? See if you can get me some free copies."

"I'll ask him tomorrow."

"What else are you taking," Justine asked.

"My third course is Problems in British Imperialism. I like it, except the professor and I don't agree about what the problems are. . . and I have to go to David's classes because I'm his teaching assistant."

"Must be alot of work."

"It's not too bad. Last semester I helped David research a paper on the Mexican Revolution and that took up most of my time. But it's finished now, and I use that time to work on the women's course. The library work for David's paper was brutal."

"But as long as you were being paid to do it. . . Paul might have to do research next year instead of teach."

"Well. . . I wasn't actually being paid. . ."

Justine stopped sewing. "Are you kidding? I wouldn't do anything I wasn't paid for." She glanced at Terry and said: "Terry pays me to come over and visit her, otherwise I wouldn't do it."

"You're full of shit," Terry retorted, and said to Becky: "The only reason she comes over here is to mooch my food. Did you ever taste Justine's cooking?"

Becky shook her head.

"It's raunchy."

"That's not fair!"

"Her specialty is Tuna Noodle Disaster. . ."

"Of all the nerve!"

"What kind of tea do you want," Terry asked.

"Anything's OK," Becky said.

"I want Salada!" Justine demanded.

"Ooh, you're being awfully aggressive, Justina. Charlie! Attack!" The dog looked up, yawned, and lay back down. "See that? That's why I'm going to take karate."

"Karate?" Becky said. "What are you going to take karate for."

"So she can take over the women's group," Justine teased. "She already infiltrated it, now she wants to take power."

At the word "infiltrated," Terry blushed. "Not me. Not yet." The kettle whistled and she went into the kitchen.

"What do you want in your tea?" she called. "I have everything but lemon." They heard the refrigerator door open. "Scratch that. I have everything but lemon and milk."

"Sugar's OK with me," Becky said.

"I want lemon and milk!" Justine called.

"You'll get sugar and like it," Terry said, and brought in three steaming cups. They rattled unsteadily on the saucers as she bent over the coffee table. "How do you like that balancing act. You ought to see me at work."

Justine giggled. "Yeah, you ought to see her—she wears this cute little striped uniform and this cute little striped hat. . ."

Terry sat down. "Hey, that uniform's no joke. Franklin's on my back to shave my legs, the bastard. I don't know what his problem is. I told him I'd wear a hair net."

The phone rang. "Damn," Terry said.

"Tell him I already left!" Justine called. "I really have to go soon. I told the invalid I'd be home."

"I have to go too," Becky said. "David's coming over at six."

They sipped the tea. Justine put down her cup and placed her hands on her belly.

"Is it the baby?" Becky asked shyly.

Justine nodded. "He's going to be a little devil."

"She!" Terry called from the kitchen, and they laughed.

"God, she's pushy, isn't she?" Justine asked. "Paul wants a boy and Terry wants a girl."

"What do you want."

"Oh. . . just a healthy baby. As long as it's healthy and happy, that's all I want."

Becky smiled. "You're not asking for much. Do you need alot of things, baby clothes, things like that? It's too bad my family lives so far away, my brother's wives are always having babies."

"I think I have a crib. This guy Joe who owns the 24 hour store down the street, he says his wife has a crib in the attic I can use."

"That's good. Have you picked out any names?"

"Lots of them, but we can't agree on any. I want to name it Rita after my mom or Charlie after my uncle Charlie. . ." Charlie raised his head and Justine murmured: "No pal, not you. . . And Paul wants to name it Haydi if it's a girl."

"That's pretty."

"But the reason he wants to name it Haydi is because it was the name of a woman who fought alongside of Castro in the revolution. See, Paul missed this chance to go to Cuba. . ."

"On the Venceremos Brigade?"

She nodded. "So I guess if he can't go down there, he's going to bring it up here. He hasn't picked out a boy's name yet. It'll probably be Mao."

"Mao's his last name."

"Is it? They have their last names first in China? Paul never told me that. How weird. Well then Tse-Tung. That's even worse. Mao Denton I could live with, but Tse-Tung Denton? No way. I told him we either name it after my family or his, but not after his revolutionary heroes."

"Maybe he feels closer to his revolutionary heroes than he does to his family," Becky suggested.

"You're probably right, Becky, 'cause if I had his family, I'd feel closer to Castro, too." She stuck the needle in the material and looked up. "I guess I shouldn't be talking like this. . . but Paul knows how I feel. . ."

"That's pretty material," Becky said.

Justine smiled. "It's a dress for my brother's wedding. He's getting married next month."

Terry came in and sat down.

"I can't wait," Justine continued. "Most of my family's never met Paul and they haven't seen me since I got pregnant. So it'll be like. . ." She looked at Terry and asked: "What's it called? A coming out party?"

Terry nodded. "That's what I need: a coming out party."

Justine smiled.

"That was my sister on the phone. Her sitter cancelled and she's bringing her kids over at eight. You know what she said? 'You see, if you lived at home with Mom and Daddy, you wouldn't have to baby-sit.' "

Becky smiled. "Interesting logic, but I don't quite understand it. . ."

"Family," Terry complained, "what a hassle. You're always obligated for something. You know?"

Justine smiled dryly. "Last night Paul was explaining to me that when you live in a collective, those obligations are supposed to be fun. He didn't say 'fun,' but I think that's what he was driving at. He said people give each other support, and it's supposed to give you a sense of security. Wouldn't he shit if I went off and started my own collective instead of joining his?"

"Are you and Paul joining a collective?" Becky asked.

"He wants to," Justine began. She and Terry exchanged glances. "With Susan and George," she said carefully, "and David and Elizabeth."

Becky stared.

"Didn't David tell you?"

"Oh. . . that collective," she said lamely.

Justine and Terry looked at each other again and Terry

said: "Does anybody want anymore tea. . ."

Justine glanced at her watch. "No. I have to split. Paul's probably having kittens by now."

Becky stood up. "I have to go too," she said, gathering her things together. "David. . ." She put on her coat.

"Hey Becky, why don't you stay awhile," Terry offered. "I'll cook some supper and we can watch tv. . . I think there's some good movies on, and the kids are usually pretty quiet. . . Nothing exciting, but at least. . ."

"No, I have to go."

"Why don't you stay," Justine urged. "Terry's a great cook. I'd stay but Paul's got some kind of dread disease and he can't stand being alone. You know, it might not be such a bad idea if you let David wait for you once in awhile."

"Yeah. You're probably right."

She said good-bye and quickly left, walking down the stairs and opening the door to the outside.

It was dusk, and the air was cold. The icicles that had dripped during the day now gleamed frozen in the moonlight. In the distance smoke churned out of the steel mills, clouding the sky with artificial weather. She walked off the porch to her car.

When Justine got home at six, David and Paul were in the living room discussing the working class. David sat on the edge of the couch, trying to convince Paul of a certain point. David always discussed the working class as if it were an exotic bird and he were a scientist who plucked its feathers to examine under a microscope.

"And I'm telling you she's not working class," David said as Justine walked into the room. Paul nodded to Justine, who stood and glared at him as if to say: I thought you were alone!

"She can't be working class," David continued. "If she's a lesbian she cannot be working class and that's all there is to it."

Justine stared at David. He reached for a cigarette. "The working class won't tolerate sexual perversions like the more bourgeois classes do. They can't afford to: they're oppressed enough as it is and won't tolerate behavior that brings down more oppression on them."

Paul shook his head uneasily. "I don't think I agree with your analysis. And I don't know if I'd call it a perversion. . ."

"Don't get me wrong, *I'm* not calling it a perversion." He lit the cigarette. "But you go into any bar in this city and you ask them what *they* call it. Besides, what the hell would she be doing at an Antonioni flick."

"Hello David," Justine interrupted.

"Oh, hello Justine, how are you." Without waiting for an answer, he opened his mouth to continue his analysis, but Justine cut in once more: "I'm fine David, and how are you."

He said: "I'm fine Justine. Now listen, Paul, I—"

"I didn't know you were here, David, I thought Paul was alone. That's why I left Terry's and came home,

Paul, because I thought you were alone. If I knew David was here, I wouldn't've come home."

"David got here a little while ago," Paul explained.

"How long ago."

"A couple hours," David said, and Paul winced.

"Oh really? A couple hours. Isn't that nice. And why the hell didn't you call me, I could've stayed at Terry's."

"Can't we talk about this later?"

"We'll talk about it right now."

"Well. . . I thought you'd already left."

"Then you were wrong, weren't you, because I hadn't already left. I'm happy that you're sitting here having such a nice talk, but I'd be happier if you had two cents worth of consideration for me and phoned. Or is that too much to ask."

He was silent.

"Well is it?!"

David looked at Paul with an all-knowing air. He had tactfully pointed out to Paul that Justine's behavior was becoming not only increasingly emotional, at times out of all proportion to what the situation required, but her behavior could also be termed irrational. Perhaps it was merely the pregnancy, but perhaps. . . He had suggested that if Paul wanted to be on the safe side, he might want to look for professional help to nip this thing in the bud.

Remnants of this conversation were in his eyes now, but Paul chose not to see. "Look, I forgot all about it. I'm sorry. Now if you don't have enough sense to wait until later to—"

"Great. You forgot about me this time, and next time I'm going to forget about you and then we'll see how *you* like it."

David stood up. "Well. . . I've got to go. I have to be

someplace at six, so I might as well. . ."

"Don't let the door hit you in the ass," Justine said without looking at him.

He looked at Paul with pity, and left. As he closed the door he heard: "Now look, Justine, David is my friend. . ."

"I don't care if he's God almighty, I don't like him and I don't like the way he treats me. And I *don't* like walking into my own house and find him talking about me as if—"

David didn't wait to hear the rest. He left and drove to Becky's. When she opened the door, he saw that something was wrong. Without a word of greeting, she turned and walked ahead of him into the living room, then turned back abruptly and faced him, hands on hips, mouth pressed into a hard line.

"Hello," he said.

"I know all about the collective. David, why did you lead me to believe you were getting your own apartment!"

"There must be an epidemic," he said wryly.

"An epidemic! I don't know what you're talking about. All I know is that I felt like a damned fool not knowing what's going on in your life when it affects *me*!"

He sighed and walked to the window, feeling both annoyed at whoever had told her, and wronged that she'd thought he'd tried to deliberately mislead her. "I didn't know how to tell you."

She waited.

He sat on the couch, and after a moment's pause, reached up for her hand.

She didn't move.

"Please. I feel so far away from you."

She sat, against her will and knowing it was a mistake, but not knowing how to refuse him. Sitting so

close, he looked like a tortured soul, and it was only
by conscious effort that she remembered why she was angry. She didn't, however, know how to form this anger
into what passed muster with the censor in her brain.
Phrases and sentences presented themselves and were attacked for one reason or another until, several moments
having passed, she could only think to blurt: "Well!"
and groan inwardly because she sounded to herself like
such a typical jealous woman.

"I don't know how it happened. I was planning on
getting my own place, and Paul started talking about a
collective. I thought it was only talk, and I told him it
sounded like a good idea. And I guess he misunderstood."

"But why can't you—"

"No. I can't. At this point I can't get out without
seeming like a liberal. Everyone will think it's because I'm
afraid it would hurt my career."

"But—"

"It's not only that. It's Justine."

"Justine!"

He nodded and lit a cigarette. "The only reason Paul's
pushing it so hard is because of Justine's pregnancy. He
thinks she can handle it."

"Handle what?"

"Everything. The baby, the responsibility. She's been
acting very . . . distraught."

"Oh come on."

"You haven't seen her."

"I saw her today."

"Today? Was it Justine who told you about the
collective?"

"Yes," she said carefully.

He nodded. "Well. . . I wouldn't put the greatest faith

in Justine's word."

"You mean you're not moving into a collective?"

"I don't know. It's all very up in the air. All I know is that I don't want to fight with you. Certainly not about Justine, of all people."

'But we're not fighting about Justine,' she thought, but didn't say this, not wanting to be guilty of further side-tracking things into an argument about their topic.

He placed his hand over hers. "We'll work it out. That is . . . if you want to . . ."

"Of course I want to. But why didn't you tell me about it before this?"

"Because I didn't know if you'd understand."

"Oh for God's sake, Dave, of course I understand. I told you that you could always come to me. . ."

When Becky fell asleep that night she dreamed that she was in the eye of a hurricane out at sea. She floated in a tiny rowboat that each battering wave could capsize. The eye was safe, calm, a bright clear sunshine yellow. Surrounding the eye was the storm, a violent turbulence of wind and rain. And beyond the storm was the unknown: perhaps the edge of the earth, perhaps land. She didn't know if she should try to row to what might be land, or stay in the eye. If she stayed, she would never be at rest, always watchful that the currents not move her to the storm. She was drifting there now. She began rowing frantically when a huge wave came down on her and she woke.

February
1970

In the beginning of February, Amos Pritchard went to a cocktail party hosted by William Schultz, the portly Chairman of the History Department. At one point in the conversation, David Sully's name came up. Sully was little liked in the Department: his contempt for his politically conservative colleagues was well known, and they in turn referred to him as their "token radical." This mutual dislike might have gone on simmering for the remaining year and a half of Sully's three year contract but for one fact. Sully had attracted attention in the University Administration. This was what Schultz confided to Pritchard, maneuvering him away from the other guests. The Administration could not overlook Sully's involvement in local university politics. The last straw was his association with the group investigating Project Rhododendron. The Department of Defense contract was a serious matter.

"I'll tell you quite frankly that they've got plans for him," Schultz said quietly, smiling to one of the professor's wives. "I myself like the man, but you can understand that I'm not about to jeopardize my own position. When I go on sabbatical next year, I want to leave with a clean slate and no enemies."

"Of course," Pritchard agreed, "but what kind of plans can they have? He can't be dismissed for his political beliefs. The only thing. . ." He paused. "You don't mean the morals clause. . ."

Schultz nodded. "Certain people have found that our little revolutionary has quite an active private life. You knew he was living with the one girl. . ."

Pritchard listened carefully, always eager for a bit of

203

gossip, especially about Sully.

"It seems that he's carrying on with another one."

"Sounds like a charming *ménage à trois*," Pritchard said, smiling broadly. "I've always been interested in that kind of thing. Of course only in an academic way," he added, and the two men laughed. "Who's the other one, do you know her name?" He raised the glass to his mouth.

"I've forgotten her name, but she's a graduate student in the Department. As a matter of fact, she's Sully's assistant."

The glass stopped at Pritchard's mouth. He lowered it. "She's doing an independent study with me."

"Well well. . . Now that's what I call interesting."

"Yes, it is, isn't it." Pritchard looked off across the room.

"There's more: they suspect him of carrying on with an undergraduate, a freshman. They've got a folder on him and if he isn't prepared to fall into line, I suppose they'll have no choice but to make the matter public. . ."

Pritchard was delighted. He would like nothing more than to see Sully dismissed. In a recent department meeting, Sully had opposed Pritchard's candidacy for Acting Chairmanship during Schultz's sabbatical. If Sully were out of the way, it would be smooth sailing for him. He wondered if Sully's student were actually doing any work, or merely sleeping her way through the job. He'd met her type before: trifling, unimaginative girls who knew only one way to further their ambitions. Well if that was what she wanted. . . And it would be one more feather in his cap. Not that he found her exceptionally attractive. But forcing Sully to resign and then having her. . .

It was this that occupied his thoughts when Becky sat across from him the afternoon of Thursday the 12th.

204

He was saying: "It might have been true that women in pre-Nazi Germany were united into a strong feminist movement, but your implication that the advent of Nazism was the destructive cause of the women's movement is a bit over-stated. I don't understand why you're concerned with this matter: it's irrelevant to your paper."

She had spent the morning in the furthest recesses of the library stacks and felt dusty. Her nose tickled and she thought she was going to sneeze. She decided that it had been a definite mistake to take this independent study with Pritchard.

He smiled. "Of course it's always important to look at the changing morals of a country when investigating its moral climate."

The change in subject made her look up. 'I must've missed something,' she thought. 'I'd better pay attention.'

"Now our morality, for example, is becoming increasingly liberal. Don't you agree?"

"Well, I don't think. . ."

"As a matter of fact, one of our professors right here in the History Department is living with a woman out of wedlock. When he came to be interviewed, he told us about it openly. He said he wanted the faculty to know where he stood. Do you know who I mean?"

She shook her head.

"David Sully. I wouldn't mention it, but it's common knowledge. Do you know him?"

"I'm his teaching assistant."

"Are you? What's your opinion of him."

"He's a good teacher. His classes are very popular."

"Do you ever see him outside of class?"

She bristled. "Of course. We have to discuss various students, or how he wants me to mark the papers, things like that."

"In my opinion he has a brilliant mind," he said, hoping to disarm her. "He's just published an article on the Mexican Revolution, and I've heard—"

"Have you read it?"

"No, but I've been told that the research is quite thorough, and the approach is interestingly fresh. . ."

"Do you have a copy with you?"

"No. But it's on sale at the campus bookstore."

She left as soon as possible, ran to the bookstore and quickly scanned the article. Finding no mention of herself, she bought the magazine, went into the lounge, read it through once trying not to hurry, and then more slowly. Pritchard was right: the research was thorough, the approach fresh, but she was not even a footnote.

She returned to the History Department, determined to confront Sully. Walking down the hall she saw the redhead, who passed quite closely. Becky did a double take. Something was wrong: that bright look of freshman innocence was unreal; under her eyes was a fine maze of early wrinkles. But she had no time to think about that now. She walked towards Sully's office. Out of the corner of her eye she saw Pritchard standing in his doorway, watching her. She stopped at the fountain, took a drink and left the building.

That night she called Sully and said she had to see him. When he arrived she pounced, demanding to know why, after all the work she had done, he had not bothered to minimally thank her in a footnote.

He slapped his forehead. Then he held out his hands pleadingly and swore that he had written a small introduction to the article, thanking her not only for the research work but for having contributed several original ideas. He hadn't told her to type it in because he'd wanted to surprise her. He'd meant to insert the introduction himself before mailing the article. but in the rush of leaving for Boston he'd forgotten.

The paragraph was in fact pinned to the bulletin board in his office and just as he said, was a short but glowing acknowledgement of her present efforts, as well as an enthusiastic prediction about the research the intellectual community could expect from this exceptional woman.

He'd written it out on the back of a pink memo slip. But in the subsequent days he'd tacked other notes over it so that by the time he mailed the article, the tribute was only a little pink corner jutting out.

She did not believe him. Here, finally, was a "legitimate" complaint as opposed to those vague nagging dissatisfactions she could never quite voice. She kept harping on the article, feeling dishonest. Though she was truly disturbed by the omission, she knew she was using it as a substitute for everything else. She was unable to stop, and listening to her voice, became deeply depressed: she felt that everything she said to him was bound to turn into a lie.

On his part, David was becoming frantic. He decided that there was only one way to shut her up, and apologizing one final time, took her in his arms and kissed her.

He led her into the bedroom. He undressed quickly, got into bed and watched as she undressed. She had been dieting and had lost five pounds. She knew she looked good, and undressed slowly, enjoying his attention. Naked, she walked to the dresser and undid her hair, placing the hairpins one by one in a small box near the mirror.

She shook her hair loose so that it fell around her face and shoulders, and got into bed. He was already excited. He gently pushed her back on the bed and ran his hands along her body: the small mounds of her breasts and the curve of her waist familiar under his hands.

She fought off disappointment. If this followed the usual scenario he would enter her before she was sufficiently aroused, and the orgasm would elude her once again. She wanted to tell him what to do but telling him didn't conform to her image of sex as being passionate and non verbal.

But she had to tell him. Each time she faked, it was worse. It was like watching the emperor prance around in his non-existent new clothes: she was cheering on a naked king. What if they stayed together? Was she going to fake for the rest of her life? She'd felt increasingly guilty about masturbating: by coming to orgasm alone, she was denying him his right to bring her there.

"Dave," she whispered, "you know what I like?" and she guided his fingers. But he was uncertain down there in that dark mysterious place between her legs. She feebly tried to tell him. He was confused about the goal of all her tense instruction.

It wasn't only his ignorance of her body, it was her own feeling that he was bored, that she was taking too much time, that she wouldn't climax anyway so what was the point of making him wait. She felt like a lost explorer and desired the security of him on top of her and in control. She didn't want the responsibility of failure, and she moved her hips against his body, trying to wriggle under him.

Relieved, he kissed and mounted her.

But it was no good. "Dave?" she whispered, "how about. . . could we try it with me on top?"

"Sure," he said unsurely, not knowing exactly what it was she wanted, and they rolled over laboriously.

Once she was on top it was easy. She rode him and

felt his pressure in her and against her. She felt the teasing growing excitement, the clenching of her muscles tighter and tighter. Her mind went blank; she only felt. Her body found its way and she went with it toward that explosion where all her gears meshed and everything was in tune; she went with her body and forgot about him until she came back.

She had hoped against hope that he had come with her but when she opened her eyes, saw that he was only an observer. She took a deep breath to quiet her pounding heart. "You didn't—"

"No, I. . . it's difficult. . . like this."

Her body felt slow and heavy, and her skin like it was at one with the air. She wanted to close her eyes and sleep. She thought of David. She couldn't leave him like this; she made herself alert and leaned down to kiss him, beginning again. But no matter how she tried to ignore it, it would not work.

She got off, the apologetic assassin. This had never happened and she felt all those encouraging words at her lips ready to rally him on to potency. But she thought it might be better to make amends, and faced in the direction of his limp penis. It lay there like an accusation: she was the castrating bitch who had devoured his strength. Before she could atone for her sin, he motioned her away with his body and got up for a cigarette.

He'd been trying to quit. She felt guilty that he lay there smoking, though at the same time, she thought: 'Fuck him. What's he acting so tragic about. I hardly ever come.' She wanted to laugh but kept silent: in this performance he was the star and she had finished the play without him.

"I'm sorry," she murmured, leaning on her elbow and

placing her hand lightly on his chest.

"That's OK," he said in a way she'd know it wasn't. "It happens sometimes." He blew the smoke upwards in a hard, straight line. "It's not your fault."

Of course it was her fault. She'd criticized him and now she had to bear his anger and resentment. All night she had done nothing but criticize him, and she thought it only fair he retaliate. She set her lips stoically, waiting for her punishment.

At first he seemed to be lost in thought; then his eyes narrowed on an idea. He stubbed out the cigarette. "I used to go with a woman who couldn't come unless we did it like that with her on top." He slid his hands under his neck for support. "She turned out to be a lesbian."

The breath went out of her. "Oh really?"

"Did you like coming that way?" he asked coolly.

"It was OK. I mean it was good, but you know. . . not fantastically good. Not as good as. . ." She couldn't complete the lie. She rolled toward him seductively, nudging him with her body to signify: not as good as with you on top.

Suddenly she couldn't stand being naked next to him. She sat up quickly. "Hey, how about going to the movies. There's a ten o'clock show downtown."

"Sure," he said without interest, "why not."

They got up to dress, hastening to leave the scene of the crime. He was clumsy. He had to maneuver himself around chairs, take care that he didn't steer his machinery into the bookcase. Becky felt like a flamboyant duchess flaunting her coordination in front of a stumbling bumpkin.

She wanted to change the subject, and was going to mention what Pritchard had said about him, but then thought of all the work she'd done on his paper without receiving any public credit, and decided to keep silent, feeling gleefully nasty that she was keeping from him something that might be important.

He was looking at her dreamily. "You know something? You're a glider. . . You know, somebody who moves. . ." He made a smooth, sweeping gesture with his hand.

She smiled sheepishly since she had glided at his expense, and went into the bathroom. She washed between her legs quickly, put on her robe, and washed her face. She hadn't worn eye liner in over a month but felt pale and naked without it now, and began to apply it unsteadily.

She was peering at the jagged line in the bathroom mirror when he came in to watch her skill. "Got to have steady hands for that," he admired.

She reached up to touch his face, looking deeply into his eyes. "Dave," she said tenderly, while inside a voice screamed: Liar! Liar! "What does one time matter, if all the other times were. . ." She shrugged, unable to find a word to describe such sexual bliss as she had known with him.

He smiled and hugged her. "You're great, Beck," he said into her hair.

His words turned her into Miss No Nonsense, who wore sensible walking shoes and was embarrased by emotion. "Oh go on, enough of that mush, get outta here so I can finish putting on my face." She smiled coyly: "Who knows? I might turn into a militant feminist any day now and then what would I do with the rest of my eye liner?" He laughed at the comment, giving her a scolding look: it wasn't politically correct for her to make fun of her sisters. "Well!?" she said, tossing her hair back like a naughty child.

"You're too much," he laughed, and left, too intent on her witticism to have trouble steering himself through the doorway.

Now she was angry at herself. 'Well,' she thought defensively into the mirror, 'what could I do?'

Her eyes filled with tears. 'Oh well,' she thought, and continued applying her eye liner. It might all be insanity, but if it was his insanity then it was her reality.

They drove to the theater and he parked the car. Walking on the snowpacked sidewalk they passed two girls and a boy in their early teens, standing in a storefront doorway. The boy was holding onto one girl's hand, making her slap her own face lightly. He was laughing. The girl was making small ineffectual sounds of protest and trying to pull her hand away. But the boy held on tighter and slapped harder. The other girl smiled faintly and tried not to get in the way.

Becky remembered that her grandfather had done the same thing to her. He'd hold her tiny hand and make her slap herself across the face. It never hurt physically, but it humiliated and frustrated her. When she cried out: "Grandpa, stop!" he'd only laugh and say: "Stop what? I'm not doing anything, why are you hitting yourself?" He'd call her his sweetheart, kiss her cheek and send her on her way, patting her bottom because he loved her.

Without thinking, she said to David: "Did you see that? Men are so oppressive, I can't believe it."

"What, that kid back there? He didn't mean any harm, he was only teasing."

"He might have been teasing, but she felt humiliated."

David snorted. "How do you know how she felt. You're always over-reacting."

"Dave, how can you tell me you agree that yes, men

212

oppress women, and then when I point out a specific example, you start to argue."

"Because not all men are oppressive to all women, that's why. Some men are conscious of their sexism. They struggle with their chauvinism, they know what to watch for. Some men are more conscious of sexism than women. Sometimes in a relationship it's the woman who's chauvinistic." And his eyes reminded her of what had just passed between them.

She thought: 'He's right. You'd better shut up. How much of that women's lib crap do you think the poor man can stand.'

In the theater they sat down in their usual positions: David resting both elbows on the armrest, Becky sitting arms to her sides. But tonight she was conscious of his moving farther and farther into her space.

She gritted her teeth and jabbed her elbow out so that his arm fell off the armrest. He jumped. "What's the matter?"

She thought: 'Right, something has to be the matter when I assert myself.' She said: "Nothing's the matter."

He shook his head and drew his arms to his sides as if she had tied a rope around him. "I don't know what's the matter with you lately. You've changed. Sometimes I can't relate to you at all."

She removed her elbow. 'He's right,' she thought. 'I am inconsiderate lately. What's the matter with me.'

Before she could apologize, he said: "See that woman over there ahead of us? The one sitting all alone?"

"Yes. . ."

"I wouldn't want to come to a movie alone. I couldn't enjoy it. Can you imagine really liking a movie and having no one to tell? It must be very lonely."

The lights dimmed. All through the movie, Becky felt the woman's presence. 'I could be like her,' she thought, 'I could be coming to the movies alone.'

She realized how precarious her situation was: she had no one else and was in no position to bargain. She had believed their relationship was held back by her reluctance to confront him; in reality, it was based on it. Now everything was shaky and she felt afraid. The fear made her take a step backwards. She told herself that it was only temporary, but she bathed in the feeling of temporality as though it were eternity.

After the movie they returned to her apartment. She hoped he wouldn't come up with her: she wanted to be away from him so she could be herself. But he invited himself up and she led the way.

Upstairs she felt like she had never left the movie. She was sitting back inside herself watching it all happen. She joked, she laughed, she gazed at him lovingly, the sweet little coquette, so very anxious to please. At one point she pretended to be a torch singer and waved an imaginary scarf across her throat as she sang tragically: "I'm a poor fool but what can I do? Why was I born: to love you."

He was amused.

She was not.

Paul had stopped talking to Justine about the collective. They no longer discussed anything involving their future. Each harbored stereotyped images of the other in panic-stricken corners of their minds. Paul saw Justine as a smug middle class hausfrau walking her fat malevolent baby in the park, while he puttered around somewhere in the background, a stoop-shouldered, dull-brained academic, holding down a steady job, living a steady life, while inside he steadily died. Justine saw Paul as a mad revolutionary, storming from one collective and demonstration to another while she and the baby followed meekly behind, Justine overworked, faded and old before her time, the baby ragged, frightened and underfed.

One morning in the first week of February, Paul woke and watched Justine as she dressed for work, seeing that stolid aspiring suburbanite. She saw his face and thought he was comparing her with the pretty college girl he'd walked with after the movie in January. "I'll dress in the other room if I offend you," she muttered.

Paul said that he wasn't even thinking about her, and in his effort to dispel the tension, suggested that they go out for breakfast and then shop for baby clothes. "Come on, you owe yourself a morning off. I'll get you to work by noon."

She agreed, and they had a delightful breakfast, flirting like they had before they were married. The delight exploded when it was time to shop for the baby, and Paul drove up in front of Goodwill.

They were cool with each other for the next few days. By the following week their relationship had climbed to a small peak in what Justine saw as a downward spiral. Then, the Thursday before Bill and Lynne's wedding, it plummeted.

That evening Justine was finishing her dress when Paul walked in the door. He was in a good mood. Rubbing warmth into his hands, he smiled at her. "Hello my little chickadee, what's all this?"

"Iff my dff," she said through a mouthful of pins. He laughed and she removed them. "It's my dress."

"Very pretty. What's it for?"

"For the wedding Saturday. I've been working on this dress for months, you've seen it before."

He had opened the refrigerator and was bending down to peer inside, but at her words he straightened. "The wedding. . . you don't mean your brother's wedding."

"Paul, I've heard of absent-minded professors, but you take the cake. Of course it's my brother's wedding, how many other weddings did we get invited to? I picked up your suit from the cleaners today. And I bought you a tie. You won't look fantastic, but you'll pass. Aren't you going to ask what we got them?"

"A suit! Justine, sometimes I wonder about you. . ." He poured a glass of milk. "I'm not going to wear a suit to the wedding. I'll go like I am."

"What do you mean, 'like I am'?"

He held out his arms. "Like I am. I'm not going to try to impress your family." He drank the milk.

"Paul, wait a minute, this is a wedding. People want to have fun at a wedding, they don't want to be bothered by you prancing around like some middle class revolutionary."

He choked. Milk spluttered onto his chin, and he wiped it away, setting the glass on the table with a loud noise.

"It's not as if we're going to some hippie wedding on a mountain top where everybody wears flowers and gunny sacks, this is a regular wedding and they won't understand. Not at *all.*"

"Justine, stop trying to change me."

"Me! *You're* the one who's always trying to change *me!*"

"Look. I'm sure you won't know what the hell I'm talking about, but what I wear happens to be a matter of principle."

"At this point, I don't give a shit about you *or* your principles. All I know is, you better not let me down in front of my people or you'll be sorry."

He made a motion with his hand, dismissing her threat.

"And before the wedding. . ." She looked down at the fabric and resumed her work. ". . I hope you'll have enough consideration to put on deodorant."

He stared at her.

"I don't know exactly when you stopped wearing it, but I wish you'd start again. And I don't care how many baths you take every day, it's not the same thing. Are you going to explain to every single person at that wedding that you stink because you're trying to change the world all by yourself?"

"All by myself! If you'd manage to read the newspapers once in awhile instead of watching the Goddamned tube, you'd know what's going on in the world and you wouldn't make an idiotic comment like that."

She let her hands fall in her lap. "In the olden days, Paul, everybody used to stink, and maybe after the revolution when no big deodorant companies want to make money by making people ashamed of their body odors, everybody'll stink then. But nobody at that wedding is going to stink, and you better not stink either."

He stepped toward her. "Justine, after that fiasco in front of Goodwill the other day—and don't interrupt me—I decided that from now on, we only have conversations when you decide that you want to be reasonable. I will not participate in another screaming match. If you want to rationally discuss the earth shattering issue of what I look and smell like at your brother's wedding, I'll be glad to sit down with you once again and try to explain it, and I said not to interrupt! The only other thing I have to say is that I can't believe you have the nerve to talk to me about consideration, because as far as consideration goes, if the way you treat *my* friends and family is any indication of how *I'm* supposed to act, then you can take your friends *and* your family, and shove them." With that, he grabbed his coat from the chair, and walked out.

Friday morning he was still asleep when Justine left for work. At lunch she got her paycheck and found a two week notice. She had been fired. Several of the women had told her to expect it as soon as her pregnancy was visible, and she was not surprised. What surprised her was the terrible feeling of dread that settled on her day.

All afternoon she was sensitive to the way people reacted to her. Some, including the Personnel Director, treated her with exaggerated kindness as though she were a crippled princess. Some stared pointedly. Others tried to look and not look at the same time. Whether they were smiling at the cute little mother-to-be, or leering because they knew what she'd done to get that way, their attention pummelled its way into her consciousness. She had to keep reminding herself that pregnancy was the most natural thing in the world, because she was beginning to feel like a freak.

Paul wasn't home when she returned, and he didn't call. Some time during the evening she fell asleep, and was awakened after midnight by Paul and David coming into the apartment, talking excitedly.

"But if someone snuck into Ward's office," David said, bending down to remove his boots, "they could've gotten them easily."

Paul stamped his boots on the mat. "Impossible. It'd be locked. Why would somebody go to all that trouble?" He walked to the couch, little chunks of snow trailing behind him. "And how could they? The locked building, the locked office. . ."

David sat down. "Maybe it was an inside job. Maybe it was Ward's secretary, maybe she's disillusioned with the power structure or she's angry at Ward and trying to get back at him."

"I don't know. I don't think she'd jeopardize her job like that, she's been around a long time. And I can't get over the feeling that we're being manipulated."

"Paul, this is a fantastic opportunity, and if you don't take advantage of it, you're out of your mind."

When Justine walked into the living room, they were deep in thought. Glancing at Sully, Paul said to her, "I didn't think you'd be up this late." He was sorry about their argument, and his tone was soft. "You'll never believe what happened."

David looked at his watch.

"In my school mailbox I found an envelope filled with xerox copies of letters between Ward and some Pentagon big-shot. They're incredible." He motioned to a sheaf of papers on the coffee table. "What we thought all along was true. Project Rhododendron is researching nerve gas, and the university has covered up the whole—"

David had cleared his throat and looked again at his watch. "We don't have much time," he added in case Paul had not gotten his point. "We've got to outline a strategy. Do we want to use these letters to educate the university community, do we want to collect signatures for a referendum, do we want to confront Ward immediately. . . What are we going to do?"

"You're right. First of all we should call a meeting for nine tomorrow. We'll have to start phoning people either tonight, or early in the morning so that—"

"Paul." Justine stood before him. "Did you forget about the wedding?"

"The wedding? The wedding! Oh no. . ."

"You're not going to the wedding," she said.

Disconcerted, Paul looked at David and back at Justine. David picked up the letters and rattled them, reminding Paul of his political commitments.

"Look, Tina. . . I don't know why this wedding is so important to you. Ok, Ok, I know it's your brother, but you've told me over and over that you never got along with him. And you only see Lynne at work. I hardly know your family, and I'm sure they won't care one way or another if I'm not there. This way, you can go and have a good time and not worry about what they think of me." He smiled unconvincingly. "Anyway, it'll solve the problem of what I wear." He saw she wasn't listening. "Tina?"

She smiled strangely, and before he could say anything else, she walked into the bedroom and closed the door.

The two men stared at the door. Paul sighed. "I think she's really upset. Maybe I should talk to her. She's been looking forward to this for months. It's not so easy for her. We're older, we've already made the break, but Justine's still tied to her family. She's just a kid. Maybe I can swing both things, there's no reason why I have to be there for the entire meeting. Either I could leave the meeting early and go to the reception, or go to the wedding, and come to the meeting late."

David frowned at this. George was in Cuba, and he did not want the responsibility for their actions to fall primarily on himself. "Paul, would she feel any better once her family met you? I'm convinced it's more than the wedding. And whatever else is bothering her won't be affected by your presence for a few hours. We've got to make alot of heavy decisions tomorrow. I think you ought to weigh those decisions against the wedding of some people you hardly know. She'll forget all about it, take my word for it."

"I'm not so sure. . ."

"Besides, it wouldn't be a correct move to let your personal matters come in the way of politics."

Paul would have liked to say all that was in his mind, but this seemed an inappropriate time to introduce criticism. They discussed strategy until four in the morning when David left.

Justine was awake. She lay staring at the wall, and as Paul got into bed, she felt the mattress sink under his weight.

On the third Saturday in February, the women from the group met at Elizabeth's apartment for a pot-luck dinner.

Because of the increasingly businesslike atmosphere of what the women had come to refer to as "General Meetings," several had voiced the need for a more informal gathering. The group numbered almost fifty, and the women channelled their energies into four committees, three of which reported back to the General Meeting.

The Course Committee had fleshed out their original idea into what would be a comprehensive, one semester women's course planned for the following September. The Storefront Committee was looking into rental space; the group hoped to move its base from the university to the community. The Daycare Committee had reported only once, having found the laws concerning the setting up of daycare centers to be exceedingly strict.

The Abortion Committee did not report to the group, and its existence was never openly discussed. Several women were trying to compile a clandestine list of doctors who would perform safe abortions. Abortion being illegal, the discovery of this group by the authorities could mean prosecution and potential jail sentences. Elizabeth reminded the women that no matter how they disliked the idea, there was always the possibility of paid political informants among them, and as their strength grew, so would this possibility.

At one in the afternoon, Becky pulled up in front of Terry's and beeped the horn. The day was warm, and the sun reflected brightly on the hard packed snow. Terry walked to the car carrying a large paper bag.

"Hi," Becky said. "What'd you bring."

Terry sighed dramatically, and from the bag removed two flat heavy looking loaves.

"Mmm. . . Looks delicious. What is it, baked leather?"

"It's supposed to be herb bread. Justine found the recipe in some magazine. But I think she forgot to read me something essential. Like yeast. What'd you bring."

"A casserole." Becky said, pulling away. "Probably that's what everybody'll bring. Does Justine need a ride?"

"No, she's not coming."

"How come."

Terry was silent. "She's going through some changes. lately. They made her leave her job, and. . .well. . . "

Becky did not pursue the subject. She wondered if the "changes" had anything to with the proposed commune.

Most of the women were already there when Becky and Terry arrived. Some were in the kitchen organizing the food, and others sat in the living room talking, or munching on cheese and crackers Elizabeth had placed on the long, low coffee table. Susan's dog Che lay under the table waiting to be fed an occasional piece of cheese.

The apartment took Becky by surprise, for Elizabeth's presence was obvious: on an end table lay letters with return addresses from Chicago and Boston, and next to them, an anthropology book with heavy margin notations. Tacked to the wall over the couch was a large water color portrait of a small-boned bespeckled figure that represented Elizabeth, sitting in a field of clover reading a book.

In fine blue print in the lower right hand corner were the words: "To Elizabeth of the morning, with love from Jeff."

When Becky pictured living with David, she imagined a separate space for her own things, a corner of the room perhaps. She wondered if this were what he meant when he told her his apartment felt "crowded."

It was Elizabeth who determined the initial tone of the gathering. Curled into an overstuffed chair at the head of the room, she informed them of the progress of the D.O.D. referendum.

At the February 14th meeting Paul attended, the small group of radicals had decided to make the Pentagon letters public, and petition President Ward to permit a referendum calling for the end of ties between the University and the Department of Defense. In the following week, over two thousand students, faculty and university employees signed this petition, which a delegation would present to Ward on March 3rd. Many of the women in the group, Elizabeth and Becky included, had spent a great deal of time talking to students and collecting signatures.

When Elizabeth exhausted the subject, Terry suggested they talk about themselves. But no one knew how to begin, and they spent over half an hour discussing what they were going to discuss and how they were going to discuss it.

Nothing resolved, they decided to eat. They broke up into groups of twos and threes, and commented on the dishes, traded recipes and diets, gossiped about school and boyfriends. There was a great deal of teasing about Terry's bread: she had bragged she was an accomplished cook.

Gradually the conversation focused on one woman at a

time. They spoke in tones of self-mockery, making carica-
tures of themselves. But when no one laughed, they became serious. Humorous grumblings about diets opened
into deep dissatisfactions with their bodies; light complaints about boyfriends opened into feelings of insecurity
and worthlessness.

In many of the narratives, Becky recognized herself.
One woman admitted that she was unable to think of the
most unhappy moments in her life without turning them
into jokes.

"It's because we can't take ourselves seriously," Becky
said. She felt as though the room were a vessel, isolated
from the world. Here they would find understanding,
and a tender ideal of sisterhood.

She wanted to talk to Elizabeth about David. Her
relationship with him was no secret, and she wanted to
admit it openly.

Before she could speak, one of the women began talking
in a loud, self-derisive voice. She told them that a few
weeks earlier she had been at the library, and had over-
heard her steady boyfriend bragging to his friend about his
recent conquest of her. The picture of her hiding behind
the stacks of books was supposed to be humorous, but no
one laughed.

Elizabeth leaned forward and described a prank she
had played during a high school excursion into Boston.
The women listened, some of them laughing, relieved at
the lighter atmosphere.

Terry didn't laugh. She despised Elizabeth's frequent
chatter about Boston. When Elizabeth paused, Terry said
quietly: "You know, I lived in Boston for a year. But
when you talk about it, it seems like you're talking about
another country. My life there was really different from

yours. . ." The women all looked at her, waiting. "I had a baby in Boston."

She reached for a cigarette from a pack lying on the floor, lit it and dragged deeply. Her hand trembled so that the smoke drifted up in a long, quivering line. "I had a job cleaning an office. I used to walk to work in the evening and walk home in the morning. Sometimes I'd see girls my age riding around in cars having fun, acting silly. . . It was springtime, and it seemed like everybody in the world was happy but me." She smiled at this, for saying it aloud she realized how it sounded.

"Where's. . . the baby?"

"Adopted. Someplace, I don't know."

They were silent. One woman said: "You know. . . I've been feeling pretty sorry for myself, but I guess compared to you, I'm lucky. Last month I had an abortion. It was pretty awful, the guy was a butcher and I got a bad infection. It's just starting to clear up."

"Why didn't you tell somebody?"

"I didn't know who to tell."

"That's why we need this kind of discussion," Terry said, then noticed, sitting next to Becky, a woman who rarely spoke. Her head was bowed, her long black hair falling around her face, and she was crying. "Diane. What's the matter."

Diane shook her head, unable to speak. Someone brought her a tissue. In a choked, almost inaudible voice, she told them that when she was sixteen, she had been dragged into an abandoned house by a group of men and raped.

There was a long silence.

"Did you know them?"

She nodded tearfully. "I knew all of them. They were seniors in my high school."

226

"Didn't you do anything about it?"

"What could I do? Who could I tell. You know what happens to a girl's reputation after she's. . .raped. I didn't do anything. I went home and took a bath and the next day I went to school. But the word got out. It was a big joke. Pretty soon all the guys thought I was a slut."

She bent her head, crying. Becky put her arm around Diane's shoulder and patted her awkwardly. The tears soaked into her shirt and touched her skin. "Shh. . .Don't cry," she said. "Don't cry."

"No," Terry said softly. "Let her cry. It'll do her good."

Becky felt that the words were directed at herself, and her own eyes filled with tears. Then she thought: 'Don't be stupid. You didn't get raped. What are you so upset about.'

Diane wiped her face. "There was nothing I could do."

"We always feel there's nothing we can do." Terry said bitterly.

"I heard there's a group in San Francisco," a woman said, "a rape squad. When a woman's raped and she knows who did it, this squad tracks the guy down and beats him up."

"They should cut off their balls."

"Cut off their fucking dicks."

"Right on," Terry said solemnly.

Diane brushed her hair back from her face. "It feels good to finally tell somebody. Thanks," she said to Becky and ventured a smile.

At this moment the front door swung open and David stepped in. looking at a piece of paper and calling irritably : "Elizabeth, where—" He stopped and looked up.

All eyes were fixed on him, united not against David himself but against what he represented.

Sensing their hostility, he forced a small apologetic smile and made his way toward the bedroom, trying to be inconspicuous as he stepped through the women. Yet at the same time he wanted to reclaim his territory, and stopped in their midst to select a piece of cheese before he disappeared into the bedroom.

In another moment he reappeared. Once again he made his way through them, this time more aggressively, repeating: "Excuse me, excuse me," in a resentful voice.

At the front door he paused to stare at Elizabeth. "What time. . ." he said, motioning at the group.

"I told you six o'clock. You said you wouldn't be home until then," she reminded him coldly. More subdued, she answered: "Six."

He left.

During this interchange, Becky had looked at neither of them; her eyes were fixed on the dark blotch of tear-stains on the front of her shirt.

"It's the only time in his life he's ever been early," Elizabeth remarked, and the women laughed.

Diane smiled. "Let's clean up. If somebody stacks the dishes, I'll wash 'em."

"I'll throw away the garbage," Terry said dryly, and they laughed again.

By five they had all departed, having decided to form a weekly discussion group. "A consciousness raising group," Terry said, adding: "Next week we'll meet at my place."

Becky took Terry home. On the way they drove through the park, passing a large hill which was in the daytime dotted with sleds. Becky remarked that she hadn't been sleigh riding since she was a child.

"I wanted to go the other day," Terry said, "but there were too many damned kids. Hey, let's go now."

Becky objected that the idea was insane but Terry persisted until she agreed. At Terry's they changed into warm clothes and returned to the park, Becky muttering that Terry's slacks were too tight, and bound to split.

In spite of her protests she was glad that they were going to do something as simple as ride down the hill on a sled. She had felt lately that her life was a mass of contradictions, and unless she clung to daily routine and simple experiences, they would crash into one another. She'd told herself she was being foolish; nevertheless, the feeling of chaos remained.

Though it was night, the moon illuminated the hill. For the first few runs they took turns on the sled, but on the next they went together, Terry in front, Becky behind. Everything was going smoothly until they neared a bump. "Turn right!" Becky yelled. "No, left! Turn left!"

Terry swerved right, left, and the sled tipped, toppling them onto the snow. Becky rolled over and came to rest on her side. Terry was sprawled face down in the snow, looking bewildered. "What happened."

Becky laughed. "Talk about women drivers. . ."

Terry threw a handful of snow at her. "If you weren't such a lousy co-pilot, we wouldn't've fallen."

Becky ducked to avoid the snow. "We wouldn't've falled? You've got to be kidding!" She lay back laughing and closed her eyes, opening them to find Terry poised above her holding a mass of snow.

"Ten. . . nine. . . eight. . ." she said.

Just as she was about to drop it on the count of seven, Becky kicked out and Terry collapsed, laughing.

The two of them lay in the snow and looked off across the park. The full yellow moon stood out against the dark sky, the bare branches of the trees against the white snow.

They stood and walked up the hill, dragging the sled behind them, but halfway up they noticed four figures standing off to one side, watching.

"Hello girls," one called, "having a good time?"

"Can we come and play with you?" the tall one yelled suggestively, and they laughed.

"Come on," Becky said, nodding in the direction of the car, "let's go."

"I'm not ready to go."

"Terry, please. . ."

"Oh, all right," she said and they headed toward the car. The four figures saw them change direction. "Aw, come on back. . ."

"Hey, don't go away, let's get it on."

"Here pussy pussy. . ." the tall one crooned, and the others laughed.

Just as they reached the car, one called: "Why don't you chicks come on back. You want it, you know you do."

"Go fuck yourself!" Terry yelled.

They were momentarily stunned. The tall one said: "Hey, you can't talk to us like that," and they walked toward the car.

"Come on," Terry said, throwing the sled in the back seat, "let's get the hell out of here."

Becky started the motor. They heard: "Come back here, you cunt, we'll show you!"

Terry rolled down her window. "Drop dead, you prick!"

"Terry!" Becky said, so shocked she almost sideswiped the car in front.

"Cocksucker!" Terry yelled, leaning out the window and making an obscene gesture.

"Terry, shut the window!" Becky hissed. "God damn it! Shut that window. I'm freezing. You'll get us into trouble!"

230

She rolled up the window, swearing.

"I don't know what's the matter with you, you must be crazy. You shouldn't sink to their level."

"Why not? Why should I pretend they're not there? Why should I pretend it doesn't bother me? We weren't bothering them, why the hell did they have to lay that goddamned macho trip on us, showing us they're such big men." She spat the word out scornfully, and Becky looked at her. "Why shouldn't I sink to their level. I mean if that's where it's at, if that's the level they're at, then fuck'em, I'll sink to their level, I'll sink lower than them, the bastards."

"Take it easy. Relax, It's all over."

"That's what you think. It's never over. And you can go on pretending it's not there and spending your life hiding, but not me. The bastards. Let's go back."

"What!"

"I wish I had a gun."

"Terry!"

She laughed. "I'm sorry. I'm a maniac. But I don't care. Fuck'em. Fuck everybody. I don't care."

"I'm sure they wouldn't have done anything."

"That's not the point! The point is that they felt they could have, and we felt they could have. You can't even go for a fucking sleigh ride in this goddamned city without. . ." She sighed. "Well, I went for my first karate lesson last week. Wait'll I get my black belt. I'll show 'em. Wham! Pow! Drop kick to the neck! Wheel kick to the—"

"Terry," Becky admonished. "Come on now. . ."

"Oh all right. But you'll see. . . I feel great! Come on. let's go back. My adrenaline's flying! We'll drive by, real close. . ."

"Forget about it. Tell me about karate. How was it."

"It was great, really great. I'm the only woman in the class, but you better believe I did the warm-up exercizes better than all the other white belts. Of course I was crippled all week. . . You should've seen me hobbling around. I could hardly move, I was in such pain. I'm going again tomorrow. Why don't you come?"

"Who, me?"

"Sure. Why not."

"I don't know. Karate's so. . ." She wrinkled her nose: "unfeminine."

And at that, the two women burst out laughing.

She dropped Terry off and drove home. As she unlocked the door, the phone started ringing.

It was David. "I've been calling for over an hour," he complained. "I thought we could spend some time together but it's too late now."

"Why don't you come over?" she offered, though she did not want to see him.

"No, it's too late. If you were home when I first called I could've come over. But it's too late now."

Becky sat down at the kitchen table and stared blankly across the room. The line was silent. "Where are you."

"I'm standing in a phone booth," he accused.

She sighed, and chided affectionately: "Poor baby, must be cold."

He was not soothed. "Where were you."

"Terry and I went sleigh riding. . ." She laughed but he did not respond. "What a spill we took. . . But we had alot of fun. . ." He was silent. "We went to the park, you know that big hill? It was nice, but. . . but we decided to leave."

His silence was intimidating.

"Terry wanted me to come up, but I figured: enough is enough!"

Silence. She knew what he wanted. She roused herself and said in a hard, malicious voice: "I see you stumbled into our little hen party."

"Yeah. . ." He chuckled.

"Poor David, you're lucky we all didn't jump up and hit you with our purses."

He laughed, and joining the game, asked sarcastically: "Did you have a good time, dear?"

"Oh lovely. That is, as good a time as anybody could have sitting around all afternoon listening to a bunch of sob stories."

He laughed again.

She stared at the floor and forced herself to say: "I mean it was like a goddamned soap opera. Pregnancy, abortion, rape. . ."

"Oh? Who raped somebody, Maggie?"

"Maggie. . ."

"You mean she didn't confess?"

"What was she supposed to say?"

"Tell me you haven't heard that your little friend Maggie's a lesbian."

Becky had always imagined that if she met a lesbian, she would be nice to her; she'd pictured herself smiling graciously at some faceless figure. But she already knew Maggie.

"David, you shouldn't say that without proof. I mean if it ever got around. . ."

"It's true. Paul saw them. She was with her 'girlfriend,' if you'll pardon the expression."

"Maybe it was her sister."

"Or her brother."

She giggled uneasily.

"You'd better watch out," he teased, "she'll turn you

all into a bunch of bull-dykes."

"Ooh, are you kidding? Hey, that's a little too much liberation for me to handle, thank you. No, I'm going to be a nice married lady. . ." She stopped: she had mentioned the forbidden subject. "No, I'll tell you what I'm going to be: a revolutionary gun moll. I'm going to be the Florence Nightingale of the Revolution, soothing fevered brows behind the barricades. . ."

"Will you take care of me?"

"I certainly will."

"No, you'll be off with all your new friends, and I'll be dying somewhere and you won't even notice."

"Oh don't be silly."

"It's true." He sighed, half teasing, half serious. "If your behavior today was any indication. . ."

"Oh David, come on. What could I do? You think I wanted them to beat *me* up with their purses? Hey, I was a prisoner of war. . ."

When they hung up she walked into the bedroom and sat listlessly on the bed. She started to cry.

Two tears had made their way out of her eyes when, as if activated by the tears themselves, her mocking thoughts began: 'There she is, the asshole, crying. I don't know what the hell you're crying about. I don't feel sorry for you, it's your own fault. You're stupid, that's all. You're just stupid.'

She clamped her hands over her ears to stop the litany of self-hatred. "Stop it!" she screamed out loud, and broke into tears.

She cried until her face was swollen and blotchy. Slowly she calmed down, and as she did the thoughts returned: 'Finally. What the hell took you so long. . .'

"Shut up!" she said aloud.

234

And there was silence. She was stunned. She listened to her thoughts and heard nothing. There was no mocking, no self-hatred. Because it was gone, she understood for the first time that it had existed. She didn't know exactly what it was, only that it was a part of herself that had learned to hurt her. She also knew for the first time that she wouldn't let it.

She took a deep breath, and another, and looked out the window at the tree standing silent and intact before her.

Her face had become tight and cold from the dried tears, and she walked to the bathroom. Before she bent over the sink, she caught her own eye in the mirror. She stared. Not at her nose or her mouth, not at the way her eyebrows arched or any artificial expression in her eyes. . . but herself. She stared into her own eyes, and it seemed that layers and layers had peeled away and she was staring directly into herself. She was shy, like someone who had touched her lover's hand for the first time.

February came to an end. Justine had gone to the wedding and reception alone. It had been worse than she'd expected. Most people were polite, sorry that Paul was "ill," and hoped he'd get well soon. But she knew they didn't believe her. They felt sorry for her: what kind of husband did she have. And pregnant too, poor thing. She saw it in their eyes. One malicious cousin suggested that Justine was not married.

She left her job and after that stayed home. She saw no reason to go out, or for that matter, to get out of bed. She watched tv until it went off at night and never changed the channel. Often she did not bother to comb her hair or dress, but sat around the house in her old terry-cloth robe and slippers. Paul watched her and worried.

She was lethargic. The stove became crusted from two weeks of Paul's hasty cooking, and the floor in front of the refrigerator was spotted with stains from drops of milk, juice, and an egg he'd dropped and wiped up hurriedly. The cigarette filled ashtrays sent a stale smell into the room. Dr. Spock's book lay beside her bed unread.

She called no one. Becky phoned once to ask how she felt; she answered in monosyllables. Terry called every day, gently trying to persuade her to come shopping or to the movies; she said no. Her Aunt Connie called and was so upset by Justine's response that she insisted she was going to bring Justine to stay with her. After that she didn't answer the phone, and told Paul to tell all callers she was sleeping.

This new Justine frightened him. He tried to persuade her to see a counselor. He tried to snap her out of it by caring for her, babying her, finally by trying to pick a fight one evening. She watched him be nice or sarcastic and waited politely for him to finish. For the first time she looked at him without feeling that painful mixture of love and hate. She felt detached. At night he clung to her tightly, desperately, until she became uncomfortable. He went out less often though it was a crucial time for the radicals: they had collected almost five thousand signatures on the D.O.D. petition and the following week were to meet with Ward. Paul resented the fact that he had to devote so much time to Justine and the apartment, but nevertheless he did all the shopping, cooking, cleaning and laundry, for his resentment was overshadowed by his fear.

She had a recurrent nightmare: she was lost in the city at night. She wandered through unfamiliar streets looking for a way home. When she turned a corner at the top of a hill, she saw a bus pull away at the bottom. By the time she got to the bus stop, the route had changed and the bus no longer came to that place. The streets kept changing too: as soon as she got her bearings, the entire geography of the city altered and she was once again lost. She woke from the dream with a low, nagging depression that seeped into the silent moments of her day. After a few nights, she no longer remembered.

On the last day in February, Paul went out to plan the strategy for their March 3rd meeting with Ward. He left at seven, looking anxiously at Justine, who stared across the living room at nothing. A cigarette hung loosely from her fingers.

"Be careful," he said, trying to make his voice light, "don't start a fire."

She looked up vacantly. "What? Oh. Yeah, sure." She took a drag of the cigarette.

He hesitated a moment, and closed the door behind him.

She sat. The movements of the baby felt as if they were in another body, quite disconnected from her own. Occasionally the ashes from the cigarette fell onto the floor or her robe.

He was gone all evening. Her thoughts wandered on the

possibility that he had died in a car crash. She imagined the phone call from the police, the funeral. . . But no. If he died, she would grieve. There was no reason for him to die: he was not at fault.

Rather, she imagined a sunny day several months hence. The circumstances of Paul's disappearance were not in evidence. It was as though he had fallen into the earth, or never existed. She and the baby lived alone in the apartment.

Or better yet, she and the baby lived someplace else. A bright little attic apartment with white walls and a small pretty cradle beside the window.

She would have to work; maybe she could get her old job back. Or perhaps if she took a secretarial course, by the time she went to work she could get a better job. She had a few hundred dollars saved up and could pay off the hospital bills gradually. She'd sell her stereo: that would bring in something. Her father might lend her some money until she got on her feet. Or Phil and Connie. And Connie loved children and might take care of the baby while Justine worked.

It would be difficult. Connie might want her to come and live with them. She didn't want to do that. Perhaps she and Terry could get a place together. If necessary, she'd work the night shift while Terry was at home with the baby. There were plenty of factories around. . .

She lit a cigarette. It tasted bad. She went into the kitchen and got a glass of water. The small window over the sink framed the dark night. She drank the water and was about to turn away when she felt a sudden kick. It was not the slow easy turning, it was violent and angry.

Her eyes focused on her reflection: a slovenly, washed out woman with tangled hair, a cigarette dangling from her lips, her eyes squinting against the smoke.

The baby kicked again: I'm here. Take care of me.

She returned to the living room, stubbed out the cigarette decisively, and sat down to think.

It was late that night when she faced her decision: she would leave Paul.

She argued with herself, though she knew the arguments were merely a matter of form. She told herself she should wait until the baby was born, until it was older. But it would not be fair. She could not let him stay and get to love the baby and then say: I forgot to tell you but it's over. Now that I don't need you anymore, get lost. Besides, she would need him then. With an infant to care for, she'd need him more than ever. Better to do it now, to know what lay ahead, than to fool herself.

She argued that she should try again. But she knew that trying would change nothing. She would have to be what he wanted or herself, either being miserable or growing away from him, and in the end come to the same conclusion as now. Only then, through years of pain.

She tried to think clearly, concretely, to calculate her life and build her resolve.

At midnight, she heard Paul's key in the lock.

March
1970

Perhaps what happened that spring was due to coincidence; perhaps it was inevitable. Across the country a fever raged through the universities and departed, leaving most students to slide back into their familiar states of political apathy. The following year they would be studying hard for exams, going to rock concerts, or making leather belts and whole-grained bread to sell in the long halls of the student unions. But in the spring of 1970 they were striking for an end to the Vietnam war, some of them convinced that this was "it:" the long awaited beginning of the Revolution.

The afternoon of Friday, March 6th, a delegation of two walked across campus to Mellon Hall. It was windy, and Paul rested his chin on top of the cardboard box he carried, securing the flaps down. His face was drawn from lack of sleep. Mark carried a letter to President Ward stating that over five thousand people had signed the petition calling for a referendum on Project Rhododendron within the month. He was puffed up with pride at going on the mission.

In the President's office, John Frick stood at the window watching Paul as he had almost five months earlier.

Behind him, Ward sat at the desk. "I think you're wrong," he said. "The best thing would be to accept the petition and consider it for a month. By that time the students will be in the midst of exams. The whole thing will have fizzled out."

Frick's face was impassive. "Those two down there represent a minority of students. The majority aren't interested in this radical mumbo-jumbo. Those two are only after publicity."

Ward shook his head. "I'm not sure. I'm not sure at all. The fact that I postponed the meeting has already caused some commotion."

The delegation was no longer in sight, and Frick didn't want to be in Ward's office when they arrived. "You have to be absolutely firm with this kind of protest. Otherwise, it could easily get out of hand." He made his excuses and returned to his second floor office.

Within fifteen minutes he saw the delegation leave and head toward the Student Union. The younger one was excited, waving his arms, raising clenched fists in the air. Paul was calm. He walked with his head bent, chin resting on the cardboard box.

Frick buzzed his secretary. "Judy, have you typed that letter to Dr. Ward?"

"Yes, Dr. Frick, shall I bring it in for you to sign?" He did not answer. It was one of his idiosyncrasies: no response meant 'yes,' and a low grunt meant 'no.'

She came in and handed him the letter. He skimmed and signed it. "I'll hand deliver this," he said.

"Yes, Dr. Frick. Shall I file the carbon?"

After she closed the door he tore the letter into minute pieces which he threw into the basket.

Across campus, Paul and Mark entered the Student Union, where a large group waited in the lounge to learn the result of the meeting. Paul walked over to Sully and spoke to him for a few minutes. Sully shook his head repeatedly. Looking dutiful more than enthusiastic, Paul walked to the front of the room and stood on a chair, placing the petitions on the table beside him.

The people waited silently. Paul spoke: "Beside me is a box filled with signatures. Over five thousand people signed this petition, and Ward has called it illegal. And why? Because you and I are not a part of the power structure that runs this university."

He paused. The room was silent. "The ideology of this university is created by the imperialist policies of the United States government. This university is not shut away from reality, it helps create reality." He pointed in the direction of the Montgomery Science Center. "That Center is trying to create nerve gas to destroy motor control of the body. To make cripples out of people. That's what it's doing, rain or shine, business as usual."

"Business as usual. That should be the motto of this university, because the business of every department is indoctrinating the new privileged classes. The History Department doesn't teach the People's history, the history of Blacks, of Native Americans—"

"Of women!" someone from the crowd shouted.

"Right on!" Paul shouted back. "It doesn't teach the history of women, and the immigrants who built this country. It doesn't teach the history of slaves who were kidnapped and brought here against their wills, the working class who labored under inhuman conditions so the capitalists could reap such profits as to effectively control this country's resources. It doesn't teach the history of the great proletarian revolutions around the world, or how the American people have been brutally suppressed every time they threaten the power of the ruling class!"

He paused and looked around the room. "The Philosophy Department is a laugh. You can get a PhD from our reknowned Department and think that Karl Marx was Groucho's brother." There was a ripple of laughter, which he ignored. "Then what does this university do? It trains students to design weapons of war that not only destroy people, but whose manufacture and use irretrievably pollutes the earth. And instead of being punished, they are rewarded by the capitalists who care nothing about the sickness and death they cause, nothing about the ecological balance of nature, but who care only about profit."

The room was silent. "We're trained by them to do their jobs and in the process we become *like* them, caring nothing except that our own little corner is safe and comfortable. Hey what do we care about other people, just don't rock the boat, just don't make them mad at *us*."

He smiled. "But don't kid yourself, because one essential fact remains the same. We have no control over our lives. We're nicely trained to fit into a society dedicated not to the proposition that all people are created equal, but to the proposition that some people are going to be allowed to live in wealth, and others forced to live in poverty and disease and squalor."

He scanned the faces. "The rhetoric of the University Administration is democracy. That's what they preach. But in fact all decisions are taken by those in power: the Board of Trustees. And the majority, the students, have no voice in what happens. When we take a petition to the President, a petition signed by over five thousand people, a petition calling for nothing more radical than a vote, we are shown to the door. Politely, mind you, but to the door all the same."

"If the true nature of that project got out, if the tax payers of this city knew the truth, that this university is attempting to design gas whose purpose is to make cripples out of people, they wouldn't stand for it. And I want to tell you something: that gas isn't only for the Vietnamese. It's going to be used on anybody who doesn't stay in line. And that means the people of this country as well as any other country in this world. And that's where the power

244

lies: sit back and take it or get gassed. That's just where it's at."

"I want to ask you one question and one question only: whose university is this. Theirs? Or ours."

"Ours!" they shouted. "Ours!"

"Yes. It's ours. And I propose we tell them: by a strike."

And so the strike began. The students marched to Mellon Hall, demanding a meeting with Ward. They were told that he had left for the day. They mingled on the ground below, chanting slogans as they circled the building.

On the second floor, Frick phoned the Chairman of the History Department. "Bill? John here. . . I'm fine, thanks, and you?. . . Bill, that matter we've been discussing, I think you should go ahead with it. . . Yes, I know, they're milling around downstairs now. . . Well, I'm not sure how your end of it will affect this situation here, but I want you to go ahead regardless. I have full confidence in your discretion. . . Yes, I appreciate it. Give my best to Maureen. . . Yes, I'll tell her. Good-bye."

On the other end of the line, William Schultz hung up the phone, sat back and stared at the large calendar on the opposite wall. He wasn't sure what Frick was up to, but he knew one thing: Frick was going places, and as long as he did his job and minded his own business, he might in some way tag along. He buzzed his secretary. "Mrs. Parlato, send a memo to David Sully telling him I'd like to see him on the 13th at four o'clock. Make it informal," he said, thought for a moment and added: "but make a carbon."

During the first week of the strike a small dedicated group tried to persuade a disinterested majority.
Most students saw no connection between themselves
and the Vietnam war so far away. Surrounded by rhododendron bushes that bloomed huge pink flowers in the
spring, the Montgomery Science Center looked innocent
enough, not a place that researched nerve gas. The Administration had not acknowledged the xeroxed letters, and
many students suspected that the radicals had forged
them. The majority continued as before: they went to
classes, studied, played cards in the Cavern, and took no
part in the strike.

But those who were involved were involved totally.
In that first week the strikers attempted to create a govern-
ing body, the Provisional Revolutionary Strike Committee,
and elected Paul the Chairman. They approved the main
strike goal: the removal of the Pentagon funded Project
Rhododendron from campus. They met to plan strategies,
and wrote up leaflets which they mimeographed and
handed out to students. They stood outside buildings,
sometimes in the rain, and spoke to students on their way
to classes, trying to convince them to join the strike.

The Administration ignored the entire situation. Frick
convinced Ward that the basic realities of self-interest
would overcome any fleeting political ideals the students
might have.

Despite the existence of the Provisional Revolutionary Strike Committee, the strike organization was loose. The leaders were sometimes those who had the most to say, sometimes those who had the least but said it loudest. At the rallies whoever wanted to speak had only to stand in line behind the podium and wait his turn. While one or two women got up to speak, it was clear that the strike leadership was all male, and members of the women's liberation group complained: the men expected them to do all the leg work, yet they had no decision making power. The male strike leaders decided they had better heed these complaints, and they asked the women's group to choose two representatives to the next meeting of the P.R.S.C.

Susan Mather felt that she was the perfect choice. Having lived in Cuba, she felt that she personally had been invested with the spirit of the Revolution. Susan and George had planned to share their experiences with others not so fortunate. They arrived back on the first of March to find that the event of the day was not the return of Susan and George from Cuba, the event was Paul's meeting with Ward.

On the evening of Wednesday, March 11th, the women's liberation group met for the first time since the strike began. As she had months before, Susan sat at the front of the room, Che beside her. He watched her every movement lest she leave him again. Susan opened the meeting. She apologized that she could not at this time make a presentation about her trip to Cuba, but they had to choose two representatives to the P.R.S.C. She expected the meeting to be short, and took it for granted they would elect Elizabeth and herself. On the contrary, the meeting was long and argumentative, and the women

247

came to two decisions: their representatives would be Elizabeth and Justine, and they would send these two women to the P.R.S.C. meeting with a women's strike demand of daycare.

When Susan called for nominations, Becky raised her hand and said: "Before we choose representatives, I think we ought to discuss if we want to be represented. I'm all in favor of the strike, and I'll work for it, but I'll work as an individual. The involvement and support of the women's group is a whole other matter. We've got alot of projects going, are we going to put them aside? The strike might carry over to next fall. I think our participation ought to be a very conscious decision, not something we do because the men say, 'Do it.' "

This point was argued back and forth, the extremes held by Susan, who wanted to support the strike fully, and Terry, who did not want to support it at all.

One woman suggested that they should benefit from their support of the strike, and Diane proposed that the women's group have its own strike demand.

Susan objected that a specific demand would detract from the main strike goal. But Becky reminded her that at last night's strike rally, Paul himself had made an open invitation to the Black Student Association: if the B.S.A. supported the strike, they could have one strike demand.

"It's not quite the same situation," Susan said.

"It's exactly the same," Terry said. "Paul talked about 'solidarity.' If he's willing to pay the B.S.A. for their solidarity, then he ought to be willing to pay us."

Susan mumbled that Terry had twisted Paul's meaning, but she was drowned out by cries of agreement from the women.

Terry went on: "Otherwise, it's discrimination."

248

"Right," Becky said. "And if we want the P.R.S.C. to be a unified, representative body, we'd better voice our objections and make our demands right now so they know where we stand."

"Right on!" the women yelled.

They voted to support the strike on the condition that they be allowed one strike demand. The next order of business was deciding on the demand. They discussed the three main activities of the group, but could come to no conclusion.

Justine was impatient with the bickering. It wasted time. And time had become important to her since Paul moved out.

Paul had responded to her late night decision much as she'd expected, but she remained firm that they separate. He was resolved that he would find another place to live. He could not stay in the apartment without her, and did not want to worry about where she might be. Angry, hurt, confused and not quite sure that she was serious, Paul left the next day to stay with David and Elizabeth.

Justine set to work. She packed away the papers, notes and clippings that cluttered his desk top and bulletin board, making sure to misplace nothing. She packed the stacks of newspapers into several cardboard boxes and shoved them under the bed. She left many of the colorful posters on the walls for she had come to like them, especially the one of Che Guevara. Throwing open the windows, she cleaned from ceiling cobwebs down to the woodwork. She worked in the chilly rooms until late that night when she fell into a sound sleep.

The next day she woke in a state of anxiety. She sat down at Paul's desk with the checkbook and savings account passbook and divided the money. If she was careful, she would have enough to hold her until the baby came and then some. The only major expense would be the hospital, and she almost wished that she were having the baby at home as Paul had wanted.

She hated the idea of money going out and none coming in. She looked in the Want Ads and made telephone inquiries, all to no avail.

Late in the afternoon she remembered the 24 Hour store; she grabbed her coat and left the house. When she arrived, she walked up to the counter and said: "Joe, I'm here to proposition you: I think you need a vacation." When she left she had a job. Until the baby was born she would clerk from seven until noon, making a little over minimum wage, a dollar fifty an hour. Joe was paying her off the books, and she'd get to keep all of the money she made, over fifty dollars a week.

Mornings she worked at the store, and afternoons cleaned or visited. Sometimes in the evenings her eyes wandered to the wallposter of Che. On an orange background, his face looked out over the words: "Let me say, at the risk of seeming ridiculous, that the true revolutionary is guided by feelings of great love." She gazed at the words and thought of Paul.

All of the women at the meeting knew that she and Paul had separated. She was seven months pregnant, and alone. Some regarded her with disapproval, others with respect.

She stood up and they gradually grew silent. "We're wasting time," she said. "And I don't know about the rest of you, but I don't have any time to waste. We've got to make a decision. Our demand has to be something that the university has the power to give us, but won't create such an uproar that it'll overshadow the main

250

strike demand. That lets out abortion, and it lets out the storefront.

"It should be something that women all over will understand and want. I think they'd want daycare."

Susan sniffed. "Daycare has nothing to do with the war."

Justine said: "I think if the women in Vietnam knew what we were doing, they'd understand too. Those women who work, a lot of them must have children. A lot of them must be just like us. . ."

She sat down, and the group voted to propose daycare to the P.R.S.C. as their strike demand.

The next order of business was the choice of representatives. Susan was not nominated. The women overwhelmingly voted Elizabeth and Justine to represent the women's group. Becky was the alternate.

The meeting ended and the women dispersed. Becky and Elizabeth leaving together. Mark was waiting in the hall for Elizabeth. and the three walked downstairs together. Elizabeth said to Becky: "I want to talk to you about our tactics at the P.R.S.C. meeting in case Justine doesn't make it. I'll call you later."

"OK." Becky waved and walked away. heading for the Cavern, where she was to meet David.

Her face was radiant. She had swung herself wholeheartedly into strike activities: she stayed on campus until two a.m., meeting and making posters and mimeographing leaflets, got to bed at three and rose at six to be back on campus ready to talk to students breakfasting before eight o'clock classes. But she was never tired.

For the first time in her life she felt she was not an individual, but a part of a movement toward a new society. She often thought of the Vietnamese woman in the film;

251

though they lived miles apart, Becky knew that they were sisters. So caught up was she that she imagined her enthusiasm would spread throughout the city and over the country. The people would rise in a great and glorious revolution. Afterwards she envisioned a productive and healthy world where not only poverty and pollution would disappear, but such evils as competition, envy and greed. And it was happening now. Someday she would sit with her grandchildren, all of them members of a classless community, and tell them about the early times of struggle.

At the Cavern she bought a cup of coffee and found an empty booth. Over the noise, she heard Bryce's voice: "That guy turned out to be a goddamned faggot. We got drunk one night and that fucking pansy told me he was in love with me, can you beat that? So I threw him out on his ass and Missie here moved in."

Beside him, Melissa sat quietly. Becky wondered if she still saved peach pits, and if she would really plant them in the spring.

The man next to Bryce said: "Funny, I never figured Tom for a fag."

"He said he wasn't before he met me," Bryce laughed. "I guess it's the old Dedham charm that turns 'em all on. Right, my little pussy?"

Melissa slapped him playfully. "Bryce, you're terrible."

He drank the rest of his coffee with an abrupt motion as though it were a shot of whisky, and set the cup roughly on the saucer. "I gotta go meet The Big Pee."

The man laughed. "Someday you're going to call him that to his face."

"No, to his face I call him Your Highness. I ought to try calling him that. He's so fucking thick he'd probably never notice."

"Can I come?" Melissa asked.

"No, my little wench. This is man talk."

"Can't I wait outside?"

"Missie," he warned. "It's all very hush hush and top secret. I have to do The Big Pee a big favor. See you guys later."

He walked across the cafeteria to the door. He opened it and started through but stopped abruptly. An expression of child-like hero worship came over his face. He stepped aside. The person in the hallway said something and Bryce threw back his head and laughed. The other person walked through. It was David Sully.

He walked toward Becky and sat down.

"Do you know him?" she asked, indicating the spot where Bryce had stood.

"Dedham? Yeah, I know him. He's quite a guy."

"He certainly is. How well do you know him."

"He started coming to my graduate seminar a couple of weeks ago. Why?"

"Listen Dave, I don't want to sound like an alarmist but I'd watch out for Bryce if I were you. He's pretty tight with Pritchard."

David recalled the long talk he'd had with Bryce. "Don't get me wrong," Bryce had confided, "she's a nice girl, it just didn't work out between us. And you know what they say about a woman scorned."

David said to Becky: "Being tight with Pritchard's no crime. He told me all about it. The guy's got to get ahead, doesn't he?"

"Yeah, but. . . I don't know. I don't trust him."

"Rebecca, you've lost your innocence. And once you lose something like that you can never get it back." With this, he stood up and walked to the food counter where he got a cup of coffee and a fluffy piece of lemon meringue pie.

He sat down across from her. She looked at the residue of cold coffee at the bottom of her cup. He ate his pie, between mouthfuls describing Paul's misery without Justine.

He seemed different to her: he looked like a stranger. His smile, his tone of voice, the way he ran his fingers through his hair had once been familiar. Now she didn't seem to know him. Was this the man she had lain with in bed? She blushed.

"At a time like this," he repeated in the same astonished tone, "she threw him out. At a time when he needs her the most. . ."

"He didn't have to leave," Becky corrected. "She offered to move out. And what do you mean, 'a time like this.' It all happened before the strike began."

"That's irrelevant. It's begun now, and she should at least have the decency to stick with him. If she doesn't, then she must be pretty low. If we don't stick together during the times of struggle, then we're lost."

"Well I think unity is important, but—"

"You don't live with him. I do. He walks around that apartment like a lost soul. He can't sleep, he won't eat. . ."

"Yes, but his life's not her responsibility, what the hell is she supposed to do, spoon feed him?"

He shook his head. If she didn't understand, he couldn't explain it to her.

He looked so disappointed that she almost said: Yes, you're right, she should think of him. She's cruel, she's heartless, oh please don't look at me that way. . . But she stood her ground and said nothing. Discussing relations between any man and woman, be it in a book or a movie or a meeting or a love affair, he defended the man and she the woman. At the end of a supposedly friendly and simple conversation, they faced each other as enemies.

"I never said she had to spoon feed him, but at least she could have some consideration. Last Monday he tried to call her all night long. And she never got home until the next day. He was going nuts worrying what happened. She stayed out all night." He looked at her meaningfully: was that any way for a pregnant woman to behave?

"Wait a minute, Dave, she was with me that night. He didn't have to go and call her Aunt Connie, it scared her half to death, she thought Justine was in a car accident or something."

"She was with you?"

"Yes, with me."

"All night?"

"We went out after the women's meeting."

"I thought the women's meeting was on Wednesday."

She sighed. "Consciousness raising meets on Monday. Do you have any other questions?"

"Who else went."

"Terry and. . ." She stopped. Elizabeth had gone with them, but David apparently did not know this, for she'd gone home early. ". . . and another woman from the group."

"Who."

"You don't know her."

"And you stayed out all night? Where the hell did you go."

"We went to a few bars. Don't I have the right to an attorney?" .

"Doesn't she know that alcohol's bad for the baby?"

"She only drank Coke."

"The bars close at three."

"They came to my place afterwards."

"Your place. And they stayed all night?"

"We got to talking and we all fell asleep in the living room."

"Sounds like a fun pajama party." After a pause, he said: "Do you want more coffee?"

"No. I'm tired. It's almost eleven. I think I'll go home and get to sleep. What with the strike going on I haven't gotten to bed before three all week."

"Yeah, the strike and the bars... I'd like to get to sleep early too, but I've got too much to do. And in the middle of everything, I got a letter from Schultz. He wants to see me on Friday. Friday the 13th, that's rich." He ran his fingers through his hair.

She stood up. "I gotta go. See you tomorrow, David."

"Sure," he said, and finished his coffee alone.

When David Sully entered the History Department offices the afternoon of the 13th, he almost collided with Amos Pritchard, who was leaving Schultz's office. David knocked on the Chairman's half open door.

"Come in, David. And please close the door behind you. Fine. have a seat. Well!" Schultz leaned back and placed his hands palms down on two folders that lay on his desk. He leaned forward and clasped his hands, looking down. He sighed. "This is a difficult business," he said, and placing his hands on the folders once more, looked David in the eye. "But it can't be avoided."

David waited.

"The administration feels you aren't fulfilling your duties in a responsible way, nor are you behaving in a manner appropriate to your position. I must say that there's been quite a bit of displeasure over your involvement in this Pentagon business." David opened his mouth to speak but Schultz held up his hand, silencing him. "And it's not only that. It's been going on for quite some time, as you well know."

As proof, he handed David the first folder. Inside, he found photostatic copies of every letter he had written to the university newspaper, all the petitions he had signed, and a record of every place he had spoken along with a paraphrase of what he'd said.

"I'm sorry about this," Schultz said. "I don't like trouble in my department."

"Sorry about what? None of these things is a crime. I'm within my constitutional rights and you and the Administration both know it."

"It isn't a question of constitutional rights. The point is that you've become an embarrassment to the Administration. They've asked me to inform you that unless the present situation is immediately rectified, your contract for the coming year will be revoked."

"Don't be ridiculous. My contract's already been signed. The Administration's embarrassment is irrelevant to my rights." He tossed the folder on the desk.

"I understand your position, believe me I do. And you in turn must understand mine." He picked up the second folder. "There are, of course, other matters to consider." He handed the folder to David, who opened it carefully.

Inside he found two typewritten pages and a large envelope. On top of the first page was written Elizabeth's name, and on top of the second, Becky's. As he skimmed the pages, Schultz said: "There are pictures, if you'd care to look."

"Pictures?" David's mouth was dry. He opened the envelope and pulled out a photograph taken at the Washington Demonstration: he was bending down to listen to Elizabeth, who was whispering to him. Becky stood to one side, watching. The camera caught the pained expression on her face.

"There are more, but it wasn't felt it would be necessary. I'm afraid you made a serious mistake when you got involved with the lunatic fringe."

"Lunatic fringe. . . Oh for God's sake. . ."

"But I do want to stress that the material here is only a sample."

"My personal life is none of the Administration's business," David said a bit more uncertainly.

"There is other evidence, given us by informants."

"Informants?"

"You've been known to smoke drugs. If that fact were to be made public. . ."

"But everyone's tried marijuana. That's hardly what I'd call a drug."

Schultz held up his hand. "What everyone tries is not the issue." He stood up. The interview was over. "You need time to think this through, and I'm sure you'll arrive at a reasonable decision."

David stood up and walked to the door. As he reached for the doorknob, Schultz said: "David, look. . . there was something I didn't want to mention. . ." He turned away, feeling it was only civilized that David had a modicum of privacy within which to react. ". . . But I think it's only fair. There's a record of that matter in '64. . ." Schultz glanced at him, then looked away. "Believe me, I don't. . ."

David opened his mouth but found he had no words. He left the office and walked down the hall. Breathing heavily, he stood in front of his desk and stared at the bulletin board cluttered with notations reminding him of the places he had to be, things he had to do. He saw that his hands were trembling. He clenched his fists and raised them to smash down on the desk in a violence of frustration, but the phone rang. In the silent office it startled him, and his fists stopped in mid-air. He stared at the phone, and picked up the receiver. It was Becky.

She had only a few hours before she returned to campus for strike activities that would last late into the night, and she needed sleep, but felt guilty about the way she'd acted toward David in The Cavern, and wanted to make amends. She invited him to her apartment, noting the tightness in his voice and attributing it to the tension they all felt. She hung up and lit a joint.

The heavy odor of marijuana greeted him when he opened the door. Becky lay on the couch, her eyes closed as she drew on the tiny roach with abrupt puffs. On the end table was a small jar containing marijuana.

David stood in the kitchen, watching her and remembering the day they'd first met, the day Pritchard had stopped in the hall.

In the living room, she stood up and stretched. As he came toward her, she held out the jar and spoke in a voice that imitated a corrupt dope fiend. "Smoke a little dope, baby?"

In one sweeping motion he raised his arm and struck her hand. The jar sailed into the radiator and shattered. Becky stared at her hand stinging from the blow, and at the flakes of glass-strewn marijuana on the floor. A burning energy surged through her body but before it could erupt he took a step and embraced her fiercely. The energy stuck in her throat to fester.

"Becky. . . Oh my God. . ." He released her and co-lapsed on the couch.

She watched him and thought, 'The next step is for me to soothe him. As in: There there David it's all right that you hit me.' She bent over the marijuana to see what she could salvage, and heard herself say in a detached voice: "What happened?"

"I just got fired. Schultz called me in. It's my work with the D.O.D. protest. Among other things. . ."

She thought, 'Good. I hope you never get another fucking job in your life, you prick.' She said, "Isn't that unconstitutional or something like that?" She continued to examine the mess near the radiator.

He stared at her hunched back, wondering why he was wasting his breath talking to someone who believed in the Constitution. "They have informants. They have pictures."

"Pictures?" She stood up and looked out the window. She had an impulse to close the curtains. She saw an image from any one of a number of detective movies: a man wearing a trench coat, collar up, hat brim pulled down over his forehead, was standing in the glow of the streetlight, staring up at the window. "Pictures of what?"

"The only one I saw was a picture of the three of us in Washington."

"In Washington. . . David. Listen. Have you ever—"

"Becky, is it you? It's not you, is it?"

"Me! *Me?*"

"I thought. . . you know, your working with Pritchard. . ."

"But I *asked* you if I should work with Pritchard. I *told* you I was thinking of working with him, why didn't you say something then!"

He shrugged. "It wasn't an issue then."

"It wasn't an issue then? When it's important in my life it's not an issue, but when it's important in your life, all of a sudden it's an issue?" She walked into the kitchen, got a broom and dustpan, and swept up the mess.

He stared across the room. After a few minutes he said: "It's just amazing. . . You do something and it seems perfectly innocent. It seems like. . . yeah, this is the right thing to do now. And then afterwards. . ."

She barely listened to him. She was wondering if she should ask him to pay for the marijuana. 'I brought that shit all the way from Portland. It was supposed to last me all year. . .'

"Those bastards," he was saying, "they lead the most Goddamned corrupt lives, and they pick out some little thing and twist it around. . ." He began pacing from one end of the small room to the other. "But if they think I'll back down now, forget it. I've struggled too long to back down. But what I want to know is, what the hell does it get me! I struggle with a reactionary Administration, I struggle to give my students political consciousness, I struggle with my own chauvinism, and what does it get me? Just one hassle after another. And nobody gives a shit. Nobody cares."

Becky sat down. She remembered her father playing the forlorn outcast. "Nobody cares," he'd tease, "I'm going

261

to go out and eat worms." As a child, she'd laugh. "You can't eat worms, Daddy, nobody eats worms." He'd sigh and say, "Yes, if nobody loves you, you can go out and eat worms."

David saw she wasn't listening. "There's talk of a Grand Jury Investigation. I could be indicted any day now and you couldn't care less. You said I could always come to you, and then when I come to you, you're not there."

There was a dull ache at the base of her rib cage. She had never seen him so vulnerable, for she believed that in spite of his self-pity he was vulnerable, and if she hadn't felt the cold urge to beat him bloody, she could have tried to soothe him. If one time in the last few months she could have screamed out at him in fury, she might now feel sympathy. As it was, she felt triumphant in his misery, and it sickened her. "I can't believe we're supposed to be friends," she said, and smiled sadly. "And 'political comrades,' whatever the hell *that* means. Not to mention lovers. We're supposed to be all those things, and look at how we act toward one another."

"Act toward one another? You're unbelievable, do you know that? I just got fired by the fascist Administration for my politics, we're in the middle of a strike, the D.O.D. is sponsoring nerve gas research to send to Vietnam, and you think the point is how we act toward one another."

"I didn't say the point of the *universe* is how we act toward one another, I merely. . ." She sighed. "This is ridiculous."

"I'll tell you what's ridiculous." He walked to the couch and stood before her so that she had to look almost straight up to see his face. "My coming here and thinking you'd stand by me, that's what's ridiculous."

"David, how can I stand *by* you when you're standing *over* me!"

He glared at her. "That's right, make a joke of it. And I'll make a joke when you can't even *get* a job because of *your* politics. You come and cry on my shoulder then, and I'll tell you how funny I think it is."

"David, I don't think it's funny that you're being fired. I'm sorry, but I just—"

"Yeah, tell me another one." He walked to the door and paused. He'd expected her to stop him, and she saw the resentment in his eyes because she would not move. There was nothing else for him to do: he walked out, slamming the door.

She stood quite still until she heard his car pull away. She was in the midst of thinking how interesting it was that she always ended up apologizing to him, when without knowing she would do it, she opened her mouth and screamed. Eyes closed, lips stretched, hands clenched, she screamed as loud as she could until all her breath was gone.

When she stopped she listened, embarrassed, expecting neighbors to come running to her rescue, and having to explain that she needed no rescue. No one came. 'Lovely,' she thought. 'I'll know if I'm ever being murdered not to waste my breath.'

It was time to return to campus. She made a cup of tea with honey to soothe her sore throat, and walked around the apartment carrying the mug as she prepared to leave.

She stood in front of the mirror and brushed her hair slowly, thinking. Then she left the apartment, closing and locking the door behind her.

The big demonstration Monday, March 16th was supposed to be peaceful. But plans of peace or violence were meaningless: no one person or group had control over what was to happen. The "leader" of the strike could not have gone up to his second in command and said: Hold back your people. There was no leader and no second in command. The strikers were not organized into tightly knit cadres, they were anyone at anytime. Occasionally, someone would laugh at the accusation that they were under orders from Moscow or Peking. They were under orders from no one, and each followed his or her own whim, conscience or inclination.

The second demonstration was larger than the first, and it was at night. Milling around Mellon Hall in the dark was exciting and dangerous. It was the closest many of them had gotten to the forbidden place, and they were bold, wanting to get inside and see what made the power structure tick. As they approached the building, Dr. Ward, under careful coaching from Frick, panicked and called the city police.

The arrival of the Tactical Patrol Unit on campus,

complete with gas masks, clubs and K-9 trucks waiting in the distance only served to provoke many of the demonstrators. A scuffle broke out when Ronnie Nye called a policeman "pig," and David Sully, trying to intervene, was arrested.

The sight of the police dragging Sully away inflamed even the non-political students. The cry went out: "They've got Sully!" They tried to get him back and failed since the police, seeing a small band of students charge at them, retaliated with gas.

After that all was chaos. The sounds and smells of tear gas filled the night air, and the familiar university surroundings were transformed into a nightmare. Unrestrained, some police responded violently.

The action continued into the night. At ten, the demonstrators regrouped in the Student Union, erecting barricades of furniture against the door. But the barricades were useless against the gas, which poured into the first floor and drifted up the staircase and vents to the second and third, forcing out the building's occupants. From there, the students ran into one of the dormitories and the police followed. The dormitory was gassed. Students who had watched from the windows ran out, many of them clad in pajamas.

At eleven the demonstrators went home to see themselves on the news, but the only mention was of the arrest of six students and an assistant professor during a small disturbance that the police now had under control.

The sun rose the next morning onto what looked like an armed camp. Police patrolled in twos and threes, and the smell of gas lingered in the halls of the Student Union and the dormitory. Red-painted slogans appeared on Mellon Hall, the Montgomery Science Center and the

ROTC building: "Strike," "D.O.D. off campus," and "Vietnamese women carry guns!" There were rumors about police guns being drawn in the dormitory halls, and talk of gunfire, but most people laughed at this and said: "Don't be stupid, man, where do you think you're at, Vietnam? This is a university, man, they wouldn't dare..."

The presence of police on campus served to immediately politicize the majority of students, and the strike was in full swing. Against Frick's professed better judgement, President Ward called a general meeting of strikers and Administration, to be held the night of Wednesday, March 17th. He called it a "pow-wow," and said that the Administration was willing to "sign a peace treaty." The irony of this was not lost on the students.

The original members of the Provisional Revolutionary Strike Committee reacted to this upsurge of interest at first with excitement, then with skepticism. The strike was not theirs anymore. The original goal was forgotten. Everything seemed to have gotten out of hand. The P.R.S.C. decided to hold an emergency meeting on Wednesday evening before Ward's "pow-wow."

Over twenty people attended the P.R.S.C. meeting, among them Paul, David, George, and Ronnie Nye, who represented the Yippies. Off to one side sat the representative from the Black Student Association. The only women attending were Becky and Justine. Elizabeth was recuperating from having been caught in the Student Union during the gassing, and Becky had taken her place. When the two women walked into the room the person Becky saw first was Bryce Dedham. He was leaning toward Sully, speaking rapidly, though she couldn't hear the words.

Overnight, those arrested had been tagged The Sully

Seven. David was anxious to keep a low profile, and out on bail the next day he'd tried to popularize The Rhododendron Seven, but it didn't catch on. He'd become a star, commanding the respect and admiration of the radical community, the sympathy of the liberals and the adoration of the Yippies. He was chain-smoking tensely, and didn't seem to hear Bryce nor see Becky and Justine, who sat down at one end of the long table.

Paul opened the meeting by asking the representative from the B.S.A. to report on their demand. The representative spoke briefly, saying that although they had several demands, they felt it would be better to focus on one, open admission for minority students. Everyone listened politely until he finished, and the meeting once more "began," as though he hadn't spoken at all.

George gave an analysis of how the situation might be handled in Cuba, and afterward said, "We've got to discuss the course of action we plan to take tonight with Ward. I think the best decision would be for this group, especially the original P.R.S.C. members, to stick to the demand of D.O.D. off campus."

"I disagree," Paul said. "We should strive for as much unity as possible without losing our original goals or weakening our principles. The students associated with the various groups are our base, and if we have no base, we're set up to be picked off. One by one."

"But how can we have unity even among ourselves when I don't know half the people in this room," someone said.

Becky cleared her throat. "Speaking of the various people, I think we all should identify ourselves. I don't know who most of you are, or who you represent." She looked at Bryce. "For example, I know you from school, but I have no idea what you're doing here."

267

"I have nothing to hide. I represent The Sully Seven Defense Committee. Certainly a legitimate group, nothing catering to the lunatic fringe."

Ronnie exploded: "Lunatic fringe!"

There was a brief argument that Paul tried to quell. Sully was silent. The phrase sounded familiar but he couldn't quite place it.

Bryce continued: "I think general paranoia is affecting everyone. I've heard there's someone in the History Department, a female graduate student, who's reporting to Ward by phone every day." Becky and David looked at each other.

"Wait a minute," Paul said. "We're not going to get anywhere with accusations. I've heard that this meeting room is bugged." He paused, and everyone looked around apprehensively. "But let's not worry about spies or bugging because we're not doing anything illegal. I propose we discuss our strike demands and then put it to a vote of the students as a body."

One of the men said, "If we're going to discuss the demands, let's leave the women until last, because once they get talking, forget it."

There was scattered laughter. Becky and Justine remained stone-faced. Justine said: "That's a stupid suggestion, and if you're worried about building unity, that's a strange way to start. *I* say we *begin* with the women's group." No one disagreed. "The women's liberation group wants a daycare center."

"A daycare center, you're kidding. . ."

David smiled, though under the table he tapped his foot nervously. "I don't think you have to go into the reasons you want daycare, Justine."

Several men laughed. Paul looked embarrassed but remained silent, afraid that any criticism of David would look like a man trying to win back his wife.

David began to speak when Becky cut him off: "I realize this issue is trivial to those of you not tied down with children, but there are women who would like to participate in strike activities but can't because they have to sit at home and watch their kids all day. Women want to do alot of things with their lives but can't."

David was about to defend himself but Bryce said. "Look, I'm sure David didn't mean any disrespect to Paul's wife. He was only trying to lighten the situation since we all seem to be a little tense."

Becky was seeing a new side of Bryce. He was trying to charm her. His face radiated sincerity and goodwill. His eyes beamed friendship and love. She saw that Bryce and David were allies, and she was furious.

"Really," Bryce said, "we should try to be friends."

"Oh Jesus," Justine mumbled, "I need a cigarette."

David said, "Bryce is right. I was only kidding. But I am sorry. My remark was uncalled for. Now, can we get on with the meeting? One thing I'd like to clear up is the name tagged onto the six people who tried to prevent me from getting arrested. It seems to me—"

"Hold it," Justine cut in. "I'm just thrilled about your ego-trip with the Seven Dwarfs, or whatever you call yourselves, but for your information, the strike, and the world, doesn't revolve around you. The charge was disorderly conduct, not murder."

"But I'm not talking about—"

"You all asked for representatives from groups," she continued, "and now you're ignoring us. The guy from the B.S.A. spoke and nobody seemed to hear what he said. And nobody seemed to notice that he left."

269

The people looked around and realized that the black representative was in fact no longer there. "I thought he went out for a cup of coffee," someone grumbled defensively.

"Just because people don't say certain words," Justine mumbled, "doesn't mean they're not prejudiced. . ."

"Look, let's get to to the point," someone said uncomfortably, "you want to talk about daycare, go ahead."

Becky said: "Justine already got a room and began a baby-sitting service in Holland 27, and we want a commitment from everyone to give four hours a week."

"How did you get the room?"

"I walked in and took it," Justine said. "Nobody was using it, so I figured why not us?"

"Yeah, but what about when the Administration finds out," someone objected.

George sighed. "Look, I think you've got a good thing going for the women. I'll volunteer four hours a week. But there's pressing business, and that is how we're going to respond to the general meeting, which is in precisely," and he looked at his watch, "fifty-five minutes."

There was general agreement.

"Can we present daycare as a strike demand?" Becky asked.

"All right, all right, it's a strike demand," George said. "We'll ask the students to vote on it."

Becky and Justine looked at each other skeptically. "OK," Justine said, "but who else is going to volunteer time."

Everyone nodded.

"OK, I'm taking down everybody's name after this meeting. Including yours," she said to Bryce. "And if you're not down at Holland 27 tomorrow to sign up, I'm going to make up my own leaflet with all your names on it."

Paul smiled proudly.

At 7:45 the group broke up, and they walked in twos and threes to the general meeting. Justine and Becky walked together; Paul walked with David behind them.

Justine said: "What do you think of that guy Bryce, I don't trust him. He's a liar if I ever saw one."

Becky nodded, and turned around to find David staring at her, and Paul watching Justine.

The Wednesday night general meeting was held in the large men's gymnasium and it was just as well, because the room was packed to capacity: people crowded onto the bleachers and jammed close together on the floor. One athletic undergraduate had climbed onto the thick metal arms that held out the basketball hoop and perched there precariously, trying to look as casual as though he were leaning against the plate glass window of a corner drugstore.

The President of the Student Association called the meeting to order. But the majority of students considered him to be Dr. Ward's favorite errand boy, and it took some amount of calling before they came to order. He introduced Dr. Ward.

Ward came to the podium amidst booing, hissing, catcalls, yells for silence and order, and general disorder. He spoke briefly, arguing that while the students were free to pursue the academic goals that they had chosen, so the Department of Defense should be free to pursue its chosen goal. There were cries of "Bullshit!" and "Off the Pig!" and "Yeah, you mother fucker, how'd you like a whiff of that nerve gas!"

Ward looked around nervously and attempted to contin-

ue his speech, but finally gave up and retreated as grace-
fully as possible, saying that it was only fair that all sides
get a chance to speak. As he left the podium, a paper airplane grazed his shoulder.

As soon as Ward stepped down, Ronnie Nye occupied
the podium. He gave a long, boring and arrogant speech
filled with vague rhetoric, the main point of which was
that anyone over thirty could not be trusted. Becky said
to Justine: "If he doesn't hurry up and finish, he'll be
over thirty before he's done and he'll have to change the
whole thing around."

When he was done, Paul Denton stepped to the podium.
He said that while he was happy to see so many students
involved in the strike, the air of irresponsible festivity
bothered him. The students must not forget the original
strike demand: the removal from campus of the Pentagon
funded Project Rhododendron. New strike demands had
been proposed: police off campus was a primary concern.
But there was too much confusion for a serious discussion
and a vote. Another general meeting was scheduled for
the following evening.

He noticed that the audience was getting jittery. He reminded them that Liberation classes had started and
schedules were posted in the Student Union. He ended
with a plea for unity and a thoughtful and serious approach to the strike.

Immediately, a man in a dirty sweatshirt stood up,
waving a clenched fist. "I had enough a' this crap," he
sneered, "and I'm gonna do me some Midnight Ramblin'.
Anybody wants to come with me, cool, we'll get down to
it. Midnight!" he screamed. "In back of the Union. Right
on!" He raised his fist in a salute, and walked away.

The rally continued. The later it got, the more confusion there was, much of it coming from the small but vocal group of men led by the man in the dirty sweatshirt.

Paul tried once again to remind the students of the original demand but few were interested. One thing was clear: they were now "officially" on strike.

When the rally broke up, Paul approached Justine and asked if she wanted a ride home. She said: "No thanks, I'm going out for coffee with Becky."

"Can I come over later?" Paul asked.

Justine nodded, and he watched the two women walk through the crowd together.

He was sitting in the darkened living room when she got home that night. She turned on the light and saw him. "Hello, what are you doing?"

"Just thinking."

She took off her coat. In spite of her pregnancy and short hair, she reminded him of how she'd looked when they first met. He came toward her and looked into her eyes. They had not been alone in two weeks. Silently, they walked into the bedroom.

It was sudden and passionate, and afterward they lay together in silence. The streetlight shone in through the small high window, illuminating the foot of the bed. Justine stared at the spot unblinking. Paul caressed her neck and shoulders. moving his lips lazily on her skin. She felt she were being touched by a memory.

Sensing her reserve. he asked, "What's wrong?"

"Paul. . ." She sighed. "This doesn't mean. . ."

He understood, and said bitterly, "Oh, you mean it's only for old time's sake?"

She moved away from him and reached down for the covers. He lay on his side. "Well what the hell, I guess we both needed a little roll in the hay, right?" He tried to sound blasé but his voice cracked. He lay back opening his mouth to let loose a stream of ugly words, but surprised himself by saying: "I want to come home."

She spread her hands over her face and looked out through her fingers at the ceiling.

"Did you hear me? I know I've been wrong about some things. All I want is a chance." He propped himself on one elbow and touched her hands. "Please."

She closed her eyes. "Don't, Paul. It's too late."

"It's not! I'll change, you'll see."

She shook her head.

"Why!"

"Because it's not that easy. People don't become what they are all by themselves, and they can't change all by themselves." She dropped her hands and opened her eyes.

"You can help me," he suggested, but she didn't answer. "At least let's talk about it."

"There's nothing to talk about."

"How can you say that! We've been married almost a year, you're carrying my child, how can you say there's nothing to talk about!" He sat up. "Justine. I love you. You've got to believe me."

She looked at his unhappy face, at his hands lying on the sheets, palms upward as though he had lost something and was powerless to retrieve it. "I believe you. And I love you too. But somehow it doesn't seem to matter. At least not now."

"What the hell kind of stupid thing is that to say! Tina. . ."

"Paul, how can you say you're going to change when you can't even call me by my right name?"

He smiled sheepishly, feeling more confident now that they were back on familiar ground.

"Why do you keep doing it? I've asked you and asked you and you don't pay any Goddamned attention to me."

The urgency in her voice shook his confidence, and he tried to explain. "I never thought it really bothered you. Why does it bother you, it fits you so well."

"No. It fits the way you see me, not the way I am."

"You don't understand what I mean," he began, but she rolled on her side and swung her legs over the edge of the bed. "Goddamn it, don't turn away from me!"

She looked back at him, her face impassive. "I turned away from you a long time ago. You were just too busy to notice."

"Oh I noticed. I noticed all right. I noticed you started changing when you began hanging around Terry."

"Terry! I knew Terry before *we* went on our first date."

"You have no idea. . ." he began, but changed his mind. He got out of bed and put on his jeans. Then he paused, and said: "No, you've got to know, because you're so Goddamned naïve. . . Your best friend Terry happens to be a lesbian, and she'd just love to get her hands on you so she could teach you all about it."

She hesitated a moment before she threw off the covers, walked to the closet and got her blue and green robe. As she put her arm into a sleeve, she said in a tired, matter-of-fact voice, "Paul, you can't teach somebody what they already know."

He looked at her. "You'd better tell me what you mean by that."

She met his eyes. "You know exactly what I mean."

"Tell me!"

She tied the long sash loosely in front. "Why should I?"

"Because you're my wife and I have a right to know."

"Why Paul," she said sweetly, "everyone knows that a marriage license is just a piece of paper."

"Justine!" He came towards her. "Tell me."

She stood before him and said: "Make me." Then she turned to leave the room.

He grabbed her arm and spun her around. Her blonde hair whipped across her face, and the sash slid to the floor. For a long time afterward he was to see that vision: her hair whipping across her eyes, the robe opening, exposing her body.

Her eyes narrowed and her face hardened. "You hit me and you better not ever close your eyes while you're in this house, or I'll shove a knife through your fucking heart."

He didn't move.

"I mean it, Paul, I don't make empty threats. You should know that by now. Let go of my arm."

He dropped her arm and watched her stride from the room, the robe billowing behind her. He picked up the sash and placed it on the dresser. He sat on the bed and stared at the mirror.

When she came back, she snapped on the overhead light, hung up her robe, and from the dresser took a large flannel nightgown which she drew over her head. She stood in front of the mirror, inspected her face, and care-

276

fully rubbed cream into her skin. Her movements were cruel: she acted like she was alone. She snapped off the light, got into bed and turned her back to him.

"Justine?"

She didn't answer.

"Justine, I'm sorry. I don't know what came over me. I love you. I'll forgive anything you've done in the past as long as you'll come back to me."

"I don't remember asking for your forgiveness." Her voice was cold.

He waited a moment before saying, "Do you want me to go?"

"No. This is your house. The next time somebody leaves, it'll be me."

He wasn't sure what this meant. He undressed and curled into the curve of her body, his one arm under her neck, the other around her belly. They lay there unable to sleep. Paul because he was too unhappy, Justine because his arm was heavy, the pressure of his body stifling. At seven months pregnant, sleep and comfort were hard to find. Several times she tried to move away, but he thought she was snuggling into his arms. She couldn't move since she was already on the edge of the bed. Finally she said, "Paul? You're too close to me."

He withdrew to the edge of the bed. "I'll apologize in advance in case I accidentally touch you in the middle of the night."

"Jesus Christ, I just don't want you laying on top of me. . . Listen, we're both upset. Let's just take it easy and go to sleep." He sighed and lay there, and after awhile he heard her even breathing.

When she woke before six, Paul was gone. She lay in bed remembering a dream, but the day had begun. She got out of bed, readied herself and left for work, not seeing the note Paul had left on the kitchen table.

After work she went to the daycare center, where Mark was teaching the children a song. He handed her the sign-up sheet, and she saw Paul's name. By five o'clock all the people at the P.R.S.C. meeting had signed up for daycare shifts except for Bryce Dedham.

She wanted to write a leaftlet, but Mark informed her that the Administration had forbidden secretaries to give strikers paper supplies or access to office machines. They made a large poster and hung it in the Student Union. Whether or not Bryce ever saw it, whether or not he cared, Justine never discovered.

Leaving campus, she took a bus to her Aunt Connie's house on the other side of town. When she arrived, Connie was sitting at the kitchen table listening to Lynne complain about Bill. The kitchen was warm with the smell of roasting chicken. Lynne drummed her polished nails on the table irritably. "I told him before we were married I didn't know how to cook, and now all of a sudden he expects a hot meal every night. What does he want, I work all day too. . ."

The back door opened. "Hello," Justine called. "It's me."

"Careful, I waxed the floor this morning," Connie said.

"I don't know about you, Auntie Con," Justine said, pronouncing the name the way she had when she was a child so that it sounded like Annie Con. "You're getting sloppy in your old age, you forgot to wax the sidewalk."

Connie laughed. "Take a load off your feet. You want some coffee?"

"Sure, I'll have a cup." She sat down at the table. "Hi Lynne, how are you?"

Lynne shrugged. "Not bad."

Connie set the cup of coffee in front of Justine and

sat down. "I'll tell you what, I'll lend you my cookbook."

"Sure, that'll do the trick. Because we never fight except for that. Those little fights don't mean anything at all, it's no reason to split up a marriage."

Her tone was vehement, and Connie looked from Lynne to Justine and back again. "How're you feeling?" she asked Justine.

"Ok. I went to the doctor yesterday."

"What'd he say?"

"Not much. I'll live. I'm too fat, but I'm healthy."

"Knock on wood," Connie said, and knocked on the table. It was formica but that didn't bother her since it was the spirit of the thing that counted.

"How's work?" Justine asked Lynne.

"It's Ok. But that was a dumb move, telling Carol you broke up with Paul. It's none of her business anyway, what'd you go and tell her for?"

"Don't be so paranoid, I ran into her downtown and we had a cup of coffee and we got to talking. You know how easy Carol is to talk to." Lynne was silent. "Well, *I* always thought she was easy to talk to. And anyways, why shouldn't I tell her, it's the truth."

"That's got nothing to do with it."

"Who's Carol?" Connie asked.

Lynne looked at her nails.

"She's a woman from work," Justine said. "You remember, I told you about her once, she lives in that big old trailer down the street from your friend that you used to play bingo with. . . Remember? She has the little boy with that bad kind of arthritis?"

Connie nodded. "Now I remember. How's her little boy doing?"

Justine shook her head and sipped the coffee.

279

"Terrible," Connie said. "Terrible."

"Carol's not the type to complain, but I don't think they can cure it."

"Terrible. Just terrible."

During this interchange, Lynne had become increasingly agitated, and now pushed back her chair. "I gotta go."

Connie looked at the two women, frowned, said something about a phone call, and left the kitchen.

Lynne stood up. "I don't know what's wrong with you, getting mixed up with that liberation group. The things you told me at work, I found out there's more to it than that. Much more."

"I don't know what you found out at work, but probably half of it's bullshit. And Ossie, you should be more cool around Connie, she's going to wonder what the hell is going on."

"Nothing's going on!"

"That isn't what I meant."

"You're the one that should be cool, you're the one that left your husband. I never thought I'd ever have to say anything to you, Justine, but things have changed. So all I have to say is, if you ever get any funny ideas about telling anybody. . ."

Justine picked up her full cup of coffee and walked to the stove. With her back to Lynne, she said: "After everything that happened, you got one hell of a nerve making a crack like that. But if that's the way you want it. . ." She picked up the coffee pot. ". . .then that's the way it is. The only way you and me ever knew each other was through Bill."

Lynne did not respond. She opened the door and left. Justine saw that she was about to pour coffee into an already full cup.

When Connie returned, she said: "What's the matter with Lynne, is she still mad because Paul didn't come to the wedding? That's not your fault. Are you all right, honey, you look so pale. . ."

"Oh, you know her, she's so moody, half the time she doesn't even know why."

Connie put on a fresh pot of coffee and sat down. "I heard Paul's mixed up in that trouble at the university. They say he's a communist. It's just as well you threw him out when you did. You don't want to get mixed up in something like that. . . you'd have the police coming to your house and who knows what. . . Maybe he'll come to his senses and then you can take him back."

"That's not why I threw him out, I threw him out because I wasn't happy."

"Happy. . . Who ever promised you happiness in marriage."

"Come on, Auntie Con, you know what I mean."

The coffee began to perk and Connie lowered the flame. "You want some cookies? I have some Lorna Doone's."

"No, I'm not supposed to gain anymore weight."

"Come on. One won't hurt."

"No."

"How about some coffee cake. Or what about an English muffin."

Justine wagged her finger: "You better cut it out. I mean it. I told my doctor all about you. . ."

Connie laughed. "Well what do you expect, you've been gone so long."

"Yeah, but you can't make up for it all at once."

"Maybe not. But I sure as hell can try."

When the coffee was done she refilled their cups. She

reached for the sugar, remembered, and frowned. "Dr. Sikorsky says I got sugar. And I read the other day that saccharin causes cancer. So what can you do? These days no matter what you do it's bad for you." She tasted her unsweetened coffee, grimaced, and put in a tab of saccharin. She tasted it again and shook her head. "Bitter." She stirred in a heaping teaspoon of sugar, sipped it and nodded, satisfied. "I don't like this business with the police at the university. He's going to ruin his life."

"It's his life. What do you think Mom would have said about me and Paul."

"Oh, she probably would've told you to do whatever's best for you and the baby. If you're that miserable with him. . . You didn't know she left your father once. . ."

"No, I didn't."

"You were just a baby. She told your father he'd better shape up or she wasn't coming back. She was no slouch, that sister-in-law of mine, God rest her soul. You haven't told your father yet. . ."

"No. . ."

"You ought to go see him. His feelings are hurt because you never come around."

Justine shrugged reluctantly.

"You know he stopped drinking."

"Did he?"

"He's got a girlfriend, a very nice woman. I met her a couple of weeks ago, she's very nice—she's got two sons in high school. Your father wants you to meet her."

Justine said nothing.

"She's divorced, too," Connie added, and Justine laughed, for her aunt's tone had implied that therefore, they would have alot in common.

"You know, baby, life goes on. You've got to forgive

and forget. I know your father treated you pretty mean after Babe died, but it was a terrible thing for him." She pushed back her chair. "I have to make the salad. If supper's not on the table by the time your uncle walks in that door, I've had it."

She took the vegetable bin from the refrigerator and stood at the kitchen counter, slicing tomatoes, radishes, cucumbers, dropping the refuse onto a section of newspaper she had spread nearby. "You know," she began, "I bet if you explained to your father about you and Paul, he'd ask you to move back home."

"No way. I'll go see him, but it wouldn't work out, me moving back home."

"You can't stay alone. Especially not after the baby's born."

"Maybe I'll get a place with a couple of friends."

"Who, girls?"

"Of course, what do you think."

"Well I don't know, that crowd you've been running around with. . ."

"No, one of them's Terry. You know her, she came to supper once."

"I remember. She seems like a nice girl."

Justine stayed with her aunt and uncle for the evening, and when she got home, she found Paul's note in the living room. It read: "Darling Justine: Thank you for last night. I love you. With all my heart, Paul. XXX OOO."

She felt sad. Once she would have been thrilled to get such a note. Now it no longer mattered. When she thought of herself and Paul, she felt a great weight on her chest; she thought of a ball of twine, impossibly snarled.

In the week following the meeting with Ward, the strike was on an upswing. Students stopped going to regular classes, and attended Liberation Classes. The most popular were Paul's courses: "Imperialism and the Third World," and "The Function of the University in a Capitalist State." The women in the group taught several courses. Elizabeth's "Anthropology as a Means to Imperialist Expansion," had caused an uproar in the Anthropology Department. Becky and two other women taught "The History of Feminism in the United States." Terry and another nursing student offered "Female Health Care."

The Daycare Center thrived despite the lack of general support. Already over twenty children came every day to the large room in the basement of the Holland building. Mark had commandeered an old refrigerator to hold milk and fruit juice, and the Daycare Committee collected toys, and mattresses for afternoon naps. Volunteers put in their four hours and sometimes more.

The Administration responded to this increased activity. At the last strike rally, Paul was announcing new Liberation Classes when a student rushed into the lounge and yelled out that the Yippies were throwing a "Strike Dance" in the Cavern. The Administration, in a sudden show of benevolence, had provided free kegs of beer. The rally emptied. The Administration was also kind enough to keep the Cavern open until three a.m. The result was that those who partied slept late the next day and missed the morning's strike activities.

And that day, an Administration representative walked into the Daycare Center and explained politely that the University was not insured in the event that one of the children were hurt.

Justine listened, equally polite.

He smiled regretfully and said that the Daycare Center was illegal and they all were trespassing.

She smiled regretfully and said that she did not care.

He stated that if they did not vacate the premises in one hour he would be forced to call the Campus Police, and she would be responsible for the consequences.

She stated that not only was she seven months pregnant but an epileptic besides. And if he called the Campus Police, he would be responsible for the consequences.

It was a stalemate. The representative left to report to his superiors. She and Mark called an emergency meeting of the Daycare Center, which now included the parents of attending children. They could reach no conclusion other than to continue daycare as planned.

After the meeting Justine hurried through the rain to the Student Union where she was due at a women's meeting. In the Union foyer she shook out her rain spattered jacket. The halls were crowded with strikers on their way to meetings, strikers putting up posters and debating in small groups, and people collecting for various causes, only some legitimate.

One straggler approached her holding out a paper covered coffee can, and pleaded: "Sister, will you give to

The Sully Seven Defense Fund?"

"Does David know you're doing this?"

"David, David who?"

"Mm-hmm, I thought so," she said, and continued on her way to the meeting. When she reached the second floor she heard the commotion coming from Room 210.

She opened the door and heard Susan's voice: "It's nothing but a deviation of nature due to the pressures of capitalist society! It's nothing but—"

In the back of the room Terry stood shifting from one foot to the other. Elizabeth stood next to Susan with a noncommittal expression on her face.

"What's going on?" Justine whispered to Becky.

"Susan wants to pass a public resolution that the women's liberation group condemns 'perverse sexual activity.'"

"What?"

"She heard some men calling us 'The Dyke's Strike Caucus,' and she says that it's preventing women from joining the strike."

Justine looked around and saw that Maggie was not present.

Susan had not paused: "They can disrupt the whole concept of revolution. Homosexuality is rooted in the dying breaths of a decadent bourgeois culture, and its only purpose is to turn people's minds away from political activity toward sexual activity."

"Wait a minute," Terry said. "Aren't you a little confused? There's a difference between what people are and how capitalism uses them. Just because it uses motherhood to spellbind women doesn't mean that motherhood itself is bad."

"I never said motherhood is bad!" Susan snapped.

"Jesus Christ. Susan, keep your shirt on," Terry said.

"You know, Terry," Susan said suggestively, "I don't know what stake you have in those kind of people, but in Cuba I kept expecting alot of trouble from them."

"You know, Susan," Terry said, aping her tone, "I don't know about your trouble and I'm not interested. Just because you maybe had some trouble with a few people is no reason to condemn a whole group. I mean, I don't go around bad-mouthing the Left because you're an asshole."

Justine coughed back laughter.

Terry continued, her voice somber: "There's only one thing I really want to say. If that resolution is passed, I'll quit this group and I'll never come back."

Susan smirked.

Terry looked around, waited a moment, and was about to speak again when a voice said: "I'll go with you."

It was Justine. She said: "It's crazy to call yourselves a liberation group and then say that not everybody can be liberated."

"Now Tina," Susan scolded, "that's not exactly the point."

"Don't you Tina me, you—"

The door opened, and a janitor looked in. "Sorry girls, I hate to break up your party, but we got another bomb threat."

"Oh no."

"You're not serious."

He shrugged and turned away, looking for the next occupied room.

Grumbling and complaining, the women left Room 210 and walked downstairs. The resolution was forgotten.

The air in the first floor was muggy from the crush of students. Outside it continued to rain and no one wanted to leave. They thought the bomb threat was a hoax: someone had called in a threat every evening at this time. Some thought it was the Administration's doing. Others believed it was the townspeople.

The local newspapers had done their best to generate misunderstanding about the strike. News articles called them "criminal anarchists" and implied the strike was caused by a small band of troublemakers from another town, diverting the youth toward violence. This device of blaming everything on outside agitators was one Becky recognized: Hitler had used it frequently in his propaganda. The newspapers also attacked David Sully, who they pictured as an evil radical attempting to corrupt the students toward a twisted, vaguely communistic end. The papers never mentioned Project Rhododendron or the Department of Defense; they ignored the Liberation Classes and the Daycare Center.

No matter who the culprit, the bomb threats were working: it was impossible to use the Student Union in the evenings.

The janitors cleared the Union. Groups of students huddled in the rain, watching the arrival of the bomb squad. The women had foreseen the possibility of the bomb threat and had made plans to postpone the meeting until the following night. Elizabeth, Terry, Becky and Justine stood there as the people moved away. "Come on," Terry said, "let's go out and get smashed."

Elizabeth and Becky agreed. Justine sighed dramatically. "I guess I have to be chauffer again. When are you drunks going to break down and buy me a uniform. I'd even be satisfied with a hat." They laughed and walked to the parking lot.

It was after three a.m. when Justine pulled up to the curb in front of Becky's apartment. On her head she wore a newspaper hat that Elizabeth had made while the four women sat in a back booth of a local bar.

Justine had entertained them with impressions: the hat sideways was Napoleon, tilted down at the rakish angle she now wore it, Humphrey Bogart. The four spent a pleasant evening, having avoided the subject of the resolution.

Terry opened the door. "Where are you going?" Becky asked drunkenly.

Terry answered: "I'm walking you to your door. You're liable to fall and incur a fibula contusion in your lobotomous poop-deck."

Becky giggled. "How can you walk me to my door, you can't even stand."

"I can stand for anything I want. Truth, Justice, and the American Way!"

Becky opened the door. "See you later, Humph."

"Hmph to you too," Justine answered. "Go on, scram, I gotta be at work in four hours."

"Be right back," Terry said and followed Becky, holding her hand out in case either of them slipped.

The rain had slowed to a thin drizzle. Becky paused at the bottom step and felt in her pockets for her keys. Terry held onto the railing. When Becky looked up, her face was serious. She spoke in a confidential tone, her head bowed slightly as though they were in a crowded room. She tried to sound authoritative, but her words kept slurring. "Listen Terry, I have to tell you: you should be careful. I know Maggie's your friend and there's certainly nothing wrong with defending your beliefs, but some of the things you said tonight might have given people the wrong impression."

"Maybe I gave them the right impression," Terry said, looking down at the rain slicked sidewalk.

Becky sighed. "You don't know what I mean."

"Yes. I do."

"You mean you want people to think you're. . . like Maggie?"

"I don't want them to think anything."

"Well then?"

She stared at Becky defiantly but spoke with difficulty: "Well then maybe I am."

"Terry, what a thing to say!"

"It's true."

"It's true?"

Terry nodded.

"You mean you've. . ."

"Well. . . I haven't actually. . ." She looked at the steps. "But I like somebody. . ."

"You mean a woman?"

Terry nodded.

"Have you told her?"

Terry shook her head.

"Why not."

"I'm afraid she'll never talk to me again."

Becky nodded solemnly. "That's heavy," she pronounced. Her voice was so serious that they broke into laughter, covering their mouths because of the late hour.

"I have to go to sleep," Becky said and hiccuped. "I think I'm drunk."

"Can you get upstairs OK?"

"Of course! My legs are as steady as. . . jello. . ." She held up one finger as if making a speech: "I'm as steady as the Rock of Gibrello. . ."

Hiccuping, she made her way up the stairs. Terry watched until she was inside the door. She had been laughing, but as she walked unsteadily back to the car, her face became gloomy. By the time Justine put the car into gear and put her foot on the gas, Terry was sniffling.

Justine shook her head. "I knew you'd end up crying in your beer."

Terry wiped her face.

"Devlin, I can read you like a goddamned book."

"Yeah, a comic book."

At the next red light, Justine said: "I'm going to give you some advice, take it or leave it, it's up to you. Things might work out in the end and they might not, but in the meantime, if you're not careful, you're going to get very hurt."

"I know." Terry nodded slowly up and down until it became a rocking motion. "I know."

The light changed and Justine pulled away. "She reminds me of Lynne. They're both smart, but not people-smart. You know, I think you should try to forget about Becky. Try to study alot or something."

"I could take cold showers," Terry said, her lower lip quivering anew.

"No, be serious."

"I could do more work in the strike."

Justine paused before saying: "I have the feeling that the strike isn't long for this world."

"What do you mean."

"I don't know. I just have the feeling."

The evening of Thursday, March 26th, one of the members of the Board of Trustees dined at John Frick's house. The man owned a chain of metal parts factories that had several large government contracts, and he was influential in state politics. After dinner Frick signalled his wife, who directed the Board Member's wife to the parts of the house they'd redecorated.

Frick led the man into the den, poured him an after dinner liquer, and gazed down at the logs smoldering in the fireplace. "My analysis of this whole situation comes down to one simple point," he said, stoking the fire with an ornate andiron. "If you give these people the illusion of freedom, you need give them nothing else. Unfortunately, Ham and I have disagreed all along on how the strike should be handled. I advised him to accept the petition, and I advised him not to involve the police. My letters are on file," he added, "but he chose to ignore them. Of course it's the man's prerogative. . ." He put a new log into the fireplace. "I've used my position as Executive Vice President as best I know how, and although it may have been wrong, I've done several things without asking him."

"Such as?"

"Two things in particular. The first was a memo I sent to university employees suggesting they not engage in strike activities. That included providing strikers with office supplies and use of machinery. I felt that while this would not have been a fruitful method of handling

292

the strikers, it was in regard to the employees. They're not organized and I knew such a memo would intimidate them."

The Board Member nodded, congratulating Frick on his good judgement.

"I also directed that beer be provided for nightly "Strike Dances." Ham was against it. You know his feelings about alcohol," he said, looking pointedly at their drinks. "I also wanted to show free nightly movies at the Student Union this past week. What student would attend a strike meeting when he had the opportunity to see James Bond for free. But. . . Ham said that we had insufficient funds." The new log caught and a bright yellow flame shot up.

Frick settled his body into the easy chair. "Well, it's what happens. A man works ten years in the same job, he gets stale. The original letters somehow got into the radicals' hands. I don't know how. There's talk it was Ham's secretary. I don't want to slander the woman, but if he cannot maintain loyalty among his staff. . . But that's beside the point. The point is that some action must be taken. Immediately. Before these groups start thinking about joining forces."

He folded his hand together. "Now. . .I've thought the matter over carefully. First of all, we could begin spring recess one week early and at the same time give in to several demands, for instance, police off campus. With the students on vacation, the strike will fold. And with no strike, there's no need for police. Another demand is the one concerning the assistant professor. He has a contract to teach one more year, and at that point he can be dismissed painlessly. The rest of it, especially that business in '64. . . I'm convinced that our making

an issue of it would only discredit the university.
After all, we hired him."

The Board Member sipped his drink. "What about
Project Rhododendron."

Frick leaned forward in a business-like manner.
"We can promise them a referendum. Next fall. During
the summer we can eliminate the trouble makers."

"The 'lunatic fringe,' as the boys in Mellon call
them," the Board Member said, smiling.

Frick laughed. The Board Member had a nasty habit of
repeating what he thought were witticisms, and Frick
had acquired the talent for realistically feigning amusement. At the same time, he was flattered that the Board
Member would comment to him about 'the boys in Mellon.'

As for the Board Member, he listened to the rest of
Frick's suggestions, which included an attempt to bolster the Administration's image by the creation of an
Administration controlled campus newspaper that would
compete with the student controlled newspaper that
had supported the strike from the beginning. He declined,
however, to read the sample article Frick had written,
though afterwards he was sorry. There was a running joke
among several Board Members about Frick's fantasies
of literary talent, and the article might have
proved entertaining.

All in all, the evening was profitable. The Board
had talked among themselves for some time about Ward's
inefficient liberalism and were in agreement about the
need to replace him. Frick really hadn't needed to go
to all this trouble. The Board Member certainly thought
his cloak and dagger mentality amusing and a bit childish, though it did make replacing Ward easier. And in
his own way, Frick would be useful. For a time.

On Friday, March 27, the University Administration issued a bulletin: spring recess would begin one week early, and as of 5:00 p.m. of that day, classes were to be cancelled for two weeks. Though the city police had been directed to leave campus, the charges against The Sully Seven were not mentioned, leading to argument among the students as to the Administration's intentions.

Neither did the bulletin mention the D.O.D. referendum. At an emergency meeting Friday morning, an up and coming administrator disagreed with Frick about the fall referendum. "It seems to me that the issue of the D.O.D. research has been obscured by both the arrests and the presence of police on campus," he said with an ingratiating smile. "If the students have forgotten about Project Rhododendron, why should we remind them?"

After the appearance of the bulletin, the strike died. The radicals were not fooled but the majority of students took advantage of the extended vacation and left town. The only students that gathered on Friday were those with suitcases waiting for the bus to the railroad station. The radicals tried to revive the strike but it was too late: slowly, the campus emptied.

By Monday the campus was deserted. A sense of dullness settled down as if the strike had never occurred. Once again it was business as usual. The rest of the world was irrelevant; here, it was spring recess.

The calls to revolution were gone. During the week-end the maintenance crews had worked overtime in the rain to remove the painted slogans since in a few days Alumni Week began, and President Ward wanted to give the alumni the impression of normalcy.

The graffiti inside the buildings had changed too. During the strike someone had written in the History Department hallway: "Take a sister by the hand." Recently, someone had crossed this out and written: "Better the ass." Becky saw it as she left the department the last evening in March.

Outside, the campus was silent. As she passed in back of Mellon Hall, a movement caught her eye across a wide expanse of lawn. When the figure got closer she recognized Justine, and waved.

Justine approached, carrying a large shoulder bag. "Hi. Creepy out here, isn't it?"

"Sure is. Where you coming from?"

"A Daycare meeting."

"Daycare. . ."

"Yeah, we decided to have a sit-in at Ward's office the first day after spring recess: parents, kids, ice cream, toys. . . I can't wait. You should come, it'll really be something."

Becky shrugged glumly.

"What's the matter with you?"

"Oh. . . I guess it's just the let-down after the strike. You know, everything was so exciting, and now it's the same old shit. And I've been hassled all day long. First I had a fight with David and then I had to meet Pritchard. He asked me to be his assistant next year."

"Pritchard. . . Isn't he the one that writes the porno books?"

Becky smiled. "Yeah, that's him. As a matter of fact," she said, looking at a book visible in Justine's open shoulder bag, "that looks like his most recent publication."

"Get out, that's one of Paul's books."

"Yeah, sure, Justine, like I really believe you. What do you think, I was born yesterday? I can see the title from here. . ." She leaned forward, peering at the book.

296

"It says. . . *The Passionate Preachings of Pritchard the Porno King.* Hot stuff."

Justine smiled.

"But it's really not his best work."

"His best work, huh. . . So what'd you tell this porno king?"

"I said I didn't think I wanted to be his assistant. That means I'll have to find another job for next year. I'd like to try and teach my own course. . ."

Justine smiled. "What about Sully."

"No. . . I don't think it'd be a good idea if I worked with him. It's too time consuming. And what with teaching the women's courses and taking my own courses and working with the group, I won't have time to do unpaid labor for Sully. He makes me so mad. . . He asked me to got out on Monday night and he knows that's when the consciousness raising group meets. I told him I'm going to start karate lessons next week and he got all upset. He says it's a stupid idea."

"Sure he thinks it's stupid. He's afraid you'll beat him up."

"I oughtta do just that. Hey, where are you going now?"

"Home."

"Want a ride?"

"Sure."

They headed toward the parking lot.

Becky said: "Hey, I heard you and Terry are getting a place together."

"Yeah. Elizabeth might join us."

"Really?"

"Mm-hmm. You know. . . we thought it'd be nice to have four people. Terry was saying that you'd make a good fourth. Of course I told her she was nuts."

"What do you mean! I'm a prize package!" They looked at each other and smiled.

"Think about it," Justine said.

"OK. I will."

April
1970

Spring was coming. Becky saw it through her bedroom window. She sat on the floor and gazed out at her tree, watching the budding branches sway in the breeze.

The radio was on, and at noon the newscast began: "Department of Defense officials told newsmen today that U.S. military advisers had been authorized to cross into Cambodia for what they termed 'protocol meetings'. . ."

Becky looked like she had come from battle: she wore old baggy jeans, a faded jersey and a worn Army shirt several sizes too large. She'd pulled her hair back with a rubber band and covered her head with a shabby blue bandana. She had just come from the store.

Yesterday she had taken her first karate lesson at a nearby studio. When she dressed to come home, she'd felt good in her body, and her bra felt so confining that she decided not to wear it. She pulled on her jeans, dark red t-shirt and sneakers.

The day was beautiful. Walking home, she breathed deeply, feeling the sunshine on her face.

Halfway down the street she saw a young man turn the corner. As he neared her, he smiled. An attractive female walking alone was his opportunity for a mild flirtation, even if she wasn't in the mood. She looked straight head, but his eyes rested on her breasts. She realized that going braless might mean a certain liberation to her, but to the world it meant something else entirely.

Just as he passed her, he said: "Hey sweetie, what'cha got there. . ." He turned his head with a smile, ready to enjoy her shame or impotent indignation.

Emboldened by one karate lesson, she whirled around. "Why don't you drop dead."

His eyes opened in astonishment. He gave a snort of laughter.

She took a step toward him, her body trembling. "Don't you laugh at me, you. . ."

Well. Appreciating a woman's body was one thing, but encountering a mad woman was another. Out of the corner of his eye he saw a man at the end of the block. "Take it easy."

"Don't you tell me to take it easy!"

Offended by her ingratitude, he walked away. She watched him. As he passed the other man he spoke, jerking his thumb toward her. The other man glanced her way and smiled, shrugging.

She walked home. Though her face was angry and defiant, she understood that her new independence had left her vulnerable. Before, she would always turn to the nearest man for protection. Now she knew that she could turn to them no longer. With the slightest twist in situation or character or mood, she was not a damsel in distress, but just another piece of ass.

When she went out this morning, she donned her oldest most shapeless clothes. And she was delighted to find that no one bothered her. At the Post Office where she mailed a letter to Ginny, a few people stared because she looked so sloppy, but no man made passes and no man made remarks. She had disguised her womanhood, hidden the beauty of her body under some baggy clothes. Though she regretted the disguise, she was euphoric, and wanted to run up to the men who ignored her and laugh right in their faces. She was playing a huge trick on them and they had fallen for it. She vowed that she would get a whole new wardrobe from Goodwill.

It would be her one small freedom: to come and go as she pleased, a sexless creature. She knew it was only for a time, but for now it was necessary. Because as well as resist those remarks on the street, she had to resist the need within her to hear them. When that weak, fawning dependent creature was gone, what she wore would no longer matter.

The phone rang and she went into the kitchen. On the table was the cardboard box filled with old letters and diaries. As part of spring cleaning, she was sorting through the contents, discarding what she didn't need.

She answered the phone. It was David.

"Hello Becky. How are you."

"I'm OK. How about you."

He paused before saying: "I'm all right. I wanted to know if you were busy. I wanted to come over and see you. There's something I want to talk to you about."

"Oh? What."

"I don't want to talk about it on the phone. Can I come over?"

"When."

"In about an hour."

"Why can't you talk to me right now?"

"I'd rather talk about it in person. Becky. . ." His voice was tender. She waited for it to pierce something in her, that big sticky balloon of soft warm feelings for him. Nothing happened. "I know that it's been hard for us lately. . . with the strike and everything. I've been under alot of pressure, and I know you haven't been yourself, either."

She was tired. She sat down and rubbed her eyes.

"Once things calm down it'll be like it was before. Won't it?"

The formica table was criss-crossed with knife marks where former tenants had sliced food, and she ran her finger over the intersecting threadlike scratches.

"Won't it Becky?"

"I don't know."

"Becky, I've been doing alot of thinking, and I've made some decisions. I want to come over and talk to you. About us."

She didn't respond.

"Can I come over?"

"I guess so."

After she hung up she stared at the cardboard box, and slowly began to sort through the letters, letters from Jack and Steve and Freddy and all the rest of her old boyfriends.

Her hand touched something hard. It was the high school diary from her junior year, a small pink plastic book with a picture of a pony-tailed "teen-aged girl" on the front. It was closed by a small lock, but the lock was broken from years ago when she had lost the key. She opened the diary. On the inside she had written and crossed out: "Rebecca Simon," "Beckie," and "Beckee," before deciding on: "Becky."

She flipped through the pages and smiled. It was all so childish, especially the index in the back where she had recorded like the lists in teen fan magazines: Jack's age, height, weight and birthday, his favorite color, food and car; his hopes for the future, and whether or not he French kissed. Then on the next page the same facts, the vital statistics for her existence, for Steve and Fred and every other one she could possibly get away with defining as her "steady."

Fred was special, for she had slept with him. When she wrote about it in her diary she called it "Heaven." She'd write: "Heaven tonight," to signify the times they had sexual intercourse in the back seat of his car. She fooled herself into thinking that they were the great romance of all time.

The last time she saw him was the week before he left for college. They went for a ride in the country, and he parked the car at the edge of a woods, suggesting they go for a walk. She knew what he meant. He made love to her on a mossy spot even though she kept whispering anxiously: "But what if somebody sees us, Freddy. . ."

Afterward, it seemed that her self had separated from her body, because she saw the scene as if she were hovering above it: the woods, and the two of them walking away, Fred ahead of her, not looking back. The leaves crunched under his feet.

It was the last time she ever saw him.

He broke up with her a month later. His letter said: "I am a rat. I'm sorry." She didn't understand the apology until she realized "I am no good for you" meant that he was dumping her.

She'd felt nothing. She didn't really care. She thought: 'Well, so I lost my virginity, it had to happen sometime.' But since he was her first and it was over, she went through the appropriate hysterics with her best friend.

She sat in the kitchen and held the diary in her hands. One entry read: "Heaven tonight, mmm. . ." She'd believed that he was The Man, the one who would cherish her always. But of course she had to believe that: she had to think of him worth the degradation she felt.

In the middle of the book she saw on an otherwise blank page the writing: "Please, don't let me forget what it's like to be *me*!!!" That frantic little jotting in the midst of all those lies about heaven made her sad.

She stood up and tossed the diary into the brown paper bag under the sink where she'd already thrown her eyeliner. 'It doesn't matter,' she thought, and automatically turned the diary into a joke which might amuse David.

In the background, the newscast began: "Department of Defense officials told newsmen today that U.S. military advisers had been authorized to cross into Cambodia for what they termed 'protocol meetings.'. . . And on the home front, the Nixon Administration, alarmed by what it regards as a rising tide of radical extremism, is planning to step up surveillance of militant left-wing groups and individuals. 'We're dealing with the criminal mind,' said a highly placed Nixon assistant, 'with people who have snapped for some reason.'. . ."

She stared out the window. The pane was flecked with dust. Blurring her vision, she looked first at the dust and then focused on the tree outside. She opened the window.

After a few minutes she went into the kitchen and retrieved her diary from the garbage. She took it into the bedroom and placed it on the window sill. She would not turn it into an anecdote with which to entertain a bored lover. It was her past. It was her life. She looked at the diary, and at the tree beyond it, waking from its winter sleep.

She heard his footsteps on the stairs.

Though the day was warm, there were few people in the State Park. Justine and Terry had walked past the empty picnic tables and stone grills to a secluded spot. They spread a blanket under an old tree, and leaned the thermos of water between two thick roots. Before them was a pond, at whose far shoreline began an expanse of trees that ended in a sharp ridge. On the other side of the ridge, beyond their range of vision, was the Expressway on which they had come and on which they would return to the city.

Justine sat against the tree, her legs outstretched. Her eyes were closed, and she was thinking about the hitch-hiker they'd picked up just outside the city. Terry leaned forward, elbows resting on bent knees, her eyes searching the near shoreline for pebbles. Occasionally she looked up at the sky and frowned.

Charlie came out of the woods where he had been exploring, trotted forward and walked into the pond.

"He's going to get all wet," Terry complained. "Charlie!" It was too late. He swam out to a log and tried to grasp it with his teeth. The log rolled over, and a branch hit him on the head. "Oh God, I hope he doesn't drown," Terry said, standing up suddenly. "Charlie, get out of the water!" He glanced at her, then lunged at the log, but it floated away. She laughed. "I hope I don't have to jump in and save him. He's awful stubborn and the water's ice cold."

"He'll be Ok."

"I guess so." Terry sat down.

Eventually, Charlie gave up and swam back to the shore where he shook himself and lay down in the sun.

Justine looked at Terry and said, "I hope that girl's careful."

"Who?"

"That hitch-hiker we picked up."

"I hope so too. She's nuts for hitching."

"Where did she say she was going, someplace in Ohio, wasn't it?"

"Oh yeah. . . She said she was a student. I think she said Kent State."

"How far is that?"

"Couple hours."

"I hope she's careful."

Terry nodded, and the two women fell silent.

"It's nice out here," Justine said. "It's nice to get out of the city."

"I know."

She gazed through the branches to the sky. "It's too bad Becky couldn't come with us."

"Mmm. . . Sully had just gotten there when I called."

"Is she coming over tonight?"

"I don't know. I don't know if *she* knows." Terry paused, and said, "The other day I talked to BJ about Becky. BJ told me I should get out and meet people." She saw a smooth white pebble flecked with brown near the tree trunk. She picked it up and rubbed off the dirt with her thumb. "BJ said alot of times when people first come out, they fall in love with straight people. She thinks it's because if you're afraid of coming out, straight people are safer to love. . ." She looked at the pebble. "She told me that when she first came out she fell in love with her best friend who was straight and stayed in love with her for years." Terry stood up. "I wonder why I never fell in love with you."

Justine smiled, opened her mouth to speak, but Terry was walking to the water. She rinsed off the stone and returned, holding it out. "Isn't it nice?"

"Pretty."

She sat down, placing the stone on the blanket.

After awhile, Justine said, "Paul came over this morning to pick up some of his things."

"How's he doing?"

"He decided not to leave town, after all. He says he wants to finish up with his degree. And he wants to be near the baby. But he's worried they'll take away his fellowship. He says there's something wrong with David's phone, and they think it's tapped."

"You're kidding."

Justine shook her head. "He said that when he thinks somebody's listening, he tries to raise their consciousness."

Terry smiled. "Did he say anything about the Grand Jury Investigation?"

Justine shook her head. "It's still only rumors. The latest is that they're going to hand down charges of conspiracy."

"He should cool it politically, at least until things calm down."

"I know. But he won't. There's that Vietnam Moratorium on the fifteenth. . . and the Panther demonstration in New Haven, he's going to that."

"Is he coming to the Daycare sit-in?"

"Mm-hmm. He was trying to kid around, he said he'd be there to protect me. and I said my two karate expert friends promised to be my bodyguards. I shouldn't've said it. I think I hurt his feelings."

Terry lay face down on the blanket, arms pillowing her head. "He should probably stay away from you awhile. . ."

"That's what he said."

Terry wriggled to mold a place for herself, and closed her eyes. Justine plucked a blade of grass, placed it between her thumbs, and blew. It took several tries before she produced the desired sound. Terry yawned. "I didn't sleep hardly at all last night. . ."

"I meant to ask you. did you talk to Elizabeth about getting a place?"

"Mm-hmm. She's still not sure. Mark asked her to get a place with him and some other people who're going to start a commune." Terry yawned again.

"Did she mention calling another women's meeting?"

"Yup, next week."

Soon Terry was asleep. Justine looked at the trees and the water, listened to the birds chirping and the faint sound of cars and trucks on the Expressway. She breathed deeply, as though it were possible to store the fresh air for her life in the city. She felt the baby moving.

Later, when Terry woke. Justine was pouring water into the thermos cup. They both drank, and Justine screwed the cup back on the thermos. Terry sat up and stretched. "How long did I sleep?"

"Oh, about a half hour."

"Did anything exciting happen?"

"You talked in your sleep."

"Did you listen?"

"Of course," Justine said, but at Terry's expression, she

laughed. "No, I didn't hear anything, honest." She paused, and said: "I was just sitting here. Thinking."

"About what?"

"Oh. . . me. The baby. Paul." She sighed. "Last time I went to the doctor's I asked him about having the baby at home. He said I was crazy."

Terry looked at her as if to say: Well what did you expect?

"I know. But I'm really scared of going to the hospital. Terry. . ." Justine brushed her fingertips lightly on the grass. "What's it like. . ."

"Having a baby?"

She nodded.

"It's hard to remember. . ." Terry looked out over the water. "They give you a drug that makes you forget. I don't think it puts you to sleep, it just makes you forget. Do you believe it, you go through all that, you really experience it, and they make you forget. Like: ha ha, it wasn't real. . . But the times I woke up, it was. . . I don't know. . ." She looked down and did not speak.

"If you don't want to talk about it. . ."

"No, it's not that. I just never talked about it before. . ." She glanced at Justine and looked back over the water. "I'll tell you, it was different than anything I ever experienced. Like, I went into the hospital all rational, I thought: '*I* don't have any romantic ideas about this. . .' or what I thought were romantic ideas. I figured, 'Well, this is going to happen, but I won't let it touch me.' You know?"

Justine nodded.

"Like, here was my head, up here, and there was my body down there, pregnant, and they were separate."

She paused. "I remember that it hurt, like being torn apart, but it seemed far away. Maybe that's because of the drugs, or maybe time makes you forget. When I woke up in

the beginning of labor everything seemed fuzzy. I kept trying to get up, and they kept pushing me back down. . . I
heard someone in another room moaning, calling out for
God, and it sounded so strange. . . Later on I woke up
again, it must have been in the delivery room because there
were these horrible lights. I heard someone moaning, 'Oh
God, oh my God. . .' and I realized it was me."

Justine waited for a moment. "Did you wake up again?"

Terry nodded. "I woke up feeling this incredible urge to
push. . . But it wasn't even that 'I felt.' Because *I* didn't
matter, it wasn't *me* anymore. It was just happening, and
that's all there was to it. Do you know what I mean? Do you
ever feel that?"

Justine nodded.

"It's not *you* anymore, it doesn't matter what you think or
want, it's happening, and you're just a part of it. It's not us
in the end, we don't control nature at all. That's what men
don't understand."

She was silent, silent for so long that Justine thought she
wouldn't speak again, but she took a breath and said:
"Then, at the end, I woke up. Really woke up. Maybe they
didn't give me enough drugs. Or maybe I wanted to wake up
and I fought the drugs. I don't know. But when I woke up at
the end. . . I felt the baby. And everything was clear."

She looked off toward the trees, and tears came to her
eyes. "I understood everything. I don't know what that
means or how to explain it to you. But I know it was true. I
understood everything. And I thought to myself. . . but it
wasn't a thought, it was more like a song: 'I'm a rock'."

"A rock?"

"Yes. It didn't mean that I was hard like a rock, or made
of stone, or that I didn't feel. It meant that I was a part of
everything. Trees, grass, animals, everything. I was a part

of the wind. the water. . . And I was a part of the rocks. I was everything. I felt myself move with the earth. I guess. . . I was life."

She stared at her upturned hands. trying to feel the very cells that composed her flesh. Then she closed her hands into fists, and looked up. "Later on I told myself that it wasn't true, I hadn't felt it, or what I felt wasn't real. I thought that maybe it was some kind of euphoric side-effect of the drugs." She smiled. "You know, some kind of patriarchal conspiracy. . ." She picked up the brown flecked pebble and rubbed it with her thumb. "But it was real. I felt it. I was there." She turned to Justine. "You know what they say about a woman having postnatal blues?"

Justine nodded.

"Well maybe postnatal blues is just coming back from that experience. It shakes your whole life. your whole center. And then you come back to the hospital: nurses running around, babies crying, people visiting. . . except with me nobody visited 'cause nobody knew. . . But there's all kinds of confusion. and you don't feel that you're a part of it, or want to be. You want to go back to that place where everything was clear, everything was right. . . everything made sense." She paused. "You experience it. . . and when you open your eyes, you're back in the world. And it's all gone. And then you look around and you wonder if maybe it never really happened. I mean, once you understand what *life* is, and then you come back here. . . I don't know, it took me so long to adjust. I'd sit in the hospital and read the newspapers, and I couldn't understand anything at all. . ."

She was silent but Justine waited, knowing she wasn't finished. Overhead an airplane crossed the sky, leaving behind it what appeared to be a trail of pretty white clouds. Terry opened her mouth to speak and Justine thought she

313

was going to speak once more of birth, but she said: "For a long time, I guess it was about a year afterwards. . ." She held her breath for a moment, then let it out in a sigh of frustration. "It's hard to explain. I just didn't feel like I was a part of anything. I'd look at the things people did to each other, the things they did to. . ." She shook her head and waved her hand vaguely, indicating the natural world around them. ". . . and I'd feel like I wasn't a part of it, like I didn't belong."

She looked into Justine's eyes. "But maybe . . . even in *this* world, we still are a part of life. Except we don't really know it. Maybe that's what people find out when they die. That they were a part of life all along and they never knew it."

Justine had been listening thoughtfully, and now she said, "Maybe people used to know a long time ago, and then, over the years everything changed and we forgot."

Terry leaned back on her elbows and gazed at the sky. The airplane was gone, but its trail had remained, like a message of deadly white chalk against the blue sky. "Yes," she said, "we forgot." Justine looked at her and saw a vein in her throat gently pulsing.

They sat in silence. Charlie crept over and lay his head on Justine's legs, pressing his nose against her belly. She pet his head, and he fell asleep.

When the sun was low in the sky, Justine said: "It's time to go home."

Terry nodded.

The two women smiled at each other, walked to the car, and drove back to the city.

314